P9-CNC-817

Dedication

To Kevin

BEYOND
THE PALE

CLARE O'DONOHUE

MIDNIGHT INK
WOODBURY, MINNESOTA

FIRST EDITION
First Printing, 2018

Book format by Cassie Willett
Cover design by Shira Atakpu
Cover art by Dominick Finelle / The July Group
Editing by Nicole Nugent

Midnight Ink, an imprint of Llewellyn Worldwide Ltd.

This is a work of fiction. Names, characters, places, and incidents are either the product of the author's imagination or are used fictitiously, and any resemblance to actual persons, living or dead, business establishments, events, or locales is entirely coincidental.

Library of Congress Cataloging-in-Publication Data
Names: O'Donohue, Clare, author.
Title: Beyond the pale : a world of spies mystery / by Clare O'Donohue.
Description: First edition. | Woodbury, Minnesota : Midnight Ink, [2018] |
    Series: A world of spies mystery ; #1
Identifiers: LCCN 2017051243 (print) | LCCN 2017054899 (ebook) | ISBN
    9780738757094 | ISBN 9780738756509 (alk. paper)
Subjects: LCSH: International Criminal Police Organization--Fiction. |
    Married people—Fiction. | College teachers—Fiction. | GSAFD: Spy
    stories. | Mystery fiction.
Classification: LCC PS3615.D665 (ebook) | LCC PS3615.D665 B49 2018 (print) |
    DDC 813/.6—dc23
LC record available at https://lccn.loc.gov/2017051243

Midnight Ink
Llewellyn Worldwide Ltd.
2143 Wooddale Drive
Woodbury, MN 55125-2989
www.midnightinkbooks.com

Printed in the United States of America

Acknowledgements

I've been living with this book in my head for about five years, and in some ways I've been researching it since birth. My parents were from the west coast of Ireland, and I spent a small portion of my childhood in Tuam, Co. Galway. Though I was raised mostly in Chicago, it was in the company of aunts and uncles, neighbors, and family friends who had been born in "the old country." Some of what I've written comes just from growing up surrounded by Irish accents, literature, folklore, and history.

But there was also a good deal I didn't know. I pored over many books, watched movies, and made two visits to Ireland specifically to walk the paths that Finn and Hollis would walk, making sure I was describing both the sights and the people fairly. I even had a Guinness or two, because it's important to get the details right. The story is fiction, but the moments that seem too quirky or funny to be real are the ones based on my own experiences. Just in case you're curious, I've provided some "behind the scenes" info and photos on my website, clareodonohue.com.

I didn't rely entirely on myself, though. My friends Eileen Lucas and Alessandra Ascoli were the book's first readers, and their insights helped me take the story in directions I hadn't anticipated. Lydia Rendon helped shape one of the characters and even lent her first name to the cause. I couldn't have managed without their cheerleading. Howard J. Dean lent his expertise in weapons, tirelessly answering many questions. And Kevin Dorff, my personal Google, offered details from his seemingly limitless knowledge of history. He's responsible for several key points in the story. What I've gotten right is because of these folks. What I've gotten wrong is entirely me.

My Mayo-born Mom, Sheila Sweeney O'Donohue, added her stories to the mix. My late father, John; my brothers, Dennis and Jack;

my nephews, Mike and Steven; and my sister by marriage, Cindy, have all been a part of this and every book I write.

And a special shout-out to all my family in Ireland and spread throughout the world—the O'Donohues, Sweeneys, Murphys, Conways, Morans, and Smiths. I hope you find I've done a good job of writing about the country we know and love.

Finally, I need to thank my editor, Nicole Nugent; acquiring editor, Terri Bischoff; and everyone at Midnight Ink, for taking on this spy story/travelogue. And especially I want to offer my gratitude to Sharon Bowers, my agent for many years and my friend, who brought her own knowledge and experience of Ireland to this book. Thank you for the help, and mostly for keeping the faith that I'd actually finish this.

And to my readers who've been waiting for a new book from me, I hope this was worth the wait. And *go raibh maith agat* (thank you)!

In Ireland the inevitable never happens,
and the unexpected constantly occurs.

—*Sir John Pentland Mahaffy*

Ireland ...

Eamon Byrnes checked his email one more time. There were no messages. He clicked to his bank's website and checked for recent activity. Nothing he didn't recognize. It was supposed to have happened by now.

"*Damnù air!*" he shouted to no one.

He tried to calm himself, take a long breath, but it did no good. He knew he was starting to panic, and that would be a mistake. Panic was what had gotten him into this mess in the first place. Panic and bad judgment. He had to be calm, think things through. That was the way he'd survive this.

It was all supposed to be simple. Easy money when he'd needed it so badly. After Nora got sick and Siobhan got into trouble, he had choices to make.

Close the business or do whatever it took to keep things running. At the time, he thought he'd chosen wisely.

And maybe he had, but somewhere he lost control of it.

Somewhere his simple idea had become dangerous. He only wanted to save those he loved, but now he was betraying them.

Eamon shut off his computer and looked out one more time. There was no one coming to his door, no one around for a distance. Still, he kept looking. There were only a few neighbors close by and only one, Mary Kelly, who would pop in for a coffee without notice. Mrs. Kelly was nearly eighty now, but nothing got past her. He'd avoided stopping by her house to let her know he was at the cottage. He was afraid she'd know straight away how desperate things were.

It was getting dark. He walked outside to get a good view of the road. There were no cars there. No bicycles. No one even out for a stroll. That's a good sign, he thought. No one had found him. Not yet, anyway.

As he stood there, he found his eyes drawn back to the house. He loved this old cottage by the sea. There was nothing in front of the place but a small patch of green and the Atlantic Ocean, wide and wild and good for the soul. The land had been in his family for more than a few generations, but now most of it was sold. What was left, this small house, was rented out to Americans looking for their roots, or needing a respite from the madness of their lives.

Eamon fixed it up to meet the clichés most Americans came to Ireland to find: a thatched roof and emerald green door, Waterford Crystal and local pottery on dark wood shelves, and worn wooden tables. He'd found a pair of overstuffed chairs at an estate sale in Donegal, and they were now in front of the stone fireplace. A Celtic cross hung above the mantel. It was the look of an Ireland that was long gone, Eamon often thought when his mood went dark, or an Ireland that never really was.

Unless he was troubled, as he was now, he preferred to be in Galway City. It was convenient for shopping and for pubs, and since Nora was gone, it was easier for him to be around people than to be alone. After the trouble with Siobhan, he'd sworn never to return here. He wondered how she'd feel if she knew he'd broken his promise.

The wind was picking up, the howling sad moan of a banshee wind, so he went back inside. He put a few bricks of turf into the fire and settled into the armchair nearest the flame. If he didn't get the email that was promised, then he would have go through with his plan. In his sixty-five years on the planet, he'd never imagined himself a murderer. But if it came to that, what choice did he have?

Nora, God rest her, would be spinning in her grave at the thought of what Eamon was about to do. But she had the comfort of being dead, and was therefore immune to the complications that life had thrown at him.

Maybe it wouldn't come to that. Maybe everything would be alright. He could go back to running his business, Skyping with Siobhan on Sunday afternoons, and having coffee with Mary as they looked out at the sea.

As he sat there, evening turned to night, and the pitch black of the ocean made his little home feel very isolated. He longed for a visit from Mary and gossip about the goings-on in the parish. But when a knock finally shook him from his thoughts, it wasn't his neighbor at the door.

One

<hr>

Hollis Larsson ran along the edge of the river. It was dark but she knew where she was going. There had been footsteps behind her a while back, but now she was completely on her own. She was struggling a bit, could feel the beads of salty sweat drip down her face, yet she had no intention of giving up. Five more miles, she told herself. And then she heard a crack... And another. A drop of water fell on her head.

She saw the car coming on the road that ran parallel to the river. The driver slowed as he got near her, passed by, and then reversed, stopping just feet from where she was. She moved closer to the river bank, slipped her keys out from her pocket, and cupped them in her hands. She pushed her car key between her fingers and made a fist.

"Hey," the man behind the wheel said. His face was hidden in darkness. "Get in the car."

She moved her body to face the car squarely, the better to attack if she needed to. The hair on the back of her neck stood up, but she felt calm. She was ready.

"Hollis," the man said, "get in. It's raining."

She bent down to get a better look and saw clearly the dark-haired man behind the wheel. "Oh, Tony," she said, relaxing her fist. "No, I'm good. I just want to get another five miles in tonight."

"Didn't you hear the thunder?"

"I'll be fine." She stood up, put the keys back in her pocket. "I'm training for a marathon."

"Finn okay with you running after dark?"

"Why wouldn't he be?"

"College towns attract weirdos," he said. "I'd be terrified if Julie were out in the middle of nowhere by herself after dark."

"I'm tougher than I look."

"You'd have to be," he said. "Well, be careful."

"Always am."

He smiled, waved goodbye, and drove off. Well-meaning neighbor assuming I can't take care of myself, she thought. I have skills.

She rolled her eyes. I *used* to have skills.

Whatever happens, I can handle it, she told herself. And then the sky opened up and she just felt foolish.

━━━━

Finn glanced up from the TV as she walked past him, soaking wet. He didn't make a comment, didn't smirk, and didn't even do a much-deserved *I told you so*, though he had warned her there was a collection of nimbus clouds heading their way. He'd seen them from the window.

"There's only a twenty percent chance of rain in the forecast," she'd said as she laced up her running shoes.

"But there's a hundred percent chance of observing rain clouds moving in the direction of our neighborhood," he'd said. "Better safe than sorry."

That was what had done it. She hated that saying, hated being safe, and was at a complete loss as to why being sorry was such a terrible thing. She went running anyway, desperate to prove that taking a chance was a good thing. So much for that teachable moment.

———

After a change of clothes and a hot cup of tea, Hollis sat in the extra-bedroom-turned-office of her tidy home. She had papers to grade, but it was Sunday and she didn't feel like working. There were bills to pay, but she didn't feel like doing that, either. She didn't feel like doing much of anything.

"Snap out of it," she said to herself.

She picked up the pile of cards on her desk—birthday cards that were now a month old. *Welcome to middle age!* one friend had cheerfully written. Was forty middle age? She dropped them in the trash can.

Something else on the desk caught her eye—a little blue booklet. She started leafing through the pages, one empty page after another, until she got to a stamp. She and Finn had flown to Toronto for a conference two years earlier, where he was the featured speaker. One stamp, and now the passport had six months until it expired. She clicked onto the To Do folder on her laptop and added "renew passport" to the list. Not that she needed to rush out and do it. She wasn't going anywhere.

This was it. This was her life. This was her *stop complaining, Hollis, there's not a thing wrong* life. A tenured professor at Bradford University, a small but prestigious institution in Southwestern Michigan. A husband of nearly fifteen years who was faithful, decent, smart, and well-meaning, if not particularly romantic. Her parents were still alive and healthy. She had a network of friends. She'd kept herself in shape with running, yoga, boxing, and anything else she could make time for. She had a nice home and money in the bank. She'd published a couple of books on global political interdependence and was even on CNN once. It was a good life, she told herself as she got up from the desk. It was enough, wasn't it?

She dropped the passport back on her desk, but her aim missed and it fell into the trash can with the cards. She stared at the blue folder for a few moments before reaching in to retrieve it.

No, she thought. It isn't enough.

Two

The Cubs–Brewers game was on when Hollis walked into the room. Finn was staring at the flat screen as if the outcome depended on him. He'd been like that for over two hours. Two hours and twenty-three minutes, not including the pregame. And Finn always watched the pregame. He said it provided the right "context" for the matchup, whatever that meant. Finn didn't just *enjoy* baseball—or anything else, for that matter. He studied it. Once he set his sights on a topic, it became an obsession.

Three years ago it was archery, followed by Middle English poetry, then tarot cards. This winter it was John Wayne—three biographies and every movie he could get his hands on from *The Big Trail* to *The Shootist*. She watched most of the movies too, hoping it would bring them closer. But while Finn explained, in great detail, the evolution of Westerns from the silent movies to the 1970s, Hollis found herself dreaming of being swept off her feet by a handsome cowboy.

Now, while the game plodded forward, she closed her eyes and waited for a commercial. She was trying to decide whether to be cute and funny, or annoyed and stern. She was trying to remember what worked these days. But these days, nothing seemed to work.

When, finally, a Bud Lite ad filled the screen, Hollis turned to her husband. "We should talk about vacations."

"We just had spring break."

"That was more than a month ago."

"Right. So we just had it."

"And we didn't do anything for it, remember? You said you had things you wanted to do around the house so we stayed in town and then you mostly went into school to read."

"You said you were fine with it."

"I was," she said, though she wasn't. "But that's not the point. I'm talking about summer vacation." She tossed a blue booklet at him. "Do you know what that is?"

Finn glanced at the booklet that had landed at his feet. "I would say a passport," he said to his wife, "but I'm guessing it's a trick question."

"It's a passport that has only been used once in the nearly ten years I've had it."

"I'm sorry." It was Finn's go-to answer these days.

Hollis stood looking at the man she'd once described as obsessed with her. But that was back in the days when they couldn't stop touching, couldn't stop talking, couldn't stop staring at each other. That was when … She couldn't quite bring herself to think it: that was when we were in love.

But they were still in love. They just weren't... She didn't know what they weren't, frustratingly, but they weren't something that they used to be.

Hollis moved toward him, standing between her husband and the television. "On my thirtieth birthday you told me that once we had tenure we'd spend our summers traveling the world."

"How old are you now?"

"Forty. My birthday was last month. You had one too many whiskeys and threw up in a plant."

"I thought that was my birthday."

"Yours is in July. Also forty, in case you've forgotten that too."

"Forty. Geez, and we're still sexy as ever."

"Are we? We used to spend hours staring at each other."

"No need." Finn pointed to his temple. "I've got you memorized now."

She knew he was trying to be funny, but the idea that there was nothing more to learn about her just made her sad. "I'm changing, Finn. You might want to look again."

"You look the same as you always did—medium height, skinny, with dark brown hair. Although you are getting gray around the temples. It's cute."

She tucked a few strays from her hair behind her ear and made a mental note to call her hairdresser. She tried to make eye contact but was competing with a forty-inch flat screen. And losing. "Are you even listening to me?"

He let out a grunt. "We'll see the world, Holly."

"When?"

"After the game." He leaned forward in his chair and pushed his wife's slender hips slightly to the left.

She stood her ground for a moment then decided to change tactics. She slid next to him on the chair.

"What now?"

She kissed his neck. "I just miss us."

"We're right here."

"We're always right here. That's the problem. I want to go somewhere. I want to see the world before I'm too old to enjoy it."

"Call your sister. She's always taking off for some exotic land. Didn't she go to Marrakesh or something last year?"

"She went to New Mexico."

"I knew it was somewhere. Maybe you can go with her this summer. Or go by yourself. You'd have fun."

"No, I wouldn't. I want to go with you. I want us to do things together. Finals are over in a few weeks and we've got months of free time."

Finn took a deep breath, then said quietly, "I'm teaching this summer."

Hollis pulled back. "No, you're not."

"I told the dean I'd do an Intro to European Literature," he said. "It's sort of an overview for incoming freshman who want to get a jump on their courses."

"Why do you have to teach that? You're a nationally recognized expert in European literature— "

"Internationally," he corrected her, then smiled a little.

"Okay, *internationally* known expert," she said. "Why waste a whole summer with incoming freshman?"

"I think it would be fun to get back to the basics. Maybe you could teach this summer too, and we could hold hands on our way to class." He patted her thigh. "That way we could spend more time together."

He had not once during the entire conversation turned his head from the game. The Cubs were losing by six runs. It was a bloodbath, and a meaningless bloodbath at that. It was late April, just three weeks into the season, and plenty of time for the team to prove themselves a powerhouse or go down in a blaze of glory. But whatever happened, it wouldn't be decided on this day, with this game. And yet, knowing this, Finn still did not turn from the TV.

There were times in the last few years when she'd lay awake in bed, wondering what it would be like to get in her car and drive away, never to return. To start over completely with nothing of her old life, even Finn. She'd never do it, of course. And she'd never tell Finn even if it was a harmless fantasy. She felt just thinking it was a betrayal somehow.

"Every fall I teach the same subject to a group of students who look and act the same as the students the year before," she said, instead of admitting her daydreams. "I put the same decorations up at Christmas, plant the same flowers in the backyard every spring, and every summer I tell you I want to travel. And you know what you say, Finn? 'We will.' But we don't." Her eyes were watery as she tried to explain.

He was silent for a moment. "We don't have to be one of those couples that's always doing stuff to spice up their marriage, do we?" he said finally. "I love you, Holly. You're the only woman I ever want to be with. That's enough, isn't it?" He squeezed her thigh. "Take a class in something. You once said you wanted to learn pottery." He leaned forward in his chair. "Run, idiot," he yelled at the TV.

"That's your answer?"

"I was going to suggest you start work on a new book. You've been talking about doing something on the United Nations," he said. "But the last time I asked you about your writing, you bit my head off."

"I know," she admitted. "But I can't find a fresh approach. That's another good reason for a vacation. It will help me take a step back and get perspective. Maybe you could help me brainstorm on some topics."

Finally he looked at her. "Seriously, Hollis, can't this wait until after the game?"

"Because the game is more important than me?"

"Because the game is live. I only have one chance to watch it. But we're going to have this conversation about thirty times between now and summer break, so I can catch it the next time you get in one of your moods."

Hollis jumped off the chair. "You don't even see the problem. I want to do things, and you want to sit in that damn chair watching other people do things."

"I'm sorry," he said, but she wasn't really sure if he was talking to her or the batter who had just been tagged out.

Three

Operation Gladio was a paramilitary group, created as a stay-behind mission by Allied forces in Italy
after World War Two," Hollis told her class. "The
group's original mission was to work closely with intelligence agencies as a kind of check on potential So-
viet aggression during the Cold War. Over the years,
according to some sources, it spread from both its
base in Italy to most of the NATO countries, and it
also changed its mission. Rumor has it, Gladio members have worked to affect the outcome of elections,
committed murder, and perhaps even acts of terror-
ism. Though there's no way to prove it."

A student raised her hand. "They don't still exist,
do they?"

Hollis shrugged. "After the existence of Operation Gladio came to light in 1990, the European Parliament passed a resolution calling for an investigation. We're still waiting for that investigation to be carried out."

Another student jumped in. "It sounds like the plot of a thriller."

"In many ways, the real-life world of spies is so much more than any thriller writer could imagine. Whether Gladio still exists or not, it's certainly not the first or last group with vague ties to intelligence, looking to change world events. There are many covert operations, secret organizations, and paramilitary groups operating right now throughout the world, affecting our lives in ways we cannot know." She could feel a thrill running up her spine just thinking about it. "But if you read the assigned chapters, you'll at least learn a little more."

She glanced at the clock. Perfectly timed exit line. She sat at her desk as the students left the room, trying to determine if any of them had gotten worked up over the topic. Mostly they seemed to be talking about the drink specials at a local bar. The only comment about Operation Gladio she heard was one student speculating on whether the information would be on the final.

Just as she was about to walk over to her office, Finn appeared at the door. He had a sheepish smile on his face. In the week since their argument about summer vacation, conversations had been limited to discussions of grocery lists and laundry. It was polite, even occasionally warm, but it was lacking connection. His sudden, and rare, appearance at her classroom made it seem as though he were looking to break the ice.

"Hungry?" he asked.

"Actually, yes. Okay if we go to the Indian restaurant on Main? I know the service is a little slow…"

He looked relieved. "It'll give us a chance to talk."

"That sounds serious."

"I hope not." The sheepish grin returned.

Once settled at the restaurant, Hollis scanned the menu and decided on a dish she'd never tried, while Finn ordered his usual Chicken Tikka. He hadn't spoken much on the drive over, and once in his chair he seemed more interested with the décor than with her. The center wall had a large painting of the Taj Mahal that took nearly the length of the room. Every time she saw it, Hollis made a comment about wanting to see for herself the world's most famous tribute to love. She noted that this time Finn had taken the chair that faced the painting, leaving Hollis without her usual comment, and only her tired reflection in the window.

"I was thinking about what you said last week about getting away," Finn said. "You're right about that. We do need some time away, a little adventure for two."

"Really?" She felt an odd burst of nervousness, the first date kind. Love is weird, she thought. There were moments after all these years when Finn was a stranger to her, and moments, like now, when she felt closer to him than anyone on earth. "What did you have in mind?"

"Let's go to Chicago and stay at a really nice hotel. There's a double header at Wrigley Field on the twentieth," he said. "We'll watch the games, grab a bite somewhere, and then go back to the hotel."

Hollis was silent.

Finn moved in closer to make his point. "It will be a nice romantic vacation before I start my summer class, just like you wanted."

Hollis stared at her husband a long time but couldn't bring herself to say anything.

"I'm trying, Hollis." The optimism in his voice was now being replaced by irritation.

She didn't want to fight, but ... baseball?

"It sounds great." She'd said the words he wanted to hear, but her voice was flat.

"I love spending time with you."

"As long as it's doing something you want to do."

Finn bit the inside of his cheek. One of the many tells that he was annoyed. "Okay, well, you can go to a spa or something and I'll meet you after the games," he said.

"So you watch a game, and I get a massage, and we meet up for a hot dog and beer? That's a romantic getaway? Why don't you go to Chicago for the games, and I'll go to Mackinac Island and stay at the Grand Hotel. That way you won't have to spend any time with me at all."

The food arrived and the pair fell into silence, each taking their own piece of naan instead of tearing off the same piece as they usually did.

"I thought that would make you happy," Finn muttered.

"I know." She took a breath, and answered in a half whisper, "That's the problem."

Finn stabbed at his chicken, taking a large piece on his fork and into his mouth. "Spicier than usual," he said. He drank his water in one gulp, so Hollis moved her water glass toward him while she looked to get the waiter's attention.

"Thanks," Finn said, finishing her glass just as the waiter came over with refills.

"Of course."

Then they returned to silence for a while before Hollis remembered that a colleague's retirement party was at the end of the week and they needed to decide on a gift. It wasn't much, but it was, at least, the kind of comfortable, if somewhat dull, conversation that could carry them through dinner.

This is the life I wanted, she thought when the waiter brought over mango kulfi with two spoons. She dug in, and let the ice cream soothe her tongue, still tender from the highly spiced dinner. All of the choices I've made up until now led me here, she thought, and I've got to stop blaming Finn for it.

"Maybe a baseball game would be fun," she offered.

"It will be really romantic, you'll see."

She looked up at her husband and did her best to smile.

Four

Hollis let her class go early. It had taken until now, in mid-May, for Michigan to shake off the winter chill. The sun was warm on her skin and for the first time she'd left her jacket at home. As she walked, she saw most of the students were taking advantage of the warmth, sitting under trees on benches to study for their upcoming finals. The school year was an enticing three days from being finished, and everyone was just looking to get it over with. Including her.

The campus at Bradford had a timeless quality to it. The buildings were nestled together, not spread out like at the larger universities. A student could walk to all his classes and back to the dorms in between. In the quad, the benches had plaques from graduating classes going back to the founding in 1903. A few of the buildings were still covered in ivy, though the administration fought the romantics every year as more was removed, citing damage to brickwork and plumbing. Finn was on the side of those who wanted to keep it. No surprise there, Hollis thought. But she wanted it gone ever since a family of rats had made a home outside her office, nestled in the ivy. Now when she passed a building covered in the stuff, she wondered what was hidden beneath the green.

She walked over to Mason Hall and up one flight of stairs to her office. She was required to do two hours of office time three days a week, and she usually spent it doing logic puzzles. She only did the difficult ones, but even then, the hardest of them took her less than five minutes. She did them anyway because she'd read somewhere you're supposed to exercise your brain once you reach a certain age. It wasn't that she minded getting older, she just couldn't get over how fast it was all going.

To the side of her desk, there was a pile of papers to be graded, but she let them sit and instead starting digging into another chapter of Lee Child's latest book. One chapter turned into two, and then ten, as she got lost in an adventure of one good man fighting against evil.

"Dr. Larsson?" The timid voice at the door belonged to Jason … Something. She used to be so good with names.

"Yes?"

"I wanted to ask you about my paper."

"I haven't read it yet."

"It's on the relationship between the United States and the USSR as the Cold War was ending, and how it contrasts with the relationship we have now with Russia."

"It sounds fascinating, Jason. I'll read it later."

"You said it's forty percent of our grade so I'm really hoping to get an A. I've applied to law schools and …"

"I don't grade papers on what students need. I grade them on what the papers deserve."

He looked stricken. "I understand."

"You're a good student. I'm sure it's a good paper."

He stood there. "I'm sorry," he said eventually. "I need a scholarship so I guess I'm just... My parents, they aren't... I mean, they don't have much." He looked about to cry.

"I'm sure it's good, Jason. Don't worry about it, just enjoy the sunshine. I promise I'll post the grades by tomorrow night." She hoped her answer would be enough, but he stayed, looking sad and uncertain. "Give me a few hours and I'll get the grades up, but no promises on what those grades will be."

He hesitated at the door for another moment before he turned and walked outside her office. She could hear him whimpering in the hall. A small part of her wanted to tell him she knew what it was like to want something badly and feel powerless to get it. It was hard enough when the dreams you had depended solely on your own actions, but when their fate rested with someone else... She didn't finish the thought.

Instead, Hollis flipped on the electric kettle she kept on the file cabinet and made herself a cup of English Breakfast. She took milk out of the mini fridge she'd bought years ago from a student, and poured a dash of it into her tea. Then she settled back at her desk.

Technically her two hours were up, but Hollis rifled through the stack of papers until she found the one written by Jason. She put her feet up on the desk and read. It was good. Not earthshattering, but a decent paper; a solid B. If she was feeling generous, a B+. There were professors at Bradford University who prided themselves on never giving out an A. Hollis wasn't one of them, but she did feel they had to be earned.

She took out her red pen and hovered it over the paper. She remembered her own panic about her future when she was his age, how she had a path laid out for herself, just as he did now. She'd veered off that path, for reasons big and small. She was tempted to tell Jason that life would happen, no matter what he planned, but that was more than he wanted from his International Politics professor. She finally put the pen against the paper, and with a sigh wrote, "A."

Then she took the next paper on the stack and read it. It would have been easier to give them all an A, but she didn't. She did, however, grade them on what she now called the Jason Curve. There was no harm in giving people the benefit of the doubt.

Before she closed up the office, she posted the grades and checked her emails. There was one from Finn telling her he was going out for beers with some of his grad students. *Join us*, he'd said at the end. The other emails were regarding upcoming events at the school. There was one from the dean congratulating her on the release of her book on the emerging Indian middle class and how it would alter India's place in global policy making. It was a dry book with a small publisher, but writing books was a necessary evil in academia. He'd ended the email with, *Can't wait to read the next book, about the UN.*

"You've got a long wait," she said.

The last email was from someone named "dagnelli." She'd known a D. Agnelli a long time ago, David Agnelli. It couldn't be him, she thought, after all these years. She hesitated to click. "You're being an idiot," she said out loud. It couldn't be him.

But it was.

Hi Hollis.

It's been more years than I want to count, but I was thinking about you the other day and I decided to say hello. I'd heard through the grapevine that you were teaching. One of your many talents was making a complex subject easy to understand—your students are lucky. I'm coming your way for business, and I was thinking I'd stop in at the University tomorrow to say hello and buy you a cup of coffee. I realize it's very short notice, but up for a trip down memory lane? Best, David.

It said almost nothing. There was no news on his own life, no explanation for why he was in town, or why he suddenly wanted to get in touch after two decades. It was just an offer for a quick hello over coffee. But her hands were shaking.

"Now you're really being an idiot," she said.

She typed, *Great to hear from you after all these years. I'd love to see you. My husband Finn and I both teach at Bradford and we'd be happy to have you to the house for dinner.*

She stared at the screen. Maybe dinner was too much. He'd said coffee. She pressed delete, and started again. *Great to hear from you. Would love to catch up over coffee tomorrow. I only have morning classes on Tuesday, and my husband Finn has only one late-afternoon class, so we're both pretty open. Let me know what works for you.*

She read it again. That sounded right. Casual and friendly, but mentioning Finn just in case David was mid-divorce and looking to reignite an old flame. She blushed at the thought. She was embarrassed and flattered, even as she knew it was all in her head. He was probably an insurance salesman trying to talk old college friends into term life policies.

Then she thought about Finn choosing his students, and the campus bar, over an evening alone with her. Again. David was an old friend, looking to catch up over coffee. Finn had never even met him. He'd be bored sitting with them as they talked over old times. No, she thought, it was worse than that. He'd be annoyed. These were old times she'd never mentioned to him. That was a whole can of worms she'd hoped never to open.

She went back to her email and deleted the mention of Finn, then pressed send before she had a chance to change her mind.

Five

When she got to Finals, a bar just off campus, Finn was holding court at a back table, surrounded by adjunct professors, grad students, and a few undergrads. Even before she reached the table she could feel the adoration. It was always like that. Back in freshman year of college she'd walked into a bar almost like Finals, and saw a fellow freshman surrounded by friends, laughing and talking. He'd looked up at her and winked, then looked away and didn't acknowledge her again until nearly Christmas. But she noticed. Tall and lean, with dark-blond hair and blue-green eyes that crinkled in the corner when he smiled, she couldn't look away. Finn was meant to be a college fling, but he'd turned out to be so much more. He was sweet and nervous when they were alone, leader-of-the-pack in front of groups. She fell for the whole package. No matter how hard she tried during those years in college, she couldn't convince herself that Finn was a man she would leave behind.

Now, rather than go straight to the table, she ordered a drink. She stood at the bar, sipping her Pinot Noir, and reminded herself that she should sign up for that wine class she'd been talking about. Getting an education in wine sounded a lot more exciting than using her non-teaching hours to write a dry analysis of the United Nations.

But she wasn't actually short of excitement, at least not at the moment. David's email was still throwing her for a loop. It was silly to imagine he was showing up after all these years looking to have an affair. It was laughable. And yet, why else would he look her up? If you just wanted to see what your old flame was up to, a quick Google search could take care of that. She'd tried searching for David right after she responded to his email. Nothing came up. It made her even more intrigued at the idea of seeing him again.

Not that she would have an affair with David. Obviously. She had never been, nor ever wanted to be, unfaithful to Finn. She'd never even flirted. But who wouldn't be flattered at the idea of it, she thought, though what she really felt was panic.

David. She was never in love with him. But she'd loved who she was during that time when she was with him. She'd loved what she dreamed her life would be ... before she walked away from all of it to come home to Michigan and Finn.

Laughter came from the table where Finn was sitting. He was having a great time, and he was creating a great time for everyone around him. She really did love that about him, even though she knew it made her seem dull by comparison. Finn was the one everyone wanted at a party, and Hollis was just along for the ride. At least that's how it felt when she was feeling sorry for herself, as she was now. But even watching him from the shadows, she didn't think she'd made a mistake in marrying him instead of following her dream. She *probably* hadn't made a mistake, she corrected herself. Anyway, there was nothing to be done about it now, so she took her wineglass, grabbed an empty chair, and sat next to her husband.

"Doctor Larsson," one of Finn's grad students told her, "your husband is just telling us about a street in Tokyo that's been written about in books more than any other in literature."

Finn blushed a little, then went back to telling his story. Years ago, he'd wooed her with his extraordinary knowledge of the greatest literature from all over the world, and now he did much the same with his students and colleagues. He had odd little insights into the lives of these writers. But it wasn't just literature. He brought history, art, music, even food, into his lectures. A class with Finn was like taking a walking tour through some of the most fascinating places and times the world had ever seen, with the best novels ever written serving as the guide.

What Hollis knew, and Finn rarely admitted, was that he had never been to any of the places he talked about. He'd read about them. He'd studied them. He'd even Google-Earthed them. But he hadn't gone to any of them. Not that he cared. He'd seen them in his imagination, and in the imagination of the writers he loved. He didn't need more than that.

Hollis sat back, sipped her wine, and listened to Finn's story. He looked over to see that she was listening, and he smiled. It was such a sweet smile that she forgot why she found him so frustrating most of the time.

———

Just short of midnight Finn and Hollis walked home, past the landscaped lawns of the campus to a neighborhood where more than half the houses were owned by university employees. Their house was the second from the end, a tan brick bungalow with square pillars on the porch and dark-green evergreen bushes on either side of the stairs. It would have looked severe if not for the pink and yellow roses that Hollis and Finn had planted when they moved in over a decade earlier.

"Have fun tonight?" He spoke in the soft tone men have around a woman they're unsure of.

"Yes. You tell great stories, always have. They're lovely to listen to." She moved her hand across his arm and down to meet his hand. He squeezed it, then let go and put his hand into his pocket. He was taller than she was by a head, and his stride was longer, so they never quite walked in sync. Finn either had to slow his natural sprint to let Hollis keep up, or she had to practically jog along beside him. Tonight, he slowed his pace and it made her happy. Grand romantic gestures are for the movies, she thought. Real love is when your husband wants to walk side-by-side.

"You're a very lucky woman."

Hollis laughed. "Don't push your luck or I might remind you that it was garbage day today and you forgot to put out the recycling."

"Sorry."

"It's fine. I did it." She leaned in and kissed his neck. She loved the warmth of his skin and the way being near him made her feel safe, even if she was annoyed or unhappy.

"We make a great team." He squeezed her hand once more, then let go again. "I can't imagine my life without you."

She bit the side of her mouth. "Neither can I."

He kissed the top of her head, then walked into the house ahead of her. By the time she'd closed the door behind her, he was already in his favorite chair with the television on.

Six

Hollis."

He looked the same, nearly.

"David." Hollis got up from her chair and reached out her hand. She felt as though she were blushing. David took it but then reached and gave her a hug. She instinctively looked around to see if she knew anyone at the Starbucks, and then silently reprimanded herself for it. She had specifically chosen one close to her office, taking a *nothing to hide* approach. So if she did run into any students or colleagues, she looked innocent. Which she was. But she hadn't told Finn about it, any of it, and that made even a hug from an old friend feel wrong.

"You haven't gotten coffee?" David asked.

"I just arrived."

"I'll get some for both of us." He started toward the counter then turned. "But it's tea, isn't it? You prefer tea, right Hols?"

She nodded. As he ordered, she studied him. David was Finn's opposite. Finn was almost a cliché Swede, tall and blond, just like his grandparents on his dad's side. David was shorter, all muscles, with black hair and dark eyes. He was in dark-blue jeans and a crisp white shirt, looking like a man trying too hard to seem casual.

She was just out of college when she met David. Finn was headed to grad school in Ann Arbor, and their college romance had come apart at the seams. Hollis was ready to move on, in more ways than one. She moved to D.C., planning for a new career and a new life. And David was one step in that direction. They were competitive, even fearless, when they were together. It was a side of herself she'd never known existed before then, and had now kept at the edges of her life. But all these years later, she felt a certain edge just being in his presence.

"You look amazing," he said as he put the tea in front of her. He sat opposite, opened the lid on his paper cup, and poured the contents of a sugar packet inside. "You obviously still work out as hard as you did then."

"Actually no." This time she knew she was blushing. "I do a spin class three times a week, and a little yoga." And boxing, and a few marathons, and her black belt in karate—but she didn't mention that. Her body was strong, she knew, but she was fighting an uphill battle to keep it that way.

"So a teacher..." He laughed. "I wouldn't have guessed that."

"A professor," she corrected him. "I got my PhD after we knew each other. How about you? Did you...? I mean, if I'm allowed to ask."

"You are, and no. I work at the State Department. Boring as hell desk job."

"Married?"

"Divorced, three years ago."

There was a knot in her stomach. A woman married for almost fifteen years can fantasize about being hit on by an old flame, but to have it happen, and in the middle of the day, at a Starbucks? Hollis sipped her tea and tried to think. She should tell him she was flattered but obviously it was out of the question. Of course, she reminded herself, he hadn't actually propositioned her.

She took a breath. "I'm sorry to hear that."

"I didn't think I'd ever be happy again, tell you the truth, but I'm getting there." He smiled and Hollis braced herself. "How about you? Are you still with your husband?"

Here it comes. "Yes. Still together."

"Finn Larsson," he said.

"You know his name?"

"I remember it from when you told me goodbye." He smiled shyly. "When you break a guy's heart, the details tend to stick."

"Oh, stop it, David. I didn't break your heart."

He gave her a half smile. "I don't know. I thought we were headed in the same direction."

"Doesn't sound like either of us went there."

"Don't you wonder 'what if'?"

She didn't answer. It was something she only barely admitted to herself; she wasn't going to start talking about it to a near-stranger. Instead she looked for the something else to say. "Finn teaches at the university too. In the Literature department."

David sort of squinted at her, then nodded slowly. Hollis thought it looked a little rehearsed. "I think I read an article in *Newsweek* about a Finn Larsson who had been brought in to consult on an unpublished Dickens manuscript that surfaced last year. He could tell it was a fraud."

"He does that kind of thing from time to time."

"Sounds fascinating."

"It is. And he's good at it."

"The article said he was one of the best."

"Then the article was lying. He *is* the best. No one knows more about writers than Finn. Name a country and he'll spend the next hour giving you a tour through every part of the place, based on its literature alone."

"But does he make you happy?"

That was a complicated question these days. "He's a good man," she said truthfully.

"That's not an answer. What's he like beyond just being good?"

"He's smart. He's kind. He's a little absentminded. He likes spinach on his pizza. He's allergic to pollen. What do you want to know?"

"It sounds like you know him well."

"I think we've learned everything we can about each other at this point."

He laughed. "So you're bored."

"No."

"Not the life you used to talk about."

"Neither is the State Department."

"No. I suppose it isn't. But there's time, you know, to do more with your life."

Hollis leaned back in her chair, getting a little distance from him. "What are you doing in town? Besides offering your services as a life coach."

"Looking up an old friend." He stared at her. It was flattering. It was uncomfortable. It was weird.

"Why all the questions about Finn?"

"Just curious, I guess, about the man you left me for."

He was laying it on a little thick. She looked into his eyes. He seemed worried, and trying to hide it. She'd gone to the coffee shop thinking that he might confess his love for her, or that their old attraction would still be there. But it was clear after only ten minutes that neither of those things were true. David Agnelli wanted something from her, and it wasn't to rekindle their long-dead romance.

"Why are you really here?" she asked.

Seven

Back at your office." David got up as he spoke. There was no question in what he said. It was a command. Hollis got up too.

They walked the few blocks back to Mason Hall in silence. As soon as they entered her small office, David closed the door behind them. "What gave me away?"

"For starters, why would someone with the State Department have business in southwest Michigan?"

He smiled. "You got me. I'm not with the State Department."

"So you did join the CIA."

"We both graduated the Farm at the top of our class. It would have been a shame if neither of us signed up for service. But I'm not CIA anymore, not strictly. For the last three years I've been working with

Interpol through the Department of Justice. A cooperative venture among agencies."

"Bureaucracies exist even in the spy game?"

"Yeah, can't escape that, I guess. But you'd like it. It's interesting work."

"No, I wouldn't. That wasn't for me."

"This is?" He gestured around the small room, crowded with books and papers, a worn wooden desk and a metal file cabinet, dented years before by a disappointed student. It wasn't much, and Hollis wasn't about to defend it.

"You're back to being a life coach."

"Sorry, Hols. It's just that you would have been one hell of an agent."

She laughed, but she was also keenly aware of how flattered she was. "If you're here to recruit me, I think I'm a little old for the job, even if I was number one in our class."

"Only at interrogation and weaponry. We were both good at surveillance, and I beat you on the obstacle course."

"Whatever helps you sleep." She smiled. "And it was Brad Thomas who beat me at obstacle. He was the real shining star. Whatever happened to him?"

"I guess he decided the life wasn't for him, either."

"You're surrounded by dropouts," she said. "So what does Interpol want with a dull Midwestern college professor like me?"

She tried to sound light, but she was getting excited at the prospect of being sought out by such a prestigious international agency with questions only she could answer, or even some consulting work that might require a security clearance. That was better than an old boyfriend wanting to rekindle a long-dead romance. Way better. Whatever it was he wanted from her, it could be the distraction she needed. Except, even as she asked the question, David had glanced at the floor.

"David?" she prompted. "You obviously came here in connection with your work, so what do you want from me?"

"A favor."

"What favor?"

"We want your help in getting some cooperation from your husband."

"My husband?" What a fool I am, she thought. I had a whole fantasy running in my head, and David's visit isn't even about me. "He's even more useless than I am when it comes to the spy world," she said, her voice cool and flat. She was suddenly jealous of Finn. He somehow found a way to be the center of attention even when he wasn't in the room. "But if you need a good book to read on the plane back to D.C., I'm sure he can recommend something." She crossed her arms and tried to look both tough and disinterested, but she could see in David's eyes that she hadn't pulled it off.

And worse, her surprise had made David's nervousness disappear, replaced by the swagger she'd remembered from the old days. He pushed some papers out of the way on her desk and sat down, surveying the room and taking command of it. "Actually it's a little more complicated than that. We need him to look at a manuscript. It's crucial to national security that he do this for us."

Hollis wasn't about to let him get away with this power play. "You're going to have to do better than that."

David paused. "I can't."

She didn't move. She stood there until the silence became uncomfortable, waiting for him to want to fill the space with noise. He'd probably assumed that mentions of the CIA and national security would send her bored professor brain into a tailspin. It had, but she took a cleansing yoga breath and stared him down.

He shitted his weight on the desk. "There's an original manuscript available for private sale in Dublin. A play said to have been written by Brendan Behan."

"Finn wrote an analysis of *The Quare Fellow*," she said. "But I'm guessing you knew that."

"It was very insightful," he said. His mouth curled a little at the edge, making a slight smile, but his eyes were tired and stressed.

"What does the sale of a manuscript have to do with Finn? Do you want him to authenticate it?"

"Yes."

It didn't make sense to her, not any of it. "Why would Interpol need it authenticated?"

"That's classified."

"And if for some reason you do, why not use someone from Ireland?" she continued. "There have to be a few Behan scholars at Trinity College. He only died in 1964, so come to think of it, there might be people who actually knew him living right there in Dublin. Why can't one of them do it?"

"That's a lot of questions."

"I'm only getting started."

"Hols, it's very important or I wouldn't be here. I'll give you what details I can," he said, then hesitated. It all seemed overly dramatic to Hollis. Maybe that's what spies are like, she thought. Maybe she would have been like that too, had she stayed. "The manuscript is in the hands of an antique dealer in Dublin," David continued. "And we need someone with your husband's background to get it. That's all I can say. I promised my superiors I wouldn't share everything with you until I had your husband's commitment to help us. We can't risk this getting out."

"You can't risk what getting out?"

"I can't say."

"Then I can't help."

Hollis and David stared at each other. It was a contest of wills that had been the hallmark of their relationship. As he had moments before, and when they'd known each other years ago, David blinked first. "I hope I can trust you." He hesitated. Hollis said nothing even though she was aching for information. Finally David spoke again. "The play isn't actually by Behan, just written as if it were. There's an undercover agent working with a very dangerous group of people. That manuscript surfacing is a signal that he's in trouble. We think it contains clues to some of the individuals involved, and their recent activities. And hopefully some information on the agent's whereabouts."

"It's in code."

"Exactly."

"So go look at it yourself."

He was growing impatient, she could tell, but she didn't care. "We can't. Someone leaked word of it to the world of high-end collectors."

"Which play is it?"

"There's a rumor it's an unpublished play, written just before he died. It's something that no one has ever seen or read. All I know is it's type-written, with handwritten notes that would look like Behan's scribbled in the margins. It's the only copy in existence."

"That must have drawn a lot of interest."

"Too much interest. The dealer is a man named Eamon Byrnes. A week ago he let the agency know it had been passed to him. One of our guys was supposed to go to Byrnes's shop to quietly buy it, but once word got out, Byrnes got paranoid and the price went up."

"But if Eamon Byrnes is one of yours..."

"He isn't working with us, not strictly. He's just a man looking to make some extra money. And Interpol has money."

"He sells to all sides?"

"Unfortunately. After the Irish economy went south in 2008, Byrnes became a fence for some thieves and forgers."

"The dangerous people you were talking about?"

David nodded. "Word is that Byrnes is afraid that if someone from Interpol comes by his shop, the bad guys will know he sells to us too. So, at the moment, the only people who have a shot at even looking at that play are people with the money to buy it, or the credentials to vouch for it."

"Like Finn."

"Yes. In a perfect world, we would use one of the experts in Ireland, but unfortunately we're no longer sure who we can trust."

It was one heck of a story. The kind of international intrigue she once imagined she'd be involved in. For a moment she was swept away by it. But then she came crashing down. There was still a part of David's story that didn't make sense to her. "Why approach me and not just go to Finn directly?"

David sighed. "He said no."

"When?"

"On Friday. Someone from the agency called him, but they didn't have any luck convincing him."

For a moment Hollis couldn't believe what she'd heard. Finn shared every moment of his day with her. At least she'd thought he had. When the deli forgot to add lettuce to his tuna salad sandwich, he texted her regular updates about it. But when Interpol needs his help, he doesn't think to mention it to her?

"If he said no," she said, trying to remember that Finn wasn't the only one who kept secrets, "he must have had a good reason."

"Hols..."

"I'm sorry."

"So that's a no from you too."

"It's not my decision to make. It's Finn's."

"I understand." The tone in his voice had softened, taken on the gentle whisper of memory. "I'd forgotten what it was like back then.

How excited we were by the classes and drills, how much we couldn't wait to be out there in the real world of spies."

"We were kids," she reminded him, and herself. "In the real world of spies, people are separated from the ones they love, they get hurt or killed. They don't know who to trust. But you don't need me to tell you that."

He rolled his eyes. "Can I tell you something? I've never run a field mission, never created an asset. My office is about the size of yours, though not as finely decorated." He laughed a little. "I hunt down thieves and killers online, looking at the Internet back channels for unusual sales or rumors. The only danger I face is carpal tunnel syndrome."

"So why did they send you?" As the words were coming out of her mouth, Hollis figured it out. "Your bosses thought that since the pitch to Finn didn't work, you could use our shared past to have a crack at my changing his mind."

Now that she'd had a moment to get used to it, instead of being embarrassed that she'd been wrong about David's intentions, she was actually relieved. She could put that whole chapter of her life back in its box as soon as he left her office.

But he didn't look in a hurry to leave. "Dumb as it sounds, I was thinking of this as a bit of an adventure," he said. "I'd see you again and actually have something to do with a real-life mission. We challenged each other back then to be better, didn't we? I thought we could do it again."

"It was a long time ago," she said, purposely keeping her tone neutral. "It was good to see you, but it sounds like this was a waste of your time." She took a few steps to the door, but David didn't follow.

"Stupid, maybe, for a middle-aged man to be looking for excitement," he added. "I'm not asking you to understand. Your life is exactly the way you want it. You're a lucky woman, Hols. You made all the right choices. It's not your responsibility that I didn't."

That did it. First Jason, and now David. She was a sucker for people who were as lost and confused as she was.

She told herself not to, but she turned toward him. "What do you need me to do, David?"

She could see the relief in his eyes.

"Talk to your husband. A man's life is at stake. Finn can help us save him, but we're running out of time."

Eight

No." Finn said the word over and over. Hollis and David sat at the kitchen table, watching as Finn paced back and forth across their kitchen.

"We don't have a choice," Hollis said.

Finn stared at her. His concern would have been obvious to David, but the twitch in his left eye, the one that signaled his growing annoyance, was meant entirely for Hollis. "Of course we have a choice," Finn said. "They can get one of their agents to pretend to be an expert on Brendan Behan and he can go to Ireland."

"We can't do that," David said. "It's already a problem that word got out. It means someone leaked it to create exactly the kind of chaos we're facing."

"Which means someone in Interpol is working for both sides?"

"We have to assume that, yes," David said. "Which is why we want an expert from the outside, a person with no connections to the agency. We don't have the time to find the mole before we get our man back. And we don't have time to put together the kind of cover Eamon Byrnes would believe. We need someone to go over now. You take an overnight flight the day after tomorrow and land in Dublin Friday morning."

"I have classes."

"No, you don't." Hollis jumped in. "Finals end tomorrow and your summer class doesn't start for two weeks."

Finn shot her a look that made Hollis feel she'd betrayed him somehow.

David chimed in. "You wrote that amazing paper on *The Quare Fellow*. You have a well-respected reputation as a literary expert. You're exactly the sort of person who has the credibility to do what we need."

Finn smiled at the compliment, but then his lips tightened. "It's dangerous."

"It's not," Hollis countered. "It's just picking up a play. That's it."

"That's not all it is."

"Hollis was the best in our class," David said, and Hollis could feel her face turn deep red. But not from humbleness, though she knew that's how David would see it.

"She was?" Finn looked over at Hollis, who refused to meet his eyes.

"She was headed for a top career at the Company. We were all surprised when she turned it down and went back home. But she had more than just career plans to think about." He smiled at Finn, who grimaced back. "I'll bet she can still handle any trouble that might come your way."

"I thought there wouldn't be any trouble," Finn said.

David shifted in his chair. Hollis could see he was growing impatient, but she knew Finn couldn't be rushed. He liked time to weigh over decisions, to imagine all outcomes. She'd stopped sending him to the grocery store years earlier when a trip for ice cream took three hours.

"As I told Hols," David said, "there's a group of people around the world, a new kind of criminal network. They call themselves TCT. We don't know what it stands for. We don't know much about them because they connect through back channels on the Internet. We don't believe that most of them have ever met in person, but they do manage to wreak havoc. What we do know is that they've stolen billions from banks and corporations, have blackmailed more than a few political figures, and are responsible for a fair number of art thefts. They're branching into forgeries now. That Dickens manuscript you exposed was one of theirs—"

"So they know who I am," Finn cut in. "I ruined one of their scams. Doesn't that make me a target?"

"Actually, that makes you even more credible," David said. "If people are watching the shop where the manuscript is, your showing up doesn't raise alarm bells. Especially if the agency floats the idea that you're working for an American buyer. We'll contact Eamon, let him know you're coming. You just have to take the manuscript and meet our contact. You stay a few extra days in Dublin as a vacation. All on the feds."

"What's the contact's name?"

"It's better if you don't know."

"Then how would I know who it is?" Finn asked.

David pulled a green leather purse out of his briefcase and set it on the table. It wasn't large, and would have looked stylish, Hollis thought, if not for the black piping and handles. "Hollis will put the play in this bag, and our contact will find you," David said. "Then just hand it over. That's all you and Hols need to do."

Finn glanced at Hollis. "Hols." He said it slowly … Hols … and she blushed. It was just the signal Finn needed that there was more to the story than an agent asking for a favor. She wished she'd just told him everything years ago.

"Finn," Hollis said, "David has explained it again and again. The undercover agent used a forged manuscript to send messages in the event he couldn't report. There's mission critical information in that manuscript, about the organization and its members. And if there's something in it that could save a person's life …"

"I'll be your handler," David jumped in. "I'll monitor everything from D.C. and you'll be perfectly safe the whole time."

"I thought you were an Internet guy," Hollis said. "Now you're our handler too?"

David nodded. "It's a promotion. But I do know what I'm doing and the whole office is in this, as well as several good people in Ireland. Look, the chatter we're picking up said our agent could be dead by Monday," David said, for at least the fifth time. "It's Tuesday. Dr. Larsson, we have less than six days to save a man's life." He seemed to run out of steam. Frustrated and tired, he turned to Hollis, who could only shrug.

Finn picked up the documents David had shown him when he first arrived, a passport with Interpol emblazoned on the front and David's picture inside, and a Justice Department badge. He held them for a moment, seeming to consider what to say, and then he handed them to David. "I get it. I'll tell you in the morning. That's the best I can do."

David was about to launch into another pitch, but Hollis shook her head. "We'll call you first thing tomorrow."

"Talk him into it, Hols. And when you get to Ireland, do me a favor: remember your training."

Nine

She let David out and returned to the kitchen just as Finn was making tea. She saw the green purse was still sitting on the table where David had left it. She took the milk out of the refrigerator and found some lemon cookies to add to a plate. When the kettle boiled, she watched Finn grab two mugs and two teabags, so she sat at the table and waited. When he was quiet like this, it was usually a bad sign. She'd tried to talk David out of coming home with her, figuring if she had a chance to talk to Finn first, to explain, to make the case for him, it would be better. But David had insisted, and now Hollis knew it had been a mistake.

Finn put two steaming mugs of Earl Gray on the table and sat opposite her. "You're not happy with me," he said as if it were an obvious truth.

"I'm perfectly happy."

"You lit up around that guy. I can't remember the last time I saw you that excited."

"Not because of *him*," she said. "Because it's a chance to do something, something that's not theoretical."

Finn crinkled his eyes a little, but he didn't smile. "Well at least you're not hiding it from me for fifteen years. I guess that's something."

There it was, the conversation that they should have had when she first returned to Michigan. "When we were in college it was my plan to join the CIA. I told you that when we got married."

"But not before you went."

"You don't tell people you want to join the CIA. It sort of disqualifies you." She tried to make it sound light, but there was pain in his eyes.

"Okay, but what's disqualifying about telling me the truth after you got back? The whole truth?"

"I didn't tell you about David because he didn't mean anything. You and I had broken up."

"You broke up with me." Finn's voice had an edge. "I couldn't figure out why you were suddenly so unhappy with everything in our senior year." He paused. "Like you are these days."

"I guess I did pick fights with you back then, maybe to get some distance from my feelings for you. I wanted a chance to follow through on what I'd been planning since I was a kid. It was always my dream to join the CIA. Then we met, and I wanted to be with you. I didn't think I could have a normal life and be a spy."

"So you made some grand sacrifice?" His voice was calm and quiet, but Finn clenched and unclenched his jaw. And the twitch was worse. They were about to have the kind of fight that required closing all the windows so the neighbors didn't hear.

"It wasn't a sacrifice. It was a choice," she said.

"So why didn't you tell me? And not just about David, but about being top of your class? You gave the impression you bombed out."

It was a complicated question and even after all these years, Hollis wasn't sure she had an answer. "I get that you're mad," she said instead. "And you can be mad at me all you want, but there is a real person in trouble."

He made that face, where his eyes squinted and his mouth moved to one side. It was the one that said he found something utterly ridiculous. It was a facial expression she loved, because it was usually aimed at politicians making promises or grad students making excuses. Aimed at her, she wasn't crazy about it. "You just want to use your passport. Pretty handy that the minute you start going off about wanting to travel, just like that"—he snapped his fingers—"we have to go to Ireland."

"Not just like anything. I've been talking about how much I wanted to travel since the day we got married. You just haven't been listening."

"I've been listening." He sipped his tea, though Hollis couldn't figure out how he managed to drink through a clenched jaw. "There's more to this than some agent sending secret messages. There's something that guy's not telling us."

"Maybe we can reach out to some of your friends in the literary community to see if they've heard about the play. David said it had gotten out—"

"I already did. When I got a call from some guy at Justice on Friday, I looked into it. There is some talk about an unpublished Behan play. Not a lot. No one has seen it, just rumors."

"So David's telling the truth."

"But even if it were real, it would only be worth about forty or fifty thousand. Not big-time collector stuff. There's talk that a Francis Bacon painting was sold in a private sale for a hundred and twenty-five million just a few days ago. That's the kind of real money that gets people excited. This Behan play ..."

"I thought Behan was having a resurgence. And the idea of an unpublished play by one of Ireland's top playwrights—don't tell me that wouldn't bring a lot of interest."

He nodded, a slight concession to her point. "Hols?"

"I hated that nickname," she said.

"Does he know that?"

"This really isn't about David. I hope you know that."

"I just don't see why we have to get mixed up in it."

"I keep telling you why. There's a man's life at stake."

He sighed. "You know I'd do anything for you, Holly, but ..."

Without meaning to, she rolled her eyes.

"You don't think I would?"

"You haven't once picked up your socks off the floor in fifteen years," she said, "despite at least three thousand requests."

He laughed. The twitch faded. "Fair point."

"You're not going to do it."

He shook his head, then looked at her. Studied her. Instead of getting angry, Finn sounded tired. "This would make you happy."

"We help someone and we spend time together in Ireland. Of course it would make me happy."

He nodded and fell silent. They drank their tea, and Hollis gave up waiting for an answer. She went upstairs and changed for bed.

———

It was nearly an hour later when Finn appeared in their bedroom doorway. "I'm a dull guy, Holly."

"No, you're not."

"I'm not putting myself down. I'm just making a point. I don't lift weights, unless you count the abridged version of the *Oxford English Dictionary*. I've never once wanted to climb Mount Everest or backpack

48

in a war zone. I contribute to PBS, I vote in off-year elections, I call my mother every Sunday and promise her I'll eat more vegetables. And then I do, because you can't lie to your mother. The closest I've come to imagining what it would be like to be a spy is when I read the complete works of Ian Fleming."

"Okay." She didn't want to say anything else because she didn't want to sound disappointed.

"You said you made a choice to give up on being in the CIA and come home. Maybe you've finally realized this isn't enough for you," he said. "Now you're unhappy."

She could see the pain in his eyes, hear the hesitancy in his voice. "Maybe," she admitted. "But if I am, it's not with you. It's with me."

"Then why am I the one you're always yelling at?"

She smiled. She felt selfish for being unhappy, and angry that he so selfishly wanted her to be happy doing only what he wanted. "I wanted to be with the man I loved, and I have never regretted that," she said, mostly meaning it. "Except when you came up with that idea about a weekend getaway to a Cubs doubleheader."

He smiled back at her. "You're not the romantic I am." He draped his pants and shirt across the chair and dropped his socks on the floor. He caught her eye, and instead of leaving them there, made a show of putting them in the hamper.

"I love having been with you all these years," she said. "I love the idea of growing old with you. But I feel—and I know this sounds awful—I feel like I'm keeping myself ready, mentally and physically ready, for an adventure I never have. It's not that I want to give up what we have, the security we've built; it's that I also want something dangerous and exciting."

"In life you make choices. And 'all of the above' isn't one of them."

He was right. He was *probably* right, but it left her with a painful question she couldn't leave unasked. "Why not?"

He didn't answer. Instead, he took off his watch and put it on its usual spot on the dresser, plugged his phone into its charger, and walked to the edge of the bed, in the same order and at the same pace as he did every night.

"If you want to yell at me," she said, "go ahead and I'll listen."

"'A man is already half in love with any woman who will listen to him.'" He looked at her, as if he were expecting something, but she didn't know what. Finally he said, "That's a Brendan Behan quote. You should know that stuff if you're going to try and flatter me into helping on this idiotic mission."

"If I were the Behan expert, I wouldn't need you for the mission. I'd go on my own."

"Would you?" He sighed. "You probably would."

"Okay, so we won't go." It wasn't as if she was expecting him to go along with David's plan. But it still stung.

He looked at her for a long while, then took a deep breath. "This is next year's birthday present," he said as he climbed under the covers and turned off the light.

"Really?" She thought it was impossible for Finn to surprise her.

"Did I get you something this year?" He had turned his back to her, a signal, she knew, that all was not yet right between them.

She put her hand on his back. "No."

"I meant to," he said. "Okay, happy birthday then."

She moved closer and kissed his neck. He rolled onto his back and she rested her head on his shoulder. "This will be good for you, for us both. It will get us out of our comfort zone. And it will be so much more fun than baseball."

He put his arm around her. "That depends on your point of view."

Ten

Ireland appeared as dots of green surrounded by waves that shaded from cobalt to baby blue. It seemed, at least from the vantage point of the plane's tiny window, to be untouched, almost ancient. Hollis imagined a place not unlike the one John Wayne found in *The Quiet Man*—quaint and beautiful, full of colorful characters and inviting cottages. Or perhaps it would be the literary salon Finn craved, where writers and artists crowded into pubs for long discussions on Joyce and Beckett. Or maybe it would be dark and gritty, like a Ken Bruen novel come to life. But whatever it was like, she was sure it wouldn't disappoint.

Hollis had spent the entire eight-hour plane ride alternating between a guidebook on Dublin and the latest Tana French novel. Though between long periods of reading and naps, she kept going back to a nagging detail: Finn's warning that there was more to the story of a missing agent than David had let on. It wasn't that she thought Finn was being paranoid; it's that she knew he was right. There would be no reason for David to tell them the whole story. In fact, it would be against instinct for an intelligence agent to give away more information than was absolutely necessary. She hadn't shared that with Finn, though, knowing it would have meant the end of the trip. But she found herself scanning the faces of passengers and flight crew, looking for an Interpol agent among them, or perhaps someone with more sinister designs. She had been preparing herself for decades for an imaginary mission. Now, faced with a real one, she was painfully aware how little her amateur training would help if they got into real trouble.

Finn, in his own way, seemed also to be readying himself for a mission more intense than the one David described. He spent the flight reading and re-reading *The Quare Fellow*, and every other work by Behan, as if there was going to be a quiz.

"I'd forgotten so much of this," he mumbled, before turning back to the start of a play and re-reading it.

"We're landing," she said, and squeezed Finn's hand. He just grunted.

"The Westbury Hotel, please," Finn told the taxi driver at the airport.

"First time in Dublin?" the cabbie asked.

"First time in Ireland," Hollis answered.

"Ah well, then, you have a lot to do, and you'll be dead in the center of town."

"Excuse me?" Finn sat up straight.

"He's talking about the hotel being centrally located," Hollis said.

"I hope so."

Hollis looked out at the city they were crawling through. Traffic was heavier than she expected. People were running across the street, eyes fixed on their cell phones, just like at home, she thought. And they were dressed in jeans and t-shirts, business suits and A-line skirts. Not a tweed cap or fisherman's sweater in the bunch. From out the window, Dublin was like any city in the U.S., except for the Georgian architecture and the friendly cab driver, who was chatting up Finn about a visit he'd made to New York a few years earlier.

"Have you been to New York?" the cabbie asked.

"A few times."

"It's mad, isn't it? There are loads of people everywhere you turn. You can't get away from them. And Dublin's getting just like it. Nowhere quiet where a man can sit with his own thoughts. Not like in the country. Are you going out west while you're here?"

"I don't think so," Finn told him.

"We might," Hollis jumped in. "We haven't firmed up our plans."

"Do yourself a favor and see the countryside. You won't be disappointed, and it will give ya a chance to get some rest."

With that advice, he pulled up in front of the Westbury, an elegant hotel just off Grafton Street. David had certainly spared no expense, but that had more to do with Finn's cover as the expert paid by a rich collector, Hollis reminded herself, than with any desire to show them a good time in Ireland.

The lobby was long and filled with stuffed chairs in muted colors, a marble floor punctuated with wool carpets, and beautiful wood beams that looked polished to a high gloss. Hollis heard the click of heels moving toward her and spun around from the reception desk, but it was only two women in business suits rushing toward a conference room.

"You okay?" Finn asked.

"Perfectly."

Once they'd checked in, Hollis took a quick shower. Even though her head was spinning from jet lag, she felt energized and whatever nervousness she'd been feeling had left her.

"This is amazing," she said, as she walked into the bedroom wearing one of the hotel's robes.

Finn looked up from his computer and the emails he said he had to check. "We've stayed in nice hotels before."

"Not in Ireland, we haven't." She grabbed some clothes from her suitcase. "It's eleven, and we have until three before we get the manuscript. What do you want to do?"

"We should probably nap. I didn't sleep well on the plane."

Hollis frowned. "What's your second choice?"

"Sex."

"What's your third choice?"

"Why don't you just save us both some time and tell me what we're going to do?" he asked.

"I thought we could start at Trinity College, go see the Book of Kells, and then make our way over to Merrion Square. Then we can get some lunch and come back here to freshen up before we head to the shop." She searched through her suitcase for a cardigan to put over her t-shirt.

"*We* head to the shop?"

"I have to go," she said, lifting the green purse from her suitcase. "I have to carry the play." She took her wallet out of her handbag, and put it in the green purse, then took it out again. "Do you suppose the contact will want the purse or is he just using it to recognize us?"

"Probably just to know it's us. It would look odd if you handed someone your purse."

"Right." She put her money, sunglasses, and a guidebook in the bag. "I'm ready when you are."

But Finn stayed seated, the reading glasses he'd just started needing perched on his nose. He reached beneath his chair and pulled out a box wrapped in light green paper with a white ribbon.

"Did you get me a present?" Hollis asked.

"It came when you were in the shower. There's a note."

For a moment she wondered if it was a little joke to break the tension they'd felt since David showed up, something silly to mark their first day in Ireland. But Finn was terrible at hiding his emotions, and all she could read on his face was annoyance.

She took the package and read the note. *To Hollis. —D.* The package was about half the size of a ream of paper, and weighed a couple of pounds. She sat on the bed, looking at it.

"Think it might be a bomb?"

That hadn't occurred to her until he'd said it. "Who delivered it?"

"No one. There was a knock on the door and when I went to answer it, this package was there. I guess someone could have been waiting around the corner to make sure I picked it up, but I didn't see anyone."

Hollis rushed to the door and listened. She could hear the ding of the elevator but nothing else.

"I already looked," Finn growled.

She opened the door anyway. The hallway was empty.

"What now, Natasha?"

"What?" She closed the door, locking it with both the deadbolt and the safety latch.

"I assume I'm Boris."

"You realize that makes David our Fearless Leader."

Finn threw his glasses on the desk and rubbed his eyes. "Are we opening it or calling the bomb squad?"

"You moved it and it didn't blow up. I say we open it." She put the package on the bed beside her, pulled on the ribbon, and carefully unwrapped it.

"Saving the wrapping for your scrapbook?" Finn asked.

"Just being careful, in case there's a clue."

Finn rolled his eyes.

The box was ordinary brown cardboard. The kind you would pick up at an office supply store, with no writing or labels—nothing to betray its contents. She lifted the lid, and let out an involuntary, "Oh."

Finn got up from the desk and took the box from her. "Euros?" He pulled bundles of cash out of the box, spreading them on the bed. She watched as he counted the hundred-euro notes—ten thousand then twenty then thirty...

When he'd finished he looked at her. "Fifty thousand euros." He turned the box over and shook it but there was nothing else. "Why did he have fifty thousand euros delivered to our hotel room?"

Hollis remembered what David had said to her—*Remember your training*—so she examined the wrapping paper but there was nothing. She looked at the ribbon. Nothing there either. She went back to the note and looked closely. It was possible there was something underneath the note, so she picked at the edges with her fingernail and lifted a corner of the paper. Working slowly, she carefully peeled the top layer back. There were two words printed underneath. *Only Eamon.*

"This is what I was worried about," Finn said. "He tells us all we have to do is walk into a shop, pick up a manuscript, and hand it over to his contact. He tells us nothing about the money until we're here. Then some lackey drops it off in front of our door without further explanation. What's next, we find out we have to kill a guy?"

"Don't be ridiculous."

"No, of course not. Everything so far has been perfectly reasonable." He tossed the bundles of cash back in the box. "Are we supposed to walk around Dublin with that in our pockets?"

She was as annoyed as he was that David had played coy, but if she admitted it now, Finn would throw it at her in every argument for the next thirty years. "Well, it only makes sense," she said. "Eamon must expect to be paid, and David knew we couldn't travel with this kind of cash. What if we got stopped at Customs?"

"Then why didn't he tell us?"

"I don't know," she admitted. "He must have had a good reason."

"Assuming the money came from David."

It was a good point. But Hollis couldn't imagine who else would have arranged for them to get the money. However it arrived, it must be necessary to complete the mission. On day one at the Farm the instructor had admonished them always to remember that, in intelligence, trusting others is both crucial and risky. Was that what David's advice had really been about?

"I was thinking I could get the manuscript, come back to the hotel, and get you," Finn said. "Then we'll go meet the contact together. Just in case something goes wrong at the shop."

"I'm CIA trained. And don't roll your eyes at me again."

"Trained or not, there's no point in both of us being in danger."

"Someone obviously knows this is our hotel room," Hollis pointed out. "It's probably David, but as you pointed out, what if it's not? How am I safer alone in the room than with you?"

Finn didn't answer. He grunted, but otherwise he just stood there, his eye twitching. Hollis took that as agreement and put the box into the hotel room safe. There was no sense in carrying it around until they were ready to go to Eamon Byrnes's shop.

Once she'd locked it, Finn started to say something, then seemed to think better of it. "This was a dumb idea," he finally got out. "This whole thing." But even as he said the words, Finn looked to Hollis like a man defeated. He put on his jacket.

"Are we going to have this argument again, or are we going to see an eight-hundred-year-old book?" There were two ways to end a fight with Finn, she knew from years of experience—kissing him, or baiting him with a piece of wrong information.

"The Book of Kells is nearly twelve hundred years old, as best as scholars can tell," Finn corrected her. "And it's not a book. It's a collection of folios divided into four volumes."

Hollis smiled and grabbed the hotel key card. Nothing made Finn happier, or distracted him quicker, than teaching.

"Promise me this is going to be over in a few hours and we'll be back to our lives," he said.

"I promise." She took one last glance back to the room safe and wondered if it was a promise she could keep, then kissed Finn on the cheek. "Tell me more about the folios."

So he did. And he kept talking as they left the hotel room, rode down the elevator, and walked out of the hotel lobby onto Grafton Street. "It's believed to have been made at the Abbey of Kells just north of Dublin. Extraordinary artwork. It's amazing to think of the hundreds of hours a monk had to put into just one page of illumination. You think of what someone could do with calfskin and inks made from plants." He smiled, his shoulders relaxing. "The pictures I've seen are out of this world."

"Now you get to see it in person."

He rolled his eyes, but this time looked more playful than sarcastic to Hollis. He was nearly over, at least for the moment, their disagreements about David. "The pictures are pretty good. And you can see it really close up."

"Next time you want to have sex, I'll show you pictures of me instead of the real thing," she teased.

"You're kind of making my argument for me, Holly. They're both good."

She laughed. She felt tension release from her shoulders. Maybe it wasn't all going according to plan, but that was half the fun. For the first time in a long time she felt lighter, even giddy. She was in Ireland, with Finn, having an adventure. She was never a believer in those woo-woo self-help gurus who preached that all you had to do was want something and it would manifest. But this trip, this moment, felt like something she'd dreamed up. And nothing was going to spoil it.

Eleven

The sun hit them as they walked the wide pedestrian-only street. Not a hot sun, but bright and temporarily blinding. Enough that Hollis didn't see the twenty-something man staring at his cell phone until she bumped into him.

"Sorry," he said, before she had a chance to apologize.

"My fault."

"Ah, you're fine," he said, his face breaking into a wide, friendly smile. Then his phone pinged and he went back to texting.

Grafton Street was a mix of high-end stores and tourist shops, and packed with people. With every step they risked crossing someone else's path. Some were clearly tourists, given away by their accents and shopping bags of souvenirs, but most seemed to be local, and in a hurry.

"Dublin is more than a thousand years old," Hollis read to Finn from the guidebook. "Founded as a Viking settlement in about the ninth century, it quickly became Ireland's largest city and its capital. After Ireland won independence for its lower twenty-six counties in 1922, it remained the capital city for the Republic of Ireland."

"I read that nearly a third of the country lives in the greater Dublin area," Finn told Hollis.

"No wonder the cabbie said the rest of Ireland was quieter." Hollis paused and looked back. "I think it's the other way." She flipped to the back of the guidebook to a map of central Dublin. As she did, a stern woman dressed in an expensive-looking black coat stopped.

"Are you alright dear? You seem a bit lost," the woman said.

"I'm fine, yes. We're looking for Trinity College."

"American?"

"Yes. We're visiting, seeing the sights."

The woman looked over at Finn. "Isn't that lovely. I've lived in Dublin my whole life and I hate to say it, but I never bother to see anything but work and home. And we've so many lovely places here."

"Do you know where Trinity is?"

"Back the other way. You can't miss it."

"We'll be looking for a place to have lunch soon," Finn told her. "If you have any suggestions..."

"There's good pizza at a shop just down the road," she said.

"We want something a little more Irish."

"Ah, you would do. Let me think..."

An older man standing near her chimed in, "You need to go to a pub, if you want authentic. This is a bit touristy round here, but there's some nice places. The Duke Pub is up the street."

Finn's face lit up. "Didn't James Joyce used to go there?"

The man nodded. "Sure, but he drank everywhere, didn't he? If it's a good craic you're after, there's where you'll start."

The man headed off toward a bus and the woman smiled and wished them luck before walking in the other direction.

"What's a *craic*?" Finn asked.

"No idea. But apparently that pub has good ones."

———

Hollis stopped for a moment at the main entrance to Trinity College on College Green, a university founded more than five hundred years earlier. Past a tall wrought iron fence was an enormous sand-colored building with columns running along it and a bright-blue clock at the top. In the center was a carved wooden door about twenty-five feet high.

"The guidebook says that the door is almost a hundred and forty years old," she read to Finn. "In 2014, a man smashed his car into the door and they had to take it down, strip it to the bare wood, replace the broken parts with matching timber, and rehang the whole thing. Can you imagine the work involved in that?"

"They would have to, wouldn't they? You can't just patch something like that."

"I guess not."

"Besides," he said, "there's pleasure in putting the time into something and getting it right, rather than just giving up on it."

He smiled at her, and for a moment he looked like the nineteen-year-old boy who'd smiled at her years ago and changed the course of her life. She wasn't sure, but she thought she might have blushed now as she did then. Then he grabbed her hand and they moved passed a crowd of college students, through the wooden door, and onto the campus.

As they walked, Hollis saw a pretty woman in a red trench coat glance at Finn. She smiled at her, but the woman didn't smile back or even seem to notice. Her eyes were fixed on Finn. "I think someone finds you attractive," she said, nodding toward the woman.

Finn just blushed. "Let's get tickets to see the Book of Kells," he said, "and afterward we can walk around campus."

He stood at the back of a long line of tourists waiting for tickets while Hollis walked a few yards away to snap pictures. The sun moved behind clouds, leaving a slight chill in the air, so she was glad she'd brought a cardigan with her. Other than the weather, which she'd been warned would be cooler than she was used to for May, everything was perfect. The campus was gorgeous—more sand-colored buildings, wide spaces, and cobbled streets. And though the buildings reeked of centuries-old tradition, the place was alive with youthful energy.

"I'm in Ireland," she said under her breath. She could hardly believe that less than a week before she'd been staring at a nearly unused passport.

David had given them scant details about the missing agent, or about the undercover job the man was on. She knew Finn's part in all of it was small, and hers even smaller. But still—she was in a foreign country, working a mission to save a man's life, and she felt the reality of it all through her body. She'd spent so many years wondering whether she would have made a good agent, and now that she was having a taste of it, she was on edge—excited and terrified and overwhelmed, and hoping more than anything that she and Finn would actually do some good.

"Ready?" Finn put his hand on her back.

She nodded, curled herself in his arm, and let him lead her to the library.

———

They started in a room filled with displays explaining the history of the Book of Kells. Finn read each panel carefully, his smile widening. He was in learning mode, and Hollis enjoyed watching him almost as much as reading the panels. The Book of Kells, the panels explained, was an illuminated manuscript of the four gospels, written on treated calfskin and elaborately decorated. Like Finn, she'd seen pictures, but when they walked into the darkened room that held the real thing, she was overwhelmed.

Only about ten inches by twelve and encased in thick glass, the folios were both smaller and more astounding than she had imagined. Finn peered down through the glass, shaking his head.

"So cool," he muttered.

Behind them a line of tourists, anxious to have their look, was growing. Hollis kept them off as long as she could, but finally she nudged Finn that it was time to move along. They went upstairs to the Long Room of the library, and Hollis's jaw dropped. The room was all wood, with carved columns reaching up two stories to a paneled, domed ceiling. And there were rows and rows of books, bound in leather with busts of philosophers and writers guarding each aisle. In the center of the room were glass cabinets displaying priceless letters and artifacts from Ireland's past. Among them was a harp believed to have belonged to Brian Boru, the last great high king of Ireland.

"Wow," Finn managed.

"Better than a picture?"

"Much better." He took her hand and squeezed it tight.

They walked the room several times, marveling at the details in the wood and the painted letters to mark where books were housed. Though they were surrounded by tourists, Hollis felt like they were sharing this moment just with each other.

"Excuse me," a woman with an American accent said to Finn as she moved past. The same pretty woman in the red coat from outside. She was petite with long black hair and large brown eyes, probably in her early thirties. This time she smiled at Finn and touched his arm.

Hollis tried not to laugh. One of Finn's best qualities was how oblivious he was to his own attractiveness.

"I'm starving," Hollis whispered to Finn.

As they went toward the exit, Hollis noticed the woman was now watching a tall black man with a shaved head and a muscular chest. I guess she found someone else, Hollis thought. You have to admire a fast worker.

Twelve

The Duke Pub was crowded, but they were able to get a small table, just enough room for their meal of fish and chips with Guinness. Hollis noticed a couple at the table next to them speaking German. She couldn't remember enough of her college German to understand more than a word here and there, but she did hear the man say, *"Ich liebe Dublin,"* and almost leaned over to tell him she did too.

Behind them was a rowdy group of university students, male and female, who were drinking and laughing. She'd been around enough to recognize students celebrating the last of their finals.

"It really does taste better here than at home," Finn said as he raised his glass. "You know that Guinness is good for you?"

"That's just an advertising slogan from the 1920s."

"Maybe at the time, but there've been studies in the last few years that show a pint of Guinness reduces the risk of a heart attack. It's the antioxidants."

Hollis lifted her glass. "Well then, doctor's orders," she said, before taking a drink. Heart-healthy or not, Finn was right about the taste. It was better than anything she'd had at home. It was smooth and silky and went down easier than she expected for such a dark brew. "Glad we came?"

"I will be when we're done with the manuscript."

"Just remember what David told us. All you have to do is ask for Eamon Byrnes. We give him the money, he'll give you the play, I put it in the bag, and we walk out. We go down the street and hand it to David's contact here, and we're done. Twenty minutes at most."

"Nothing to worry about." Though he sounded worried as he spoke.

"Nothing." She reached across the table and put her hand on his. "I think it's really sexy that you're doing this."

"You thought it was really sexy when I cleaned out the gutters, and when I organized our tax receipts."

"So?"

"It's just that whenever you get me to do something I don't want to do, you say it's sexy." He smiled. "So either you think I'm still an adolescent boy who will do anything to impress a girl, or you find dominating me a turn on."

"Which do you think it is?"

"Doesn't matter. Either way, you owe me for this." He swallowed the last of his beer.

The students finished their pints, slamming them down on the bar. "We're off," one of them said. "See ya next term, Sam."

The bartender nodded and gave the students a quick wave. As they left, Hollis noticed a man who had been standing at the bar behind them, halfway through a pint. He was a tall, bald, black man. He looked just like the man at Trinity College, she thought, but that would be too much of a coincidence.

Unless it wasn't.

"Let's get going," she said.

"I was going to have another pint."

"We need to be on our toes for this afternoon. We can have another afterward, to celebrate."

"I can manage another one. Besides we've got plenty of time." He got up and went to the bar, while Hollis watched the bald man. He glanced Finn's way but didn't seem to pay much attention. He looked to be reading something on his cell phone. Maybe it was just a coincidence, Hollis decided. They were only blocks from Trinity, and the Duke was a famous pub. But just in case, she grabbed her cell phone and, pretending to be reading an email, snapped a quick picture of him.

When Finn returned with two pints of Guinness, he was frowning. "I was just thinking... why Monday?" he asked.

"Today's Friday," Hollis told him.

"I know, but your boyfriend said that their agent could be dead as early as Monday. It's been bugging me since he said it, and the closer we get to being in the middle of this, the more it doesn't make sense."

"Why not?"

"If whoever took him—"

"We don't know that anyone took him. He's missing, but that could mean he's hiding."

"Okay, fine. But either way, why Monday?" He took a drink and seemed to forget his point for a moment, lost in the taste of his beer. "That is really good."

"You were saying about Monday?"

"Something else is going on." A young man sat at the table next to them, and Finn leaned forward to whisper. "And it's going to happen Monday."

She had to admit there was something to what Finn was saying. "Maybe there's an exchange," she offered, "the agent for the manuscript. And it happens Monday."

"Or maybe the manuscript contains a code to defuse a nuclear bomb that's going off on Monday."

She laughed. "Yes, that's it. We're going to save the world. I'm glad to see you're getting caught up in the excitement."

"I'm not. But there's something, Holly. I can feel it. It's like when I read that Dickens play and it was good, really good. Perfect, really. But I knew that it wasn't real. There was something just off about it, and I could feel it in my bones. That's how I feel now." He finished his beer with one long swig. When Hollis caught his eye, he shrugged. "I've only had two beers. I can handle two beers." Then he reached for hers.

She slapped his hand, grabbing her full Guinness and getting up from the table. She tapped the young man on the shoulder. "I didn't even touch this, but we have to leave. Would you like it?"

He smiled. "That's grand, yeah. Be a shame to let it go to waste."

She noticed the man at the bar had his phone turned at an odd angle, pointed toward her and Finn, and it seemed, possibly, as if he were taking pictures of them. Had he seen her take his picture, she wondered. Hollis turned back to her husband. "We're done this afternoon, so whatever happens Monday, we'll be clear of it. And we should go."

Finn held onto his empty glass for a few moments, seeming to consider the matter. Then he let go of the empty pint and stood up. "Where to now?"

"We still have more than an hour before it's time," she said. "Let's go see the Oscar Wilde statue in Merrion Square. And there's a church on Whitefriar Street that has the remains of Saint Valentine enshrined there. Couples are supposed to say a prayer that he'll bless their love and watch over them."

"Do we need someone watching over us?" Finn asked.

"It can't hurt."

As they passed the man at the bar, Hollis moved closer to him. He didn't look up or make eye contact, so it gave her a chance to get a good look. He could have been a tourist enjoying a midday beer, but she could feel a cold chill in her spine as she passed him. There was nothing casual about the way he was standing. His whole body was tense, ready for action. His left hand rested on the bar, almost in a fist. And she felt sure there was a bulge under his jacket, just where someone wearing a holster would carry a gun.

Thirteen

They seemed harmless enough, the Americans. Their identities had checked out. Two college professors on a weekend to Ireland attracted by word of the Behan manuscript. Irish scholars had been enquiring, but these were the first international visitors to want a peek. Still, it wouldn't have been suspicious, except for one thing: they had attracted attention.

He walked slowly, watching the woman try to take her husband's hand and his seeming disinterest in it. Another reason to avoid long-term relationships, he thought. They were lonelier than being alone.

But his main interest wasn't in watching the pair from Michigan. It was in the others who were watching. Clearly the couple was useful, but to all the wrong people. Perhaps they could be useful to him as well.

As he watched them take holiday snaps, he wondered if they had any idea what would happen when that usefulness was at an end.

Fourteen

Merrion Square had been lovely, quieter than she'd expected. The statue of Oscar Wilde was playful and irreverent, like the man himself. Hollis had stopped to take photos of all the sayings engraved in a base nearby, but as she snapped the camera on her phone, she looked around. It felt as if someone was watching. She almost asked Finn if he felt the same way, but he'd returned to his concerns about Monday, and she knew there was no good that would come in suggesting someone might be following them.

"This was all a mistake," he said.

"You've said that before."

"It bears repeating. And if whoever is behind all this would kill an Interpol agent on Monday, there's no reason to think they wouldn't kill us today. Friday is just as good a day to kill someone."

Finn's obsessive need to understand was a double-edged sword, Hollis knew. It made him an extraordinary scholar, but it also made him, at times, a relentless worrier. "You're just nervous."

"I'm not nervous. I'm looking at this with a cool head instead of getting myself caught up in ancient fantasies about adventure."

Instead of taking the bait, Hollis walked away from him, heading toward the edge of the park with Finn, a few steps behind, still talking. He was scared, and he was right to be, but everything would be fine. Their role was so small. They would have the manuscript for ten or twenty minutes at most. Just long enough to walk from the store to the restaurant and hand it over. What could happen in twenty minutes?

She hated to even imagine the possibilities. Someone was watching them. She was sure of it now. But when she spun around to where she thought the person would be, there were just kids playing. Maybe she was just imagining things. Maybe the man at the bar didn't have a gun.

It would be over soon. They would have helped on an important mission, maybe save a man's life, and she would have had her little adventure. Then the rest of the weekend would be theirs. It would be nice to see another part of Ireland. They were scheduled to return home on Monday, and Finn would probably be happy to spend the rest of the trip somewhere else. Newgrange, the Stone Age temple older than the Pyramids of Giza, wasn't too far, she thought. She decided to ask at the hotel for suggestions on the best way to get there.

"Are you listening to me?" Finn asked.

She hadn't been. "Those homes are really beautiful," she said instead. The Georgian homes near the square were no-nonsense brick buildings set off with playfully colorful doors. Just like the Irish people she'd met—serious until approached, then smiling and happy to help.

"I'm getting tired," she said. "Maybe we should skip the church and head back to the hotel."

"That's what I was just saying." He smiled. "And you accuse me of not listening to you."

At least in the room they'd be safe. She couldn't tell Finn about the people she thought, or maybe just imagined, were trailing them. He'd head to the airport immediately and wait for the next plane home. Instead, she kept her guard up until they were back in their room. The jet lag was getting to them both, but while Finn nodded off almost immediately, even behind the locked door, Hollis felt on edge.

It made sense, she decided, that other Interpol agents would be watching them, making sure that everything went smoothly. But it made just as much sense that whoever was behind the agent's disappearance was aware that an American college professor was in Dublin to collect the manuscript.

At ten minutes to three, she put the fifty thousand euros in the green purse. As they left the hotel for their appointment, Hollis took one last moment to catch her breath. She stopped in the lobby at the travel brochures hoping it would turn her thoughts to what they would do after they finished their task.

"We should take a tour of the Guinness factory tomorrow," she said as she grabbed a handful of brochures. "And you can have as many beers as you want." With nowhere better to store them, she put them in the green purse. She put the bag's strap over her shoulder and her arm across the bag. The money weighed the purse down, so she held it so close to her body and let the strap dig into her skin.

She could see that Finn was more anxious than before, and she wondered if he'd noticed the man in the pub, or felt the presence of eyes watching them in the park. But if he had, he wasn't any better at sharing than she was.

"Okay?" she asked.

He nodded. "Let's just get this over with."

They walked out of their hotel back onto Grafton Street and the swarm of people who passed through it. Even without the cars, Grafton Street was still hazardous to anyone not sure of their destination.

"There's Brown Thomas," Hollis pointed toward the upscale department store that dominated a full block. "David said that Lemon Street is between our hotel and that store. We must have passed it somehow." She looked around and was nearly hit by a woman carrying a large shopping bag. "I wish I could see street signs somewhere."

Finn walked a few yards away from her, toward a narrow street that jutted out like a tree branch from the main road. As he moved, a crowd of tourists walked past, and Hollis lost sight of him. But she did glimpse—or thought she did—a woman in a red trench coat.

Hollis pushed through the crowd until she caught sight of Finn's blond hair. "What are you doing?"

"I found Lemon Street," he said. "There's a sign halfway down the street for Byrnes Antiques."

She followed him down the narrow road, looking around for another glimpse of the red coat, but there wasn't one.

"What's wrong?" Finn asked as they reached the shop. "You look scared. You want to back out?"

"No. I'm not scared. I'm …" She thought for a moment, then admitted the truth. "I just … I don't know. I thought I saw someone, maybe."

"What do you mean?"

She took a breath. "Last-minute jitters, I guess."

"So much for CIA training." He stopped and grabbed her by the shoulders. "Hollis, honestly, do you really think our doing this could save someone's life?"

She looked into his eyes. "Yes. I do."

He nodded slightly. "Okay. Twenty minutes from now we'll be done."

A few feet later, they were at the shop. Finn pushed open the shop's door and walked inside. Hollis took one more look around, but saw nothing on the street except shoppers walking briskly to get out of a sudden downpour.

Fifteen

Byrnes Antiques was small and dark with a musty odor that hit as soon as they stepped inside. Every inch of floor and wall space was packed with furniture and artwork, but it was hard to see the details in the dimly lit space.

A thin man with gray hair wearing a black overcoat was talking with the shop's clerk. While they waited, Hollis glanced at the display case of jewelry and buttons, trying to look casual, though her heart was beating fast. Once he entered the store, Finn seemed to relax. He loves to perform, Hollis thought, as her own palms covered in a film of sweat.

"I'm sorry we don't have what you're looking for," the shop clerk said to the man in the overcoat. The clerk, a twenty-something man with spiked dark-brown hair was wearing a worn t-shirt and jeans. He looked out of place in an antiques shop, but his words had the confidence of someone who knew every inch of the place.

"He was very clear that I should come..." the man said, his voice half insistent, half desperate. "I don't know what I should do."

"Well, it's beyond the pale, I admit," the young man said, glancing toward Finn and Hollis, his voice getting louder. "But I can't help you here."

The gray-haired man only nodded at the young man's impatience, then took one last glance around. As he did, he caught Hollis's eye. He smiled and she smiled back. Such a friendly country, she thought. Even someone as upset as that man still offered a warm smile. "What am I supposed to do?" he asked.

"As I said," the young clerk said, his tone getting sharper with each word, "I can't help you. Perhaps you should look to the source for your item."

After a moment, the man seemed to give up and he walked out of the shop, leaving Hollis and Finn alone with the clerk.

"Can I help you?"

"I'm here to meet with Eamon Byrnes," Finn said to him.

"He's not in at the moment. Can I be of help? I'm Kieran O'Malley, Mr. Byrnes's store manager."

"I'm afraid not. It was suggested to me that I speak with Mr. Byrnes." Finn turned to Hollis. "What now?"

"When will he be back?" Hollis asked Kieran.

"I can't say. He doesn't keep regular hours here. He comes and goes as he pleases with no notice at all."

"Was he in earlier today?"

"He wasn't. He hasn't been here all week."

"That's odd," Finn said.

"Is it?" The young man took a long look at Finn. "Are you a friend of Mr. Byrnes?"

"No … I was told to speak to the owner, that's all. Can you call him?"

"Ah, well. That's a difficult situation. He didn't answer his mobile earlier, so I'm waiting for him to ring back."

"We'll just look around then." Hollis grabbed Finn's arm and pulled him toward a display of books. "This doesn't make sense," she whispered.

"Shouldn't we just leave and tell David's contact what happened?"

"Not yet. Let's just take a moment."

"To do what?"

"I don't know."

She could feel adrenaline pumping through her, making her a bit queasy. But, she told herself, they'd come this far. It felt silly to just walk away. Like Finn had said about the gate at Trinity, there's a pleasure in doing something right and not just giving up on it, especially when the stakes were so high. Besides, what was the point of all of this—the trip, the arguments with Finn—if they walked away empty-handed?

Kieran stepped forward. "Mr. Byrnes has entrusted me with access to all of the valuable items of the shop. We have lovely pieces of jewelry you might like, missus, and a fine watch that just came in yesterday from an estate in Cork."

"That's very kind, but we're not looking for jewelry," Hollis said.

"Right then, my mistake. Americans usually want the smaller stuff they can bring home with them from holiday. But if you don't mind shipping, we have some nice furniture."

Hollis moved toward a large cabinet. Kieran was about to follow her, but Finn stepped in front of him.

"The Pogues," Finn pointed toward the band name on Kieran's t-shirt. "That's a bit before your time."

Kieran laughed. "It's my dad's actually. He saw them in the eighties."

"I hear they're still playing. Hard to believe McGowan is still alive."

The young man laughed. "He'll outlive us all."

While Finn and Kieran talked about Irish rock bands, Hollis wandered the shop pretending to be interested in a rolling desk top and then a large mirror. She could see toward the back that there was a door with a sign that read OFFICE. She glanced back at Finn, who was asking the kid about the best pubs to hear music. As usual, he'd found his audience's soft spot, because Kieran grabbed a pen and paper and was writing a list. Finn had moved slowly so that Kieran was facing away from the back of the store, and by the sound of it, had forgotten that Hollis was there.

Finn caught Hollis's attention. She pointed toward the office door, and he shook his head. She widened her eyes and nodded. He shrugged, then turned his attention back to Keiran. They could even argue in pantomime, but at least she'd won. She took a deep breath to calm herself. Before she could talk herself out of it, she ducked through the door, closing it lightly behind her.

———

It wasn't really an office. It was a small storeroom with a desk and a stairway, littered with boxes, that must have led to more storage above. Even the desk had items piled on top of it. Walking more than a foot in any direction was going to be a challenge. Hollis moved as quietly as she could toward the desk. The first drawer opened easily but contained only blank shipping labels and a receipt book. The other two drawers were equally unimpressive. On the other side of the desk was a small file cabinet. She tugged gently. Locked. Hollis looked around for keys, but no luck. She found a sterling silver antique letter opener with a price tag of 160 euros attached to it.

"And to think I've been opening my mail like a peasant," she whispered to herself.

When she was training at the Farm, she was taught how to pick a lock, but it had been a long time and it wasn't something she'd kept practicing, much to her currant annoyance. She tried the tip of it in the lock, but no luck. She pushed it into the edge of the file drawer and tried to force it open, but all she succeeded in doing was bending the letter opener and scratching the cabinet. Her heart was beating loudly, at least to her ears, and she tried to calm down by focusing on the task at hand. She tried again, kneeling on the floor and putting all her strength into it. This time the drawer gave way, though it creaked as it opened, and she held her breath, waiting for the clerk to discover her. "I just got carried away by all the beautiful things and wandered back here to see what else you had," she said in a whisper. She rehearsed her excuse as she worked, hoping to sound calm if she got caught.

Inside the drawer were a few letters addressed to Eamon. Two electrical bills and an invoice for some items bought at an estate sale. A fourth letter was addressed to a Siobhan Byrnes. It was unopened, but the return address was *Probation Office, Department of Justice*. Next to the letter was a small leather address book. Hollis opened it and saw that *Eamon Byrnes* had been scrawled across the inside cover. She flipped through the pages, and at first nothing seemed out of the ordinary. Then she noticed the names—DeValera, Pearse, Connolly ... One last name that matched a famous Irish rebel was a coincidence, but three? She flipped to the Bs and saw it: Behan, with what looked like a phone number.

Leaving the cabinet open rather than risk the squeaking sound again, she stood up and looked around. "Where would someone keep a forged play?"

She put the address book into the green purse and moved slowly toward the other end of the room. She could hear Finn's laugh. Thank heavens he's so charming, she thought.

There were more pieces of furniture with boxes piled on them. She twisted around to see behind a dresser and knocked a small ceramic vase over, catching it moments before it smashed into the floor.

She took a deep breath. Finn couldn't keep Kieran occupied for much longer. She felt guilty for lying to the young man, who was probably desperate to make a sale. On the way out she would buy something. Maybe she could get a discount on the bent letter opener.

As she stepped back toward the door, Hollis heard a rustle from the stairs. She stood perfectly still, waiting, but there were no more sounds from the stairs. From the front of the shop, though, she could hear new voices. Both angry, but both with Irish accents. Then suddenly the voices stopped. They'd been found out. Finn was in trouble. Her head was spinning with scenarios, one worse than the other. David's advice came back into her head. *Remember your training.*

"Stay calm," she told herself, as she reached back for the bent letter opener, the only weapon within reach.

But then she heard a familiar laugh. Finn wasn't in trouble. Whatever had happened, whatever the angry voices, it wasn't about him. She put the letter opener back on the desk.

She took one gentle step forward and saw a bulletin board crowded with notices, pictures, and cards. In one of the photos there was an older man, maybe in his sixties, in front of the shop. He was elegant-looking, with trimmed gray hair and a tailored black suit. Next to him was Kieran, equally well-dressed.

There was another picture of the man, though he was clearly fifteen or twenty years younger in it. This time he was standing in front of a cottage, with one arm around the waist of a woman and a little girl mugging for the camera. A shy boy about the same age as the little girl peeked out from behind the man's leg. They must be photos of Eamon Byrnes, Hollis thought, feeling a certain satisfaction in having put a face to the name. But it explained nothing about why he hadn't shown up at work.

"That's an amazing piece of art," Finn was saying, his voice a little loud.

Hollis made her way back toward the door, gingerly opened it, and peeked out. Kieran's head turned toward her but Finn grabbed his arm, pulling him in the other direction. "Is that a John Lavery?" he asked, pointing toward a portrait of a woman in a white shirt. "He did wonderful portraits."

"He did yeah, but that's not a Lavery. Local man did that well after Lavery's time."

"It looks just like his work."

"Ah no. If it were, it'd be worth nearly a million euros. We wouldn't hang it in the corner, I assure you."

Hollis slipped out of the office, closing the door as quietly as she could. Then she walked quickly toward the door, just as Kieran turned toward her.

"You have some lovely things," Hollis said. "That's a nice chain you have on. What's the charm?"

Kieran reached up for the chain around his neck and held it out for her to see more clearly. "It's a luck stone. If you find a stone with a hole in it, it protects you from evil. That's the story anyway. The hole is supposed to represent a passageway, so it's especially good luck on a journey."

"Perfect for us," she said. "Us, or any tourists."

"It would be yeah, but not the sort of thing we sell here. A bit down market."

"I was really taken by those earrings," she said pointing toward the jewelry display.

"Ah, grand. I knew I was right about you wanting to bring some Irish jewelry home to America. Which ones caught your eye?"

Hollis scanned the inventory and choose a pair of pearl cluster earrings with a pink sheen. "He forgot my birthday this year," she said. She knew she was talking too fast, but she couldn't help it.

"Did I?" Finn said. "I thought I'd gotten you exactly what you asked for." Finn frowned when he looked at the price tag. "On the other hand, you can't get enough presents for your wife, can you?" he added, as he handed over a stack of euros.

"I wouldn't know. I'm not married," Kieran said.

"No girlfriend?" Hollis asked. "There's no nice girl working here you can date?"

"You sound like my ma. No, the only girl who worked here was Mr. Byrnes daughter, Siobhan, and she went off to Australia after her mam died."

"How sad. No other family?"

"Lots of family. None close. Just Mr. Byrnes and me, of course, running things. I've taken on a lot of responsibility, I don't mind telling you."

Hollis took the earrings the moment Kieran had wrapped them. "I'm sure you have. I think we've taken enough of your time."

Kieran looked toward the back of the shop, but Hollis knew she'd closed the door, so everything looked the same. At least from this side of the shop. Once he walked to the back, it would be pretty obvious the file cabinet had been pried open from the scratches she'd left around the edge.

"Thanks for the list of music venues," Finn said. "I'm sure we'll hit one of these up tonight."

"Good then," Kieran said. "Enjoy your holiday."

Hollis tugged at Finn's arm until they were out the door into bright sunshine.

Sixteen

E arrings?" Finn said as soon as they left the shop.

"He probably works on commission. We did waste his time and ruin an expensive letter opener."

"What letter opener?"

"It's not important." Hollis looked around as they walked back toward Grafton Street. Just the usual crowds of tourists and locals, but no bald man or woman in a red coat. "Kieran lied. He said Eamon Byrnes comes and goes with no notice at all. But he was wearing a ratty t-shirt and jeans. I saw pictures in the back. Kieran and a man that has to be Eamon, were in front of the shop wearing very stylish suits. I'll bet he has to dress up when Eamon's at the shop. It makes sense when you see the price of the things they sell in there. They're selling an image as much as anything else. Kieran knew that Eamon wouldn't be in today, so he disregarded the dress code."

Finn stopped as they reached the corner. "I found something out too. While you were in the back, a FedEx man came in, and I thought Keiran would bite his head off. Apparently some package that was supposed to be delivered today hadn't arrived. It was from Eamon Byrnes on Druid Street, in Galway City. It was supposed to be addressed to Keiran. The delivery guy said there had been a mix-up and it had been returned to the original address. It'll be there by three tomorrow."

"Do you think it's the manuscript?" Hollis asked.

"Maybe, but that doesn't explain why Eamon isn't in Dublin."

The purse, heavy with the cash still inside it, was hurting her shoulder, so Hollis switched it to the other side. "Remember what the man was saying when we came into the shop? That someone, a he, was clear that the man should be there."

"So he was expecting Eamon too."

"Looks like it."

"Did you think the conversation between Kieran and the other man was strange?" Finn asked.

"Kieran seemed rude, pretty much the opposite of the way he was with us."

Finn grunted. "It wasn't just rude. It was weird. Kieran said it was 'beyond the pale' that Eamon wasn't there, which is an extreme way to describe his absence. If he doesn't know why Eamon isn't at the shop, he can hardly consider it completely unacceptable."

"You must remember the other meaning to the phrase," Hollis said. "In the seventeenth century, the word *pale* meant a boundary. The British who occupied Ireland used the word to describe the area around Dublin where they had control."

"They called the western part of the country 'beyond the pale' because it was, to them, an unmanageable area. And Galway's on the west coast," Finn finished her thought. "So you think Kieran was giving him some kind of clue to Eamon's whereabouts?"

"I don't know. Two strangers walked in on their conversation, maybe they went into some kind of code."

"So do you think they're protecting Eamon from TCT?"

"Maybe," Hollis said. "Or hiding him from Interpol. Maybe he sold the Behan manuscript to someone else and decided not to tell his handlers."

"Or maybe he took the manuscript and is in hiding somewhere. I'm assuming you didn't find it."

"No," she admitted, "but I found something else—an address book with an odd collection of names in it. Hopefully Interpol will find it useful."

The wind picked up, and Finn pulled his jacket tight. "Unless you memorized it, Holly, I don't know that will help."

She leaned toward him, as if sheltering herself from the wind, and whispered, "I took it."

She could practically hear Finn's jaw clench. "Of course you did." Finn took a few steps across the street. His momentary interest in the mission seemed to have passed. "We've done what was asked of us, so that's it, right? Let's go meet that agent, tell him what we know, and get this over with."

He was right. They had done what was asked and more, and it was a bit of a thrill. The only regret she had was that David would never share the outcome with her, so she'd never know if the small address book hidden in the purse would lead to their missing spy, or just be a silly distraction stolen by an overeager woman playing at intelligence-gathering. She hurried to catch up with Finn, who was taking long *I'm annoyed with you* strides, putting distance between them and forcing her to choose between sulking behind him or running to catch up.

"Sorry, miss," a man said, as his shoulder tapped against Hollis.

"It's fine," she said, but it wasn't. As he moved away from her, she felt the green purse slipping off her shoulder. Before she could stop him, it was in his hands. "Hey!"

The guy started to run. Finn turned around just as Hollis lost control of the purse. He moved toward the thief, grabbed his shirt, but the guy pulled back, slipping out of Finn's grasp. Just as he was about to get away, Hollis spun and kicked the man in the thigh, knocking him down. Five years of karate classes was money well spent. He dropped the bag and grabbed his injured limb.

"Shite!" he yelled. "Lay off."

Hollis reached down and grabbed her purse. In the scuffle one of the straps had been broken, but at least she had it back.

Finn wrapped his arms around her. "You okay?"

She nodded.

Several people stopped to help. A woman yelled, "I'm calling the guards," but the man got up and ran away before anyone could stop him. As he ran, Hollis could see he now had a limp, and that made her feel just a little proud.

Seventeen

David told them that after they left the antique shop they should go directly to Bewley's, which turned out to be a large café near their hotel. It had dark wood, exotic plants, and stained-glass windows. If not for people on their cell phones, it would have looked unchanged from when it was built in the mid-1920s.

Once they were seated, Hollis took the address book out of the purse and tucked it into the waistband of her gray jeans, then buttoned her cardigan to cover it. If anyone was going to try and steal the purse again, they would get the money, but at least they wouldn't get the book. Stealing the purse wouldn't be good either, she realized. It would mean explaining the loss of fifty thousand euros to David and his bosses at Interpol. She put the purse on her lap, with her hands on it.

Finn scanned the room. "Anyone look like an agent to you?"

Hollis looked around as discreetly as she could, trying to make it seem she was only interested in the cakes and pies of the other diners. But aside from beautiful desserts, all she could see were hungry Dubliners and tourists. "No," she admitted. "I guess we have to wait to be found."

"What should we get while we wait?" Finn asked.

"We just ate two hours ago."

"This is dessert. Besides, won't it look odd if we don't order anything? Your friend David told us to look and act like tourists."

"Will you stop saying that? He's not *my* friend David. The only reason he got in touch was because of you. And I'm still mad that you didn't tell me that you'd been approached to do this."

"I'd point out the hypocrisy of being angry that I kept a secret for seventy-two hours when you kept one for more than fifteen years..." Hollis opened her mouth to defend herself but Finn kept talking, "but I've been married to you long enough to know that somehow I'd still be in trouble."

"Then apology accepted. What are you hungry for?" She picked up the menu and scanned through.

"I'd love a drink to steady my nerves but that's probably not the best choice. My stomach is spinning."

"Really? You look so calm," Hollis said.

"I was thinking you were the one with nerves of steel. That was amazing, what you did to that guy in the street."

"Do you suppose he tried to grab the purse because he knew about the manuscript?"

"Or he saw a couple of tourists and figured we were easy prey. But in either case, keep the purse where we can see it." Finn leaned back, looking every bit an untroubled man on vacation. She envied his way of being at home wherever he was. "So, Bruce Lee, what do you want for your victory celebration?"

Hollis glanced again at the menu. "Scones. They have scones with cream and jam. And they have their own brand of tea."

As the waitress came over, Finn smiled. "Tea and scones," he told her. "Unless you would recommend something else?"

"I wouldn't," she said. "You've found my exact favorite things." She brushed his arm as she picked up the menu.

Once she'd gone, Hollis laughed. "She was flirting with you."

"Was she?"

"Right in front of me."

"Jealous?"

Hollis thought for a moment. "No. You're too smart to mess with a woman who can high kick a mugger. And besides, you've got me exactly where you've always dreamed."

"I'm pretty sure I've never dreamed about getting you into a tea shop."

"Owing you a favor."

Finn grinned widely, his annoyance with her over at least for the moment. "That is a very nice place to be."

Hollis laughed. If not for the address book pushing against her stomach and the weight of all that cash in the green purse, she could have forgotten what they were doing at Bewley's.

"Enjoying your holiday?" A man pulled up a chair and sat between Hollis and Finn. The tall, bald black man Hollis had seen at the library. Hollis tried to meet Finn's eyes. She should have told him she thought they were being followed. She really needed to learn the lesson about secrets, she told herself. But that was a problem for another day. Now the man following them was right at their table, and she hadn't even seen him until he was practically on top of them.

"Yes, we are. Thanks," Finn said.

The man smiled. "I believe you're here to meet a friend."

"Are we?" Hollis jumped in. "What's his name?"

"Eamon Byrnes."

"You're not him," she said.

The man let out a laugh. "No."

"Then who are you?" Finn asked.

The man looked at Finn, smiled slightly. "I was sent by a different friend."

"Marcus?" Finn asked. He glanced quickly at Hollis, which caused the man to turn toward her. She sat, unmoving, though she could feel her heart beating fast.

"Yeah, Marcus sent me," the man said.

His accent was different than what Hollis had been used to hearing since they'd arrived. It was slightly English, but not. Not Australian. Definitely not Irish. She couldn't place it.

"Did you meet with Eamon?" the man asked.

"No," Finn said. "Eamon wasn't there."

He turned his gaze back to Finn. "Where was he?"

"No idea."

The man seemed to be studying Finn, which, though unnerving, gave Hollis a chance to study him. He was tall, muscular without being bulky. The sort of man who stays in shape without ever stepping into a gym. And he had the attitude of someone who'd seen things. Done things. Though there was also an elegance to him as well, and it wasn't just the black suit and crisp white shirt open at the collar. It was his smile, both practiced and warm. If she hadn't noticed the gun earlier, she would have been fooled by that smile. But she had, and she wasn't.

"No rush," the man said. "I suppose you'll try again tomorrow."

"The sales clerk said that Byrnes hadn't been in all week."

"Well, that's no use, is it? Looks like you've got a problem."

"Not us," Finn said. "We did what we said we would do and now we're finished."

The man leaned forward. "I don't think you're finished, Dr. Lars-son. I think you're just getting started, and that's why you're here."

"You think?"

"Yes," the man said. "I've got a lot of theories about you and your in-terest in Mr. Byrnes."

"I'm an academic," Finn said. "I don't care much for wild speculation. So you can think what you like, but my wife and I are done with this."

The man took a long breath, showing, at least to Hollis, a remark-able lung capacity. Underneath the black suit and careful smile was a man with tremendous physical power. She had never been unnerved by an exhale before, but she was now. But what frightened her more was when he reached into his jacket, at exactly the spot Hollis had thought she'd seen a bulge of a gun's harness earlier that day.

Eighteen

The waitress came over with two small pots of tea for Finn and Hollis. "Would you like a tea or coffee?" she asked the man. "And perhaps something to eat?"

"I'm not staying." He took his hand out of his jacket.

She smiled at Finn. "Be right back with your scones."

"I don't mean to be rude, Mr. ...." Finn poured his tea. Hollis was shocked by how steady his hands were. Under the table, hers were shaking.

"Peter Moodley. And you are Finn and Hollis Larsson. So now that we know each other's names, no reason we can't all be great friends. Which is what I want, honestly. It's the way we can help each other." He looked over at Hollis's green purse on her lap. "That's a shame." He picked up the bag by the broken handle before she could stop him. "How did that happen?"

"I got it caught in something and pulled a little too hard," Hollis said. She reached for the bag, but Peter moved it just out of her grasp and dropped it on the floor between their chairs. As he did, he opened it.

"I'm so sorry," he said. He reached in and grabbed the brochures and put them on the table along with her wallet, sunglasses, and a Dublin guidebook. He left the money in the bag and handed it to Hollis with a slight smile. She put the purse back on her lap, pressed against the address book hidden under her cardigan, but holding it tighter this time. She looked over at Finn, who shook his head. There was nothing to be done except wait to see what this man's game was.

Peter opened the wallet first, reading her license, checking through her credit cards, and even pulling out her university parking card. Nothing was left untouched. He lifted the sunglasses, but only to move them aside and leave room to spread the brochures across the table. "Guinness Storehouse, National Gallery, Killmainham Gaol, the Abbey Theatre. You're covering your bases, aren't you?"

"We're trying to see everything. We're only here for a short time," Finn said.

As the man looked at Finn, his eyes narrowed. "Very short," he said. "You almost make it seem like you're here to enjoy a romantic weekend in Dublin."

"We are," Hollis said.

He turned his head to her. "Good to get some fun in before Finn has to teach summer classes."

Hollis shuddered but said nothing. She wasn't going to indulge his efforts at torturing them with how much he knew, and how little they did.

Peter picked up the Abbey Theatre brochure. "You're going here tonight?"

"I don't know," Finn answered. "We haven't decided what our plans are."

"I'll bet. A fun weekend will be much easier to accomplish if you give me the names of everyone involved."

"Everyone involved in our weekend?" Finn asked.

"Don't play dumb, Finn. A man of your credentials can hardly get away with it."

Finn looked spooked. He needed a moment to think, Hollis knew. "Can you stop speaking in riddles?" Hollis asked. He was trying to intimidate, so she decided a display of confidence would even the playing field. "I'm pretty good at puzzles, but I can't understand what it is you're trying to imply."

His head snapped to her side of the table, his smile gone. "Then let me be clear. There are five people involved in a multimillion-dollar forgery. We know the identity of one of them. And we further know that a second person is someone who has authenticated the forgery as the real thing. Someone with impeccable credentials. Someone who might be looking to supplement his teaching income with a one-fifth share of a hundred and twenty-five million dollars. Someone who might be willing to pay a lot of money to see what the Behan play contains by way of information."

"That someone isn't me," Finn said.

"Isn't it?" Peter lowered his voice almost to a whisper, but one that still carried the force of a shout. "If you tell me where the agent is, I might be able to help you."

"How would I know?" Finn looked to Hollis, who felt her head was swimming. She noticed that Peter had never said he was with Interpol. The *we* in his story could just as easily be TCT. Either way, it was clear Peter Moodley saw himself on the opposing side of Finn and Hollis's mission.

Hollis took some strength from the fact that they were in a crowded tea room where it was unlikely Peter would want to make a scene. "Well, thank you for the information, Mr. Moodley," she said. "Whatever it is you think we're here for, right now we're just trying to enjoy a cup of tea. Tea time is a pretty sacred thing in Ireland, from what I've read. So while I hope you don't think I'm being rude, can I suggest you let us have this time in peace? If you like, I can ask the waitress to find you a table of your own." As she spoke Hollis looked around the room for someone on staff.

Peter seemed amused. "You enjoy the play tonight. It's a new playwright from Cavan. It's a comedy, supposed to be good." He got up as the waitress arrived with the scones.

"We're both a bit tired," Hollis said. "We probably won't go to any plays."

"Don't lie to me Mrs. Larsson..."

"Dr. Larsson," she corrected him. She always corrected people for that, out of habit, but regretted it this time. He probably wasn't up for a lesson in gender politics.

He leaned down and whispered in her ear. "There's a saying in Ireland, Dr. Larsson. 'God between us and all harm.' At the moment, God is unavailable and I'm the only one here." He buttoned his suit coat as he looked around, then he walked past the tables of hungry Dubliners, and out of the restaurant.

"What was that?" Finn asked after a moment.

"I'm not sure. He was either warning us, or threatening us." She took a deep breath, relieved that he was gone, at least for now. "Who's Marcus?"

"A kid I knew growing up. A bully. It was the first name that popped in my head. I wanted to see if he was expecting me to say David. And obviously he wasn't."

"No, he's definitely not our contact. He would know we're working with Interpol," Hollis said. "My instincts were right."

"What instincts?"

She told Finn about seeing the man before at Trinity and at the pub, along with the dark-haired woman in the red coat.

"If he was with Interpol, he'd have known we were trying to help find the agent. He must be one of the TCT gang," he said, "or group … or however Internet thieves classify themselves. Maybe Peter Moodley is from their South African branch."

"That's the accent! I couldn't place it." She looked around quickly, then went into her waistband for the address book, keeping it on her lap as she flipped through the pages. "There's an entry for Alan Paton. Do you suppose that's code for our bald friend?"

"A South African writer for a South African spy? Maybe. But we don't know if those names connect to agents, thieves, or buyers. Or if they mean anything at all. Maybe Eamon Byrnes liked to write down the names of famous people."

She wasn't going to argue. The address book mattered. Probably. "But if he is TCT, wouldn't he know you weren't working with them?"

"Remember what David said, that it was a loose collection of people who'd probably never met? And what's with the hundred-and-twenty-five-million-dollar forgery? What does that have to do with anything?"

"I don't know." She slathered jam and clotted cream onto her scone and took a bite. The combination of hearty pastry with indulgent cream momentarily soothed her nerves. And in that one calm second she remembered something. "Francis Bacon was an Irish painter, wasn't he? Didn't you mention a painting of his that sold for a lot of money recently?"

Finn began preparing a scone for himself. "That's the chatter among some museum friends of mine. It's one of those paintings that no one ever sees because it goes from one private collector to another. Shame really, because it belongs in a museum. It sold for a hundred and twenty-five …" He let out a gasp. "It's a forgery?"

"The missing agent must have known that. He must have put information in the Behan manuscript that could identify some of the players involved, like the authenticator."

"So my walking into Eamon's shop makes it look like I'm trying to retrieve information that could incriminate me," Finn said, dropping his scone. "Remind me to kill your old boyfriend."

"This is one of the rare occasions I don't think you'll need reminding," she said. "What do we do now?"

"We could spend the evening at the hotel, or we could see what that was all about and go to the play. Or if you want, we could just hightail it to the airport."

They were in deeper than either of them had anticipated, and nearly every part of her wanted to keep going to see where it all lead. But this wasn't a game. People were missing, and strangers were issuing vague threats. She and Finn weren't safe. "We should probably get the next plane home and turn this book over to David. He'll straighten out the confusion about why we went to Eamon's shop."

Finn frowned. "I wasn't expecting you to say that."

"You want to stay?"

"We have spent our whole adult lives building reputations as academics, and as experts in our field. You know how much gossip there is in our world. That's how I found out about the sale of the painting. If there are rumors that my integrity has a price, that I'm involved … that we're involved … in some criminal organization, then we're done. And honestly, I don't trust David to get us out of this, because he's the one who got us into it in the first place."

She was glad to see that they were on the same page about pursuing answers, but it was also slightly unnerving. Finn had the same look in his eye as when he talked about John Wayne last winter, or archery three years before.

Nineteen

They were fascinating, he'd decided. The way she'd taken the mugger down. The way they'd handled themselves at the tea shop. They could be spies. They could be criminals. It was often hard to know the difference. Americans were fond of seeing people as white hats and black ones—good guys and bad. Their confidence in their own judgement sometimes robbed them of the ability to discern the subtle differences between the two.

But these Midwestern college professors were different. Just in following them around, he'd grown to like them. Almost wish them well. Too bad, he thought. Odds were they wouldn't live to catch their plane home.

Twenty

No luck," Hollis said when voicemail picked up at David's office at the Justice Department. She hung up. There was no sense leaving another message. She'd already done that on his cell phone, twice.

"First the agent, then Eamon. And now a third man's gone missing," Finn said. "It's getting kind of monotonous."

"A fourth man if you count our Interpol contact."

"I wonder if someone was there and saw Moodley and just didn't want to blow his cover."

"So he left us to sit there, exposed?"

Finn shrugged. "Or maybe something held him up."

Hollis didn't want to think about what that could be. "Are we really going to go to the theater tonight?"

"I guess, if you're sure that's what you want to do."

"That man, Peter Moodley. It's not like he told us we *had* to go to the play. It was more like he assumed we were going."

"Maybe Eamon Byrnes will be there."

She knew this game that she and Finn were playing. Each one leaving room for the other to back out. Their first conversational game of chicken was when the wedding plans had gotten out of control. Each said they didn't need a big wedding, in case the other would take the bait and suggest elopement, but without making the kind of definitive statement that could lead to one person feeling forced into doing something they disliked. In the end, their little game had been outplayed by their mothers, who had, without asking, invited dozens of people neither Finn nor Hollis knew.

That hadn't stopped them from playing chicken, though. Instead they'd refined it over the years, learned to read each other better, finding that it was still the best way to have plausible deniability if something went wrong—the *I did it because I thought you wanted to* escape hatch.

She also saw they were each fighting a battle of curiosity verses caution. A desire to *know* was innate in every academic, though usually that knowledge didn't mean risking one's life. Still, they couldn't just sit in the room, and she saw that Finn was looking for an excuse to let curiosity win this round.

"I do know what Eamon Byrnes looks like," Hollis said. "At least I think that was him in the photo I saw at the shop."

"If we see him, we can report back to David that he was in Dublin and avoiding us. And if we don't see him, we can always leave at intermission and spend the rest of our weekend as planned."

"And we'll be in a crowd of people," Hollis assured herself as much as Finn. "It'll be safe."

"But we're not going to *do* anything," he said. "We're just going to observe and see if we're approached."

"Unless Eamon is there."

Finn considered it. "Maybe." He paused for a moment. "I feel like Michael Collins signing the peace treaty with England in 1921."

"You may have signed your own death warrant," she said, paraphrasing the famous words of a soldier and politician, whose negotiations for Irish freedom resulted in civil war and his own death in less than a year. "Let's hope you're not as prescient as he was."

"Let's do more than hope. Let's be careful." As he talked, Finn was getting his jacket. When he put it on, he stuffed his hands into his pockets. Then he paused and pulled out a small metal object. He held it in his open hand, staring.

It was a bullet.

He dropped it onto the desk and they both watched it roll harmlessly to a stop. "It's a warning. Someone got close enough to slip this in my pocket without my noticing. So they're close enough to do anything they want."

"Why threaten us?" she asked. "What do we know?"

"A lot less than people think we know, clearly."

Hollis picked up the bullet, examining it closely. "Well, we know it's an unfired nine-millimeter."

Finn let out a long breath. "Of course you know the caliber. Did you remember that from your days at the … what do they call that place where they train spies?"

"They train agents. And it's nicknamed the Farm."

"So do you remember how to identify calibers from the days when you were there, or have you been studying such things behind my back all these years?"

His annoyance sparked her own. "If you read about medieval poetry, I don't think of it as something you did behind my back."

"Because I tell you." He paused. "In excruciating detail."

She smiled at that truth. "I've read about it since my training. Not behind your back; I just thoughtfully spared you from learning all about calibers. You're welcome." She turned back to the bullet. "Do you think it could have been Peter Moodley? I know he was carrying a gun, at least I think he was, but I never saw what it was."

"He doesn't seem the subtle type." Finn sat on the bed and took a deep breath. "Besides, the bullet is an anonymous threat. His was right out in the open."

Hollis sat on the bed next to Finn, putting her hand in his. For a moment they were silent, letting the weight of the threat sink in. She found that, along with fear, she was a little angry—with herself, with David, and with whoever had put the bullet in Finn's pocket. There was something cowardly about the anonymity of it, she decided. Not that she was looking for a confrontation. "If we can figure out when it got there …"

"I think that's the first time I put my hand in my pocket all day."

It could have been anyone, she realized. Peter Moodley, the woman in the red coat who brushed against him at Trinity Library, the older man at the shop, Keiran, or anyone on crowded Grafton Street. "Do we stay here?"

"Are we safer in this room? Didn't you point out earlier that at least some people know where we're staying?"

"And we haven't exactly been hiding it. We've walked in and out of the front door of the hotel several times. We're registered under our own names." She sighed. "If we can't reach David, I don't know what to do."

Finn got up. "We don't need David to tell us what to do. The Abbey Theatre is a crowded place, and we have a plan. You still want to go?"

He was back to the *you first* game. Hollis followed him out the door. She had the feeling that what they were doing was either going to turn out to be incredibly exciting or very, very stupid. And if it was the latter, she wasn't sure that this time *I thought you wanted to* was going to be all it took to make things right again.

Twenty-One

They walked from their hotel to the theater trying to make sense of the day's events. Hollis thought they should take a taxi, but Finn was determined to see if they would be followed. He kept telling her he was irritated she hadn't told him earlier about Peter Moodley or the woman, but Hollis felt he was more upset that he hadn't seen either of them himself.

But this time, as far as either could tell, there was no one on their tail.

Dublin sparkled at night. There was laughter and the faint sounds of music leaking out from the pubs. People wandered the streets when Finn and Hollis were near the Temple Bar area, but things got quieter as they approached the river. If not for her fear about what might happen, Hollis thought it would have been fun to wander the city after dark. Finn must have felt the same way because as they crossed a bridge over the River Liffey, he stopped and kissed her.

"What was that for?"

"James Bond always gets lots of action," he said.

"You'll get plenty of action tonight, I promise—assuming we're not going to our deaths."

He kissed her again then pushed back a stray hair, using that as an excuse to lean in to her ear. "I forgot to ask what you did with the money and address book," he whispered.

"Room safe at the hotel," she said, as she nibbled on his neck.

He pulled back as two girls passed them, giggling. "We don't get separated tonight for any reason. Deal?"

She nodded. She had no intention of going anywhere without Finn.

———

The Abbey Theatre was surprisingly modern to Hollis. Large glass windows with stone pillars framed the two-story building. She knew the theater company that was housed in it had been founded more than a hundred years before by a group that included W.B. Yeats, and had showcased the talents of many of Ireland's best playwrights from J.M. Synge to George Bernard Shaw. She'd imagined a building that was steeped in history. But like so much of what she'd seen of the country so far, the theater seemed designed to look toward the future even as it honored the past.

Once they purchased the tickets, Hollis and Finn went upstairs to the bar. As they scanned the crowd, Hollis tried to steady her nerves. Why are we here? What are we looking for? She kept asking herself questions, but she couldn't imagine the answers.

The upstairs bar was intimate, with wood paneling and a long marble bar packed with young men and women in jeans, mixed with older couples in suits and cocktail dresses. What they had in common looked to be excitement at the premiere of a new play.

"I was out with Jimmy last night," a young man was saying to a girl as Hollis walked passed. "He was langered. I almost left him at the pub. Save myself, you know …"

"Ya should have," the girl said.

"Ah now, he's a good craic when he's had a few."

The young man laughed as his girlfriend rolled her eyes. Couples everywhere are the same, she thought, even if the words they use don't always translate across oceans. Divided by a common language, Hollis thought. She made her way to the bar with Finn at her back.

"What's a good white wine?" Hollis asked the bartender. He said something, but she couldn't quite make it out. "That'll be great. We'll have two."

Finn smiled. "You have no idea what you just ordered."

"None."

"Why is yes always your default answer?"

"You've benefitted." She kissed his cheek, but as she did, she scanned the crowd. No Eamon Byrnes. "I wonder what's going to happen tonight."

"I don't know. But I was thinking, if we had picked up the manuscript and given it to David's contact, maybe the next step was for him to hand it to someone who would be here tonight."

"In exchange for the missing agent?"

"Or money, or something."

"Makes sense. So we're on the lookout for anyone we recognize," Hollis said. The bartender put two glasses in front of them. They each took a sip, trying their best to look like casual theater goers instead of out-of-their-element amateur spies. Hollis smiled as she tasted the wine. "Delicious."

"Yes."

"See? Not knowing what you're getting is sometimes half the fun."

"It's the other half that worries me."

Hollis turned toward the other side of the room. No Eamon Byrnes there either. But someone else did catch her eye. "That's interesting."

Finn moved to see where Hollis was looking. "What?"

"There's a man over there," she nodded toward the window. "By himself. Gray hair, trench coat, drinking a whiskey."

"I see him. Is that Eamon?"

"No, but don't you recognize him? It's the man who was in the antique shop when we walked in."

"You sure?"

"He smiled at me. I remember he had kind eyes." She thought for a moment, then made up her mind. "I think I should talk to him."

"No."

"We can't just sit here."

"That is exactly what you promised me we would do."

He was right, and she hated it. "Maybe we wait for a while and see if he comes to us."

"Maybe." He wasn't really listening, she could tell. Finn was staring at the man in the trench coat, who, if he was waiting for someone, seemed unconcerned about it. He was looking down at the cover of his program, taking occasional sips from his whiskey. Finn gulped his wine and took a deep breath. "Here goes."

"I thought we were just going to observe unless—" Finn was halfway across the room before Hollis had a chance to finish her sentence, so she grabbed her wineglass and followed him.

"Hey," Finn was saying as she caught up. "You look familiar."

"Do I?" the man said.

"The antique shop this afternoon," Hollis chimed in, trying to sound like she'd just figured it out.

The man looked at her and smiled. "I remember you. You're Americans?"

"Yes, on holiday." Finn held out his hand. "Finn Larsson. This is my wife, Hollis."

"Liam Tierney." He shook Finn's hand, and then took Hollis's hand in his. Instead of shaking it, though, he held it for a moment before releasing it back to her. Hollis put him at about sixty, with the deepest blue eyes she'd ever seen, framed by tanned laugh lines. His face wasn't movie-star handsome, but he had a presence about him. He struck her as a man used to being instantly liked.

"Are you on vacation too?" Hollis asked.

"No, Dublin born and bred," Liam said. "I'm a dealer, mostly estate sales and the like. Sometimes I bring things to Byrnes Antiques if I think that's the right market for them in one of his shops."

"*One* of his shops?"

"Yes, the original is in Galway. This one was opened as a kind of gift to his daughter, but it didn't work out." He bit the edge of his lip. "Did you find anything that interested you at the shop?"

Hollis tucked her hair behind her ear and cupped her earlobe to show off the pearl cluster earrings they'd bought that afternoon. "Just these."

The man leaned in. "They're lovely. It's always nice to have a unique souvenir, I think, rather than some cheap mug or shamrock hat. Did Eamon help you find those?"

Hollis did her best to seem confused. "I thought the store manager's name was Kieran."

"He is. But I heard your husband ask for Eamon as I walked out."

They both turned to Finn. Once again, Hollis was impressed with how calm he seemed. "I'll let you in on a secret," he said. "I'm a professor of literature in the States and I came to Dublin because there's a rumor that there's a newly discovered play from Brendan Behan."

"I heard something about that. Lots of interest in it," Liam said. "Was it the real thing?"

"We didn't get to see it," Hollis told the man. "Any chance Eamon showed you?"

Liam shook his head. "Out of my league, I'm afraid. It was a bit of a frustration. Eamon and I grew up together, but he was determined to keep it close to the vest. How did you get wind of it?"

"A contact in the States," Finn answered, but Hollis could see he was struggling a bit.

"A collector," Hollis jumped in. "A tech billionaire. Finn's done some work for him before, authenticating manuscripts. How did you hear?"

"Word gets out."

"Eamon didn't tell you himself? Since you're old friends..." Hollis said.

"Yes, he did. But I was supposed to keep it between us." Liam glanced around the room. "If you see it, I hope you'll let me take a peek. Just as a fellow lover of Irish literature." He reached into his pocket and handed Finn a card. He left his hand out as if expecting something in return, so Finn reached into his wallet and handed the man one of his cards from Bradford University. Liam glanced at it and frowned before pocketing it.

"I've chased these kinds of alleged finds before," Finn said. "It's possible the manuscript doesn't exist at all."

"The joys and tragedies of the antiques business." Liam set down his whiskey glass. "I suppose I should look for my seat. Lovely to meet you both. Finn..."

"Larsson."

He patted Finn's arm, nodded toward Hollis, and walked away, disappearing in the crowd before they could see where he went.

Hollis immediately turned to Finn. "Why did you go over to him?"

"You took down a mugger. I just wanted to contribute."

"You were pretty smooth," she said. "I was surprised you told him we were here about the manuscript."

"If he is involved, then he already knows. If I lied, it would have been more suspicious. By telling the truth, I look like I've got nothing to hide."

She thought about it a moment. With a mix of both admiration and jealousy, she had to admit his instincts were dead-on. "So I guess we see the play and keep our eyes open," she said. "What is the play?"

Finn nodded toward a poster in the corner. "It's about the disappearance of a just-married woman, and her family's fight to get her back."

"Sounds sad."

"The review on the poster calls it a 'comedic send-up of all the Irish hold dear.'"

The lights dimmed briefly. Around them people started moving toward the bar's exit.

Hollis grimaced. "There's no intermission. No chance to leave in the middle of things."

"No chance for anyone else to leave either, I guess."

She raised her eyebrow. "You know my bladder. I won't make it through the whole play."

"What happened to not getting separated?"

Several twenty-something women passed by, headed in the direction of the bathroom. Hollis nodded toward them. "Safety in numbers. Go to the seats. If we're each with a crowd, we'll be okay."

Twenty-Two

As the crowd moved toward the theater, Hollis went the other direction, following signs for the toilet. Down one flight and to the back she found what she was looking for.

The women she thought had also been looking for one last chance at the bathroom had actually stepped outside for a final preshow cigarette. The difference between being twenty and forty, Hollis thought.

As she entered the stall, the house lights blinked a second time.

"Don't rush me," she muttered.

Until now she'd never noticed how vulnerable a person was with her panties around her knees. And it wasn't just her that was vulnerable. Even though she knew Finn would be surrounded by other theater goers, she was nervous about leaving him. Peter Moodley had wanted them at the theater. Liam Tierney now knew their names. Maybe nothing would happen, but if it did, she wanted to be with Finn. Not alone in the ladies' room.

As she exited the stall, though, she realized she wasn't alone. There was a woman at the sink staring into the mirror. Not washing her hands or applying lipstick. Just staring. And it was someone Hollis recognized. The woman with the dark hair from Trinity Library.

She almost froze in place, but somewhere in the back of her mind, Hollis remembered something from a CIA training course: keep moving. Keeping the body moving, even a little, during a potentially dangerous situation, allows the brain to adapt to the stress. Stand still and it's that much harder to react if things get deadly.

Hollis walked to the sink, washed her hands, and glanced into the mirror as if she were checking her makeup. In the reflection, she could see the woman standing just steps from the door. There was no point in pretending she could get past her, so she decided to take Finn's approach and admit as much as seemed safe. As casually as she could, Hollis looked over at the other woman. "I didn't realize Dublin was such a small city."

"Excuse me?" the woman said in an American accent.

"This is the third time I've seen you today."

The woman smiled. "You're very observant."

"It's not hard when someone is following me."

Her smile widened. She put out her hand. "Lydia Dempsey."

Hollis had one eye on the exit. With the toilets tucked away from the lobby and everyone already seated for the play, she wondered if a scream would bring help. She hoped she wouldn't need to find out. She shook the woman's hand and noticed the strong grip. "Hollis Larsson. But you probably knew that."

"Probably," Lydia said. "Though I lost track of you for a while. Where were you this afternoon?"

"Playing tourist with my husband. How about you? Did you get much sightseeing in when you weren't tracking us?"

"Actually no. I was supposed to meet an American couple at Bewley's this afternoon, but I got slightly delayed. When I arrived, they were gone."

Hollis blinked several times, trying to take it all in. She wasn't going to say anything more, she decided quickly, until she talked to Finn. "How unfortunate," Hollis said. "I hope you tried the scones. They're amazing."

Lydia dropped her smile. "I want the manuscript."

Hollis was steps from the door, but Lydia was between her and the only exit. "Did Marcus send you?" Hollis asked her. If it worked to determine Peter Moodley wasn't the contact, maybe it would also prove Lydia Dempsey was.

But all Lydia did was stare at her. Then finally she said, "No."

"Who then?"

Lydia moved closer. "I want the manuscript."

Hollis tried to move past her, but Lydia was quicker than she was. "Please excuse me, I don't want to miss act one."

Lydia grabbed Hollis's arm. "You need to listen to me, Dr. Larsson."

It was a dumb thought, but it popped in Hollis's mind that she was glad she'd gone to the bathroom because otherwise she'd probably have peed right then. "I don't have any manuscript."

"I don't believe you."

"Search my purse," Hollis said. "Search my hotel room. We don't have it. We never did. Odds are it doesn't exist."

"It exists. And if you tell me where it is now, I can help you. By Monday it will be too late."

"What happens Monday?"

"Don't play the innocent. We both know the trouble you and your husband are in."

"You must be in trouble too, or else you wouldn't be stalking Finn and me. You would have been there instead of hiding from Peter Moodley."

It had just slipped out, but it must have hit a nerve. Lydia's neck went just so slightly pink.

"I could kill you here," she said.

"But you won't. Because maybe we do have the manuscript, or know where it is. And if you think killing me will scare Finn into helping you, then you don't know us. You don't know how much we love each other."

For a moment they stood there staring at each other. Hollis was taller than the other woman by at least half a foot, but it didn't seem to give her much advantage. She widened her stance slightly and turned a little to her side, making herself harder to knock over. It was amazing what was coming back to her after all these years.

From outside the toilet, Hollis heard the giggling of the twenty-something women who must have finished their cigarettes and returned to the theater. Hollis reached past Lydia, grabbed for the handle, and swung the door wide, making as much noise as possible in the process.

Once outside the ladies' room, she took a deep breath, swore on a whisper, and headed as quickly as she could to Finn.

Twenty-Three

The play had started. Finn was ten rows back, just a few seats from the aisle, but Hollis still had to step over an elderly couple to get to him. Once in her seat she whispered in his ear about her encounter with Lydia, and in the process she was shushed by a woman seated behind her.

Finn whispered back, "So is she Interpol?"

"If she was, why act so threatening? There was something odd about it."

"Then who is she?"

Hollis shrugged.

On stage two women were yelling at each other. One screamed, "There is no God," and the other actress slapped her.

"I thought this was a comedy?" Finn whispered.

"Sssh," said the woman behind them.

"We have to sit here now, don't we?" Hollis whispered, trying to keep her voice as low as possible by putting her mouth on Finn's ear. That got her a disapproving look from the "ssh" lady.

"I think so. If we get up now, we're just drawing attention to ourselves and walking into an empty lobby."

The woman behind them leaned down. "Sssssshhh," she said in a voice that was louder than anything Hollis and Finn had said. So loud, the actresses on stage stopped and looked into the audience for a moment.

Hollis held back a laugh. We stay, she thought, and then duck out as quickly as possible as soon as this is over. At least they were safe in a crowded theater.

She had been so looking forward to a long weekend in Ireland, but now she was going to suggest that they get the next plane home. If Peter and Lydia were two TCT thieves, or rivals of the group, or rogue agents … or whoever they were, Ireland wasn't safe. She and Finn would keep trying David. If they had no luck, she would need to reach him from home. She still had the address book to turn over, and maybe that would turn out to be something. If there really was a possibility that Finn had been mistaken for a member of a criminal underground, they had a better chance of explaining themselves at home, where every turn they made didn't put them in harm's way.

She looked over at her husband, who was watching the audience as much as the play. He was the only problem with her new plan. Peter had gotten under his skin and now, just days after talking him into coming to Ireland, she'd have an equally difficult task in talking him into leaving.

On stage, the actress who'd been slapped launched into a speech about her affair with the Taoiseach, the Irish prime minister. The audience roared with laughter, but the references meant nothing to Hollis.

Maybe if she could concentrate she would enjoy it as much as the rest of the theater was obviously doing. But as the minutes ticked slowly by, she was both dreading and desperate for the end of the play. If they stayed with the crowd, she wondered, could they get out unnoticed? Could they get back to their hotel without being followed? It was foolish, she guessed, to think that the Lydia woman, or Peter Moodley, didn't know where they were staying. If one of them was Interpol, maybe she and Finn were safe. But what if neither of them were?

She pulled her cell phone out of her purse, hoping for a missed call, or maybe a text. Something from David that would let them know that everything would soon be okay. But there was nothing. Finn saw what she was doing and took her hand. Whatever was going on, at least they were together, she thought.

Hollis scanned the crowd. She realized that in her rush to tell Finn about the events in the ladies' room, she missed something just as important. Even in the darkened theater she recognized the gray hair and the trench coat. Liam Tierney was sitting directly in front of them.

Hollis sat frozen, watching Liam. He didn't seem to be any more interested in the play than she was. But he wasn't looking at the audience either. The more she watched, the more it seemed as if he had fallen asleep. His head was slightly slouched to the right.

She nudged Finn and pointed toward him. "There's something on his collar," she said.

Finn dropped his program on the floor and bent down to pick it up, resting his hand on the back of Liam's chair. He didn't look back, didn't react at all. So Finn inched his hand over to the shirt. And as soon as Finn's hand touched the collar, instead of turning to see who was touching him, Liam tipped onto the lap of a woman next to him. For just a moment she seemed confused, then she gave the man a little shove. And then she screamed.

Twenty-Four

The actors stopped what they were doing and looked down at the audience. The woman had jumped from her seat and was pointing toward a lifeless Liam Tierney. The houselights came up and one of the ushers walked over to the row and tapped on Liam's hand. "Sir. Sir. Are you alright?"

There was no response. The usher walked away and a manager came over. He also tapped Liam and called him sir. Then he whispered to the usher. A minute later an announcement was made that a man had had a heart attack, and help was on the way. The play, the announcer said, was cancelled for the evening, and those looking for a refund or exchange for another night would be helped in the lobby.

The actors went off stage and the audience either rushed closer to see what was happening, or made for the exits.

Hollis and Finn stayed in their row, where they had a pretty good view of the back of the man's head, now lying against an empty seat.

"Are you sure he's dead?" Finn asked someone. No one answered, so Finn jumped over the seats, and checked his pulse. "I'm a doctor," he explained.

Hollis bit her lip. He was a doctor twice over, technically. He'd gotten a doctorate in literature and another in art history—neither of which had so much as a first-aid class included in the curriculum.

The few audience members still standing around waited for Finn to talk. "He's gone, I'm afraid." He bent over and examined his collar more clearly. Hollis noticed what had caught his attention—small drops of blood on Liam's collar. It hardly seemed worth Finn's attention, but Finn was staring at them. There was something to it, she knew, and it had to do with why Liam was dead. While she waited, Hollis tried not to panic. If it wasn't a heart attack, then it was something else, something she didn't even want to think about.

More people left the theater. Someone said that they'd opened the bar for anyone who needed a stiff one. Someone else joked that the gray-haired man had taken the idea of "a stiff one" to ridiculous lengths, and was scolded by an older woman for speaking ill of the dead. The woman Liam had fallen on was standing in the aisle, staring down at the body, so Hollis got up and walked over to her.

"Did you know him?" Hollis said to the woman.

"He wasn't with us."

"Who was he with?"

"I don't know," she said, still staring at a dead Liam Tierney. "The seat on the other side of him was empty. I thought he was waiting for his friend, but I guess the man changed his mind."

"What friend?"

"He was talking to a man in the lobby just before we walked in. I saw him, but he didn't come into the theater with …" She made a sign of the cross and started to cry.

Hollis stepped between the woman and Liam's body, almost stepping on Finn's hand as he continued his pretense of being a physician. He was now carefully examining Liam's face. "What did the man look like?" Hollis asked the woman.

"He was black. A tall man with no hair. … I don't know anything else."

That was all Hollis was going to get. The woman started to cry again. Hollis briefly considered that the tears were just a cover-up and the woman was really the killer, but the angle was all wrong. The drops of blood were on the left side of the man's neck, and the woman had been sitting on his right.

The woman's date took her hand and she fell into his arms. As they left the theater, two Garda and several paramedics walked in. Finn moved back from the body and joined Hollis at their seats.

"It wasn't a heart attack. Did you see the blood?"

"Too small for a knife wound," she said.

"He wasn't stabbed, not that I could see. But the blood was coming from mid-neck."

Hollis looked around the quickly emptying theater. For a moment things looked hopeful, but then there she was—the woman who said her name was Lydia Dempsey. She was standing a few feet from them, right next to the exit. "Let's just go." Hollis grabbed Finn's hand and started walking toward the other side of the theater and another exit door.

In only a few feet they could be out of the theater and closer to being safe. But just as they passed the curtains leading to the exit, they heard a voice. "Quite an unexpected development."

"Mr. Moodley," Finn said, as he stepped between Hollis and the man.

"You should probably call me Peter. It's friendlier. And you're going to need a friend, given the trouble you two seem to get up to."

"We didn't have anything to do with this," Hollis said.

"You just happened to sit right behind a dead man?"

"And you just happened to be talking to him right before he sat down?"

Peter held his hands up in a mock surrender. "Maybe we should go somewhere quiet and have a chat about all of this. Before someone else gets killed."

Hollis grabbed Finn's arm, tugging him back toward the crowd. They were back in the theater, with the police a comfortable few yards away. Hollis saw Peter stop at the curtain.

They walked as quickly as they could toward the other exit. Lydia Dempsey was gone, and the police were starting to take statements. "We're not getting messed up in this any further," Finn said, and he moved toward the exit before police had a chance to speak to them.

Out in the lobby the crowd was thinning. Hollis held Finn's hand while she looked around. No Lydia, no Peter. Out on the street, three women in their sixties were talking excitedly about the events, offering theories about the death between rounds of, "Poor man, may he rest in peace." Among the group was the woman who had been shushing them earlier. A taxi pulled up, and the shushing woman opened the door.

"We'll go home now and put the kettle on," she said to the others.

But before she could get in, Finn walked past them, pushing Hollis into the cab. "Sorry, ladies. We're in a hurry," he said.

Hollis heard her say, "Americans!" as the taxi drove off.

Twenty-Five

He felt a little guilty about just walking out of the theater and leaving the mess behind him, but there was little choice in it. The Americans had certainly put themselves in the middle of it. The good news was that it was clear now what—or who—he was up against. Sides were forming. It was always good when enemies came into focus.

The bad news was, well, the rest of it. Death was hard no matter how it happened. When it happened the way it had tonight, it was especially tough. But that was, he hoped, as difficult as the road would get for him.

Finn and Hollis—he had taken to thinking of them by their first names—had handled themselves as well as could be expected under the circumstances.

"More's the pity," he mumbled as he walked into the cool night air and drew his coat close to shelter himself from the rain.

Twenty-Six

Every person they passed—in the street, in the lobby of the hotel, and especially in the hallway leading to their room—made them jump. At the door of the room, Finn told Hollis to stand back and let him go in first, just in case.

"Why should I stand back? I'm the one with the black belt," she protested.

"Fat lot of good that will do you against a man with a gun."

"But your knowledge of Yeats will protect us?"

Finn glared at her.

"Okay," she said, "I'm standing back." And to prove her point, she moved toward the door across the hall and let Finn go in to the room alone. But it was annoying. It was all well and good for Finn to want to be the protector, it was even sweet, but she was the one with CIA training. Maybe it was twenty years old, but she'd kept herself ready, and she'd proved it that afternoon when she knocked down the mugger. And more than that, this was her fault. They wouldn't be in Ireland if she hadn't insisted.

If someone was going to get shot, it should be her.

But there wasn't a gunman waiting. Finn came out after a minute with an, "All clear."

"At least something has gone right," he muttered. As soon as she walked into the room, he locked and dead bolted the door behind her.

Hollis kicked off her shoes. "It will feel so good to stop looking over my shoulder for a while."

"The next time I say let's go to Chicago and watch a doubleheader," he said, "we do it. Now let's call your boyfriend and ask him what the hell we should do now."

"You win the *I told you so* game, if that makes you happy."

"Nothing about this makes me happy."

"And you know something, I'm really getting tired of you throwing my very brief relationship with David in my face."

Finn grabbed the room phone. "Call him."

"I can't."

"Why not?"

"I was thinking, what if the phone is bugged?"

"Fantastic." Finn dropped the phone back into its stand and instead opened the minibar. He grabbed a tiny bottle of Powers Whiskey, a Carlsburg, and a small can of mixed nuts.

"What are you doing?"

"Interpol is paying for the room, aren't they? I might as well get some compensation for my trouble." He stretched out on the bed, grabbed the remote, and flipped on the flat screen.

"You're right."

"Of course I'm right. We never should have gone on this nutty mid-life crisis adventure of yours."

"I meant about having a drink. But thanks for the insult. This afternoon you were having fun."

"This afternoon nobody was dead."

Hollis looked around. Everything seemed untouched from when they'd left. She'd half expected the place to have been ransacked. It was a relief that it wasn't, but it was also unnerving. If the others thought she and Finn had the manuscript, why not look in the room? She'd all but dared Lydia Dempsey to do it. So why hadn't she? Even if she or Peter Moodley weren't sure, wouldn't they check anyway?

And then it hit her. Maybe they had. And if they'd gotten into the room once, they could do it again whenever they wanted. She checked the bolt on the door. It was locked tight, but was that enough? Hollis opened the room safe and found the money and address book still inside.

"They didn't come for it?" Finn asked.

She hated when he read her mind. "I was only worried about having it on me," she admitted. "It didn't occur to me until after we were at the theater that they could have come here."

"But they were both at the theater. It would have been hard for either one of them to leave and be back in time for the ..." He paused. "The heart attack."

"Either one of them could have sent someone else. It's a gang, right? Or a group, or a gaggle, or whatever it's called."

"Den. Den of thieves," Finn said. "Wonderful. There's more of them and we don't know what they look like or who they're working for. But they sure know who we are."

"What were they doing there, do you think?"

"Aside from ruining a 'comedic send up of all the Irish hold dear'?"

"Maybe Peter and Lydia thought Liam had the manuscript, and they were hoping to buy it from him."

"Why the theater?"

"Public place. Somewhere no one could get hurt," she said. "It's what we thought."

Finn let out a dry laugh.

Hollis opened the minibar, grabbed one of the beers and a chocolate bar, and joined Finn on the bed. "I'm sorry," she said, in practically a whisper.

He grunted. After a moment of silence he grunted again, louder. "It's not your fault. Not entirely, anyway. I wanted to go to the theater as much as you did." He put a hand on her thigh. "I feel like everyone else has the full play and we've only got the sides."

"Well, let's start there. What do we know?"

"Our careers are finished and we'll probably go to prison for being part of a criminal underground we've never heard of."

"I thought you didn't trade in wild speculation, professor."

"Fine," he said. "There's an Interpol agent missing and it has something to do with a group calling themselves TCT. Apparently they're involved with a forged painting that sold for a hundred and twenty-five million dollars to a private collector in a private sale.

"It's got to be much easier to pass off a fake on a private sale than to sell a painting at a public auction, so that makes sense."

"Also there are five people involved, and one of them is the person who falsely authenticated the painting. And I'm about to take the fall for that."

She was determined to stay on track even as the possibility of their being somehow in trouble from one side or the other seemed to grow larger by the minute. "What do we know about the dead man?"

Finn took a long drink from his beer. "His name. Liam Tierney. He's an antiques dealer who wanted to see Eamon Byrne as urgently as we did."

"He gave you his card."

Finn reached over to his jacket, thrown over the bottom of the bed, and pulled out the card. "It just says 'antiques' and has a picture of a shovel. You suppose he specialized in antique gardening equipment?"

"At this point I'd believe almost anything." She took the card from him and examined it. There was nothing special about the paper, and nothing written on it except one word and a web address. The only thing that stood out was the odd-looking shovel on the right-hand side of the card.

"He looked surprised when he saw my business card," Finn said. "Maybe he was expecting it to match his. Maybe the web address, or the shovel, is some kind of code."

"David said the group members may not have even met each other. That could be their way of communicating membership. I wonder if there are a lot of them."

"Maybe, but forgery is a very specialized skill. I remember how difficult it was for me to see the flaws in the Dickens manuscript," Finn said. "It's got to be the same with the Bacon painting. It's got to be as close to perfect as you can get. There are probably only a handful of people who could do that."

"And only a handful of people who would want to buy it." Hollis grabbed her laptop and plugged in the web address. It was a dark green page, with the illustration of the shovel at the center. She clicked on the shovel but nothing happened.

"Try scrolling down," Finn suggested.

At the bottom of the page were three words: *Druid Street, Galway.*

"That's the address of the package that didn't get delivered," Finn said. "So that package must have something to do with all of this."

"It must be the manuscript. And if what Peter told us is true, then it probably has information that could identify the three so-far unknown people in the group of five. That must have been the information the missing agent had found. Maybe that's why he's missing."

"That's just conjecture."

"This whole thing is conjecture," Hollis pointed out. "What we really know is that Eamon Byrnes is supposed to have the manuscript, but he's missing."

"Or hiding. Or dead."

"And that Peter Moodley isn't our contact. And if he's Interpol, he's somehow out of the loop on why we're here ..."

"But we can't be sure that Lydia woman is the contact we were supposed to meet," Finn pointed out. "We don't know why she wants the manuscript."

"Whoever Lydia and Peter are, they knew we were the ones collecting the manuscript, because they were following us even before we got to the shop. So how did they know?"

"Someone told them." They both sat silent for a minute before Finn said what they'd both been thinking. "Your boyfriend David."

Twenty-Seven

 avid, just David," she said "'Hollis's old boyfriend David' is not actually his legal name so stop saying that. It's old news."

"You didn't tell me about it until the other night, so it's very new news to me."

"And you've told me about every woman you've ever slept with?"

"Yes."

Hollis took a long look at her husband. "Really?" It took a moment for it to sink in. "Huh."

"What?"

"If you've told me about all the women you've been with, then you haven't been with that many. I mean, I always thought you were more experienced because you were so cute and …" She could see that Finn was blushing. "And, you know, you're so good at it."

"I was nineteen when we started dating, Holly, and I was very focused on school. Were you expecting more than a couple of ex-girlfriends? Have you got more than a couple of Davids in your past?"

"Sssh." Hollis pointed toward the television.

On screen was a wide shot of the Abbey Theatre, and then a close-up of a stretcher being removed. A news anchor spoke over the footage. "A new play at the Abbey Theatre was interrupted tonight by an unexpected death in the audience midway through act two. The man is identified as sixty-three-year-old Patrick Lahey, an artist from Inishmore. His cause of death is unknown, pending an autopsy. Garda are asking for help identifying the doctor at the scene who came to the aide of Mr. Lahey, as they have questions for him. According to witnesses, the doctor is an American man in his early thirties …"

"He was lying. His name, where he's from," Hollis said.

"Also, they have a description of me."

"They said early thirties."

"I look young for my age."

"Well, it doesn't matter. If he died of a heart attack, they're not going to come looking for you."

Finn muted the television but kept staring at it, even as the presenter moved on to a different story. "I don't think he did die of a heart attack," he said after a few minutes. "It just doesn't explain the blood on his collar."

"So it was a knife wound?"

"No. It wasn't a big enough hole for a knife, even a small one."

"It was barely any blood though. You've had more severe cuts from shaving," she pointed out.

"The blood wasn't dry, so unless he was shaving during the play, there's something more to it."

"Like?"

"Like an injection, right in the vein of his neck."

Hollis knew that it had to be, but saying it out loud made it real. "So he was definitely murdered?"

Finn nodded just slightly, then took another swig of his beer.

Murder. It was a horrible word, she realized. Horrible but terrifyingly accurate. How could she ever have seen this as a little adventure, a way to re-spark her marriage and feel, if only for a moment, like a woman of mystery? Somewhere that man had people who loved him, who were only now getting the news.

She and Finn had people who loved them, she thought, and if the manuscript was worth killing for once ...

She left the thought unfinished and tried to focus again on what they knew.

Finn was staring off into space, but she could guess at what he was thinking. He had said the wound was mid-neck. So while Patrick or Liam, or whoever he was, watched the play, or maybe just before it, someone injected a poison into the carotid artery in the man's neck. That could create a small amount of blood that could end up on his collar. Whatever the poison was, it led to a death that looked, at least until autopsy, like a heart attack.

"According to the woman seated next to him, he'd been talking to Peter Moodley just before taking his seat," she said. "I'm not saying it rules out Peter, but if it was an injection, it didn't happen in the lobby. I don't think he could have had a poison injected into his artery and then taken a seat to watch a play. It had to happen while he was seated."

"The problem with that theory is no one noticed if anyone sat next to him, even for a minute. Did you see anyone?"

She shook her head.

"Do you think it's a coincidence that Liam—I mean, Patrick—ended up sitting in front of us?"

"There were empty seats. He could have chosen his seat because of where we were sitting."

"Did he come in before or after us?"

"I dashed in just as the play was starting," Hollis said. "The lights were already dimmed. Did you see him when you took your seat?"

Finn shook his head. "I kept my eyes peeled for you. I didn't pay attention to anyone else. It must have been just as the lights went out. Perfect timing. It's dark, but there's still movement as the stragglers get to their seats. Someone could have slipped in, done the deed, and left before anyone thought to notice."

"It's pretty horrible," Hollis said. Whoever he was, Patrick or Liam, a criminal or an antiques dealer, he was a person they'd just been casually chatting with forty minutes earlier.

"At least we know that's not how we'll die." Finn pointed to the desk, and the single bullet still sitting there. "Do you suppose it's the same person? Injecting a man in a crowded theater seems so daring, so cold-blooded. Hardly seems like the kind of person who would bother issuing a threat."

Hollis grabbed her laptop again. It took several annoying minutes to find what she was looking for, but at least she had a plan. "I was going to try and talk you into leaving Ireland, but now I'm not going to persuade. I'm going to insist. The earliest flight leaving for Chicago is at eleven thirty in the morning," she said. "There's one for New York at ten. We could go there and get a connecting flight."

Finn sat up. "I was going to try and talk you into it. And actually I'd like to get out of here sooner than ten."

"Nothing earlier going to the States," she said, but kept looking. "We could go to London. The earliest flight is at six twenty. We can call David from some pay phone at Heathrow, fly to Chicago, and put this whole mess behind us."

"Buy the tickets now so we know we're on that flight."

"What if they're tracking our card?"

"You think they are?"

Hollis didn't answer the question. She couldn't. For years after she turned down Langley she imagined what life as a spy would have been like. She'd imagined danger, secrets, and foreign intrigue. She hadn't imagined being scared out of her wits. She grabbed a desk chair and pushed it under the door knob just in case someone tracking them had keys to the room. It wasn't wildly high-tech espionage stuff, but it would have to do.

"Let's just go to the airport in a few hours," she said. "We can buy tickets to London in cash, and once we're there we can buy the tickets home."

"How are we going to get enough cash to buy the tickets if we can't use credit cards or the debit card?"

"We have bundles of cash. I don't think David can begrudge us using some of it. And even if the cash has some kind of tracer on it ..."

"They do that?"

"Yeah, they do that." Spying was just like riding a bicycle, she thought, alarmed and amused at the same time. "But even if it does have a tracer, all it will tell them is we used it at the airport, not what plane we took or where it went."

Just having a plan made her feel more in control. Except for two thousand euros, she put the money back in the green purse and put the purse in her suitcase, surrounded by clothes. The two thousand euros and address book went into the black bag she carried every day. She packed up Finn's case too, since he seemed lost in thought. They were ready.

Finn lay back against the pillow. "Let's get some sleep."

Hollis set the alarm on her phone for three, turned off the lights, and climbed into bed. Both she and Finn were still dressed in the clothes they'd worn to the theater. Neither had mentioned it, but she figured it was understood. If they had to make a quick exit from the hotel, they needed to be ready.

Twenty-Eight

Hollis could feel Finn's breath against her neck. It was steady, in and out. How had he managed to fall asleep with everything going on around them? A gift of his obsessive nature, she decided. Once he put his mind on sleep, he slept.

She, on other hand, was playing a movie in her head. Trying to go through the streets of Dublin to find clues that she had overlooked earlier. She prided herself on always being on alert, even at home where nothing ever happened. But somewhere during their day she'd let something get past her. She wanted to blame it on jetlag, on the excitement of what was supposed to be an easy mission, but it was more than that. Dublin had charmed her. The formal architecture and the informal people, the lights on the bridges that crossed over the Liffey, the deep green lawns of the squares, and the dark brown, smooth taste of Guinness. It was all different than she'd expected. More. She was sure it had the same problems of any large city, not the least of which was a dead man in their national theater, but she was still sad to be leaving so soon. Under the circumstances, it was unlikely she'd ever be able to talk Finn into a return trip.

She lay in bed, trying to see past the charm, and her own fear and exhaustion. There was something she'd seen or heard, something that would make everything make sense. But no matter how many times she played the day in her head, she couldn't find the clue she'd missed—though she was sure it was there, just out of reach, taunting her.

———

She must have drifted off, because the sound of her phone's alarm startled her. Three in the morning. Still quiet and dark. She turned on the bedside light and saw that the chair she'd propped against the door was still in place. Finn grumbled but got up. Since they weren't in need of a quick escape, they both changed into clean clothes, made sure all their items were packed, and dropped the key card on the desk.

Finn picked up the bullet and put it in his jacket pocket, just where he'd found it. "A souvenir," he said. Hollis cocked an eyebrow at him. "What? You have new earrings. And this is so much more personal a memento."

All they needed was to get to the lobby, in a taxi, and to the airport. Hollis thought it should be simple enough. If Peter Moodley or Lydia Dempsey—or anyone else, for that matter—had followed them to the hotel, they would have expected Finn and Hollis to have checked out right away, or maybe in the morning, but not in the middle of the night.

At least that's what she hoped.

"Ready?" Finn asked as he put his hand on the door handle.

"Not really, but the sooner we're gone, the better."

He pressed down on the handle and slowly pulled open the door. There was a slight creaking sound from the door hinges, and in the hallway, the hum of overhead lights. But other than that, silence. She resisted the urge to say the hotel was "dead quiet" because she assumed Finn wasn't in a mood for levity, but it felt eerie to be one of the few people awake in the building.

They each grabbed a suitcase and walked into the hallway. Finn closed the door behind him as gently as he could. So far, so good. There was a bing that made them both jump, but it was just the elevator opening on the floor below. They stood, motionless, waiting for the doors to open on their floor, and for someone—maybe Patrick's killer?—to emerge. But the elevator doors didn't open.

"Should we take the stairs?" Finn asked.

"Is that safer?"

He pressed the elevator's down button. "Let's just get out of here."

It seemed like an eternity before the elevator arrived, but it was empty. Hollis told herself that it was a good sign, another hurdle crossed. She was aching to call David and ask him what was going on, but she and Finn had switched their cell phones off before leaving the room, just in case someone was trying to track them. The call would have to wait until they were at the airport in London, just as they agreed.

When they reached the ground floor, the elevator doors opened and they walked toward the lobby. It was lit, but quiet. Every step on the marble floor echoed. She hadn't worn her gym shoes because she read once that they would make her look like a tourist. Why didn't she think about making a quiet escape?

When they were about halfway to the door, they heard, "Good morning," and both spun around. An elegant young man in a black suit smiled. "Are you checking out?"

"Yes," Finn said. "We left the card in the room."

"Lovely. You have an early flight then?"

"Yes, very early."

"If you need a taxi..."

"They don't." From behind them Hollis heard a woman, an American woman. She didn't want to turn around, but there was no choice.

"Well, you're all sorted then," the young man said. "Safe home." He walked away. As his footsteps faded, Hollis noticed that the enormous lobby was now very empty.

Finn turned to face the woman first, and Hollis joined him. It was her. Lydia Dempsey, wearing jeans and a loose-fitting blue V-neck sweater. She looked so petite, barely five-three. She should be easy to overtake, Hollis briefly considered, except there was something in her eyes that suggested she was tougher than she looked.

"I don't know who you are," Finn started, stammering at first but then with a whispered anger, "but my wife and I aren't mixed up in this, and we're going home. We've got summer school starting next week."

She smiled. "Nice speech. Did you practice it?"

Finn took Hollis's hand and started to walk around Lydia, but she moved faster than they did. And as she moved, Lydia lifted her sweater slightly to reveal a gun tucked into the waistband of her jeans.

"I can scream," Hollis told her. "There's a parking valet just outside of the door."

"I'm not going to hurt you."

"Well, you're not trying to help us," Finn said. "So what do you want?"

"Eamon Byrnes."

Hollis saw the young man in the black suit reappear. "Excuse me," she called out. "We actually do need a taxi."

Lydia touched the area of her sweater that hid the gun. "You're not going to the airport. You're not leaving Ireland until you tell me where Eamon is."

"Never mind," Finn told the guy. The young man stood, looking confused. It's all about the service at high-end hotels, Hollis thought, and this poor guy is being whiplashed for just trying to do his job. As tempted as she was to tell the man to call a taxi anyway, there was no point in putting him in danger.

Hollis realized that a piece of her was holding out hope that Lydia had been their contact, but with one flash of that gun, she knew that Lydia wasn't who they were expecting to find at Bewley's. It left her wondering what had happened to their contact, what had happened to David, and mostly, what was about to happen to Finn and her. In less than a minute, Lydia Dempsey could spirit them out into the street and they'd disappear like the others.

"We don't know where Eamon is," Hollis said, talking fast. "We went to the shop yesterday and he wasn't there. The manager didn't know when he'd be in. We really don't have any way to help you. That's all we know."

"So the speech about maybe having the manuscript?"

"I was bluffing. You can search our luggage. We don't have it."

Lydia's shoulders dropped a little, and to Hollis, she suddenly seemed very tired and afraid. But as quickly as it happened, the flash of vulnerability was gone. "What about Liam Tierney? Do you know anything about what's happened to him?"

"Only what we saw," Finn said.

"You saw him?" she asked.

"Yesterday."

She looked back and forth between Hollis and Finn. "Where is he?"

"Don't you know?" Finn asked.

"I guess I don't. Why don't you tell me?"

Finn gulped. "He's at the morgue."

Lydia Dempsey reached for her gun.

Twenty-Nine

Move to the couch against the window," Lydia said. "Quietly." She grabbed Hollis's arm with her left hand and held her gun against Finn's back.

Hollis tried to figure the odds that she could get out of Lydia's grip before she had a chance to pull the trigger. Whatever they were, they weren't good enough.

"You're not getting the first plane to London today, but if you're honest with me, you'll go home eventually."

"How did you know we were going to London?" Finn asked.

"Tracker on your computer." She rolled her eyes. "It routed the hotel's WiFi through me. A pro would have known better than to do a flight search on a personal laptop."

"That's what I've been telling you," Finn said. "We're not pros. We're college professors."

"You're the last people to see Liam. Maybe you're the ones who killed him."

"We didn't kill him."

"But you know he's dead, and that's more information than I have."

Lydia pushed Hollis toward one of the tufted couches. Finn sat next to her and across from Lydia, who took a position on a couch that faced them. They all sat up straight, looking formal and polite, as if they were waiting to be served tea and petit fours. Lydia tucked the gun back under her sweater, but Hollis could see it was a Glock 9mm—the same caliber as the bullet in Finn's pocket.

"Who was he to you?" Hollis asked.

"He's my fiancé."

Hollis stared at the woman, trying to take it in. "The gray-haired man who died at the theater?"

Lydia cocked her head for a moment. For a woman trained not to be taken by surprise, she seemed completely caught off guard. "No. The missing agent. Why did you think I meant the man at the theater?"

"Because that's the name he gave us." Finn's voice was calm, even friendly. "But on the news last night they said his name was Patrick Lahey. They said he was an artist."

She rolled her eyes. "He was an art *forger*," she said, "and from what I've been able to find out, a pretty good one." She sat back on the couch, relaxing her posture and letting her hand move away from where the gun was hidden. "He called himself Liam Tierney?"

"Yes," Hollis said, but before she answered any more questions she had a few of her own. "Who told you that we would be interested in the manuscript?"

"David."

It was comforting, Hollis thought, that Lydia might actually be who she said she was. But it didn't erase the confrontation last night, or the gun. Especially the gun. "How do you know David?"

Lydia shook her head. "I don't. Not personally. Did he get you involved in this?"

"Yes."

"Why you?"

"He'd heard of my husband. Finn has a well-deserved reputation for knowing a fake from the real thing."

She turned to Finn. "What did David tell you about the manuscript?"

"He said it might contain clues that would help find a missing agent."

Lydia stared at him. "And that's all?"

"Is there more?"

"No." Lydia's voice was emphatic, but she moved her hands just slightly so that her thumbs were hidden from view. The disconnect between the strength in her voice and the passive, hidden thumbs, was a liar's tell. Hollis remembered it from research she did for an article on politicians' body language.

"You were sent to meet with us at Bewley's?" Hollis asked.

"Yes, I told you last night."

"A man named Peter Moodley was at Beweley's too. Do you know him?"

"I don't think so."

"Tall, bald black guy. South African. You've never seen him?"

"Not that I recall."

She was a smooth liar, Hollis thought, remembering how Lydia had stared directly at Peter at the Trinity Library.

"How do we know you were our contact?" Finn asked. "Where's your ID?"

Lydia's jaw stiffened. "Interpol agents don't have badges."

"Yes, they do," Finn said. "David showed me his badge."

"Well, technically I'm with a different agency," she admitted. "All my ID is fake. There's nothing I can give you to prove who I am."

"But you were our contact?"

"Yes." She was growing impatient, but she wasn't the only one. "You'll just have to trust me."

"We had something on us that was supposed to be a signal to our contact," Hollis said, thinking of the green purse now safely tucked in her suitcase. "Just tell me what it was and I'll know you're telling the truth."

"I don't take quizzes."

Hollis looked toward Finn, hoping their long-term relationship telepathy would work during stressful situations. He gave her a slight smile, and she knew that it did. "Then I guess we'll wait until we can talk to someone who can prove who they are," she told Lydia.

But Lydia wasn't backing down. "I have the gun."

Finn stood. "We have the information. You can shoot us in this echo chamber of a lobby, if you want, but it will draw the kind of attention you're hoping to avoid."

Hollis got up too, but Lydia grabbed her arm before she could take any steps away from the couch. "You love your wife, Dr. Larsson? Well, I love my fiancé. So, attention or not, I'm going to do whatever it takes to get him back."

Finn stood between Hollis and Lydia, and as he did, he gripped Lydia's free arm. "I do love my wife, Ms. Dempsey, and I'll do whatever it takes to protect her. So if you want to reach for your gun to shoot me, you'll have to let go of my wife."

There was silence for a moment as all three, linked into an odd and dangerous triangle, waited for someone to make a move. Hollis could feel her heart punching against her chest as she tried not to think about the ridiculous chance Finn had taken. Lydia was either a spy or a criminal—and in either case might be willing to kill them both.

"I guess you were right, Hollis. He does love you."

Finn looked back at Hollis, who smiled slightly. He nodded. She couldn't get over how brave he was being, how brave they both were. Or how stupid.

Lydia took a step back. "Okay. I'm not going to shoot you. I'm just going to show you something."

Finn stayed in front of Hollis while Lydia reached into her jeans pocket and pulled out a phone. "Here," she said. "This is Liam Tierney."

Finn took the phone and Hollis crammed into his side to see it. On the screen was a slightly blurry picture of a half-naked man with brown hair cut so short it looked nearly shaved. He was still in bed, with one hand covering his eyes as if he were trying to shield himself from the light, the way someone might look if he'd just woken up. There wasn't enough of his face to tell who it was, just a small dark mark on the palm of his hand.

"Is he familiar to you?"

Both Hollis and Finn shook their heads.

"He's been missing for over a week." Lydia's voice was softer as she spoke. "I don't know if he's alive or dead. And I don't know why Patrick Lahey would tell you that he was Liam. He must have been trying to pass along a message or something. I need to know what it is. Maybe it will help me find him."

"You should have led with that," Hollis told her, "instead of coming out all guns ablazing."

Lydia nodded. "In my line of work, it's safer to be tough than scared."

The young manager appeared out of nowhere, as if on cue. "Is everything alright? May I get you some coffee, or some tea?"

"Yes," Lydia spoke for them all. "We'd love some coffee. And if you have anything to eat…"

"We don't serve full breakfast until half past six," the manager apologized.

"Anything you have will do."

"Grand," he said. "It'll be up straight away."

It was such a civilized exchange coming moments after a death threat that Hollis almost laughed. They sat back on the couch, though this time there was considerably less tension. Wanting to protect someone you love was a motive Hollis could get behind. Lydia had no tells of being a liar as she spoke about her fiancé. Her breathing was normal, and her body was relaxed. She didn't move her head back a little, the way liars often do, or over explain herself. By all outward signs, she was telling the truth. But, Hollis reminded herself, it was Lydia's job to lie and get away with it.

"We met last year," Lydia explained, as the coffee and currant scones arrived. "He's with Stiúrthóireacht na Faisnéise."

"Irish military intelligence," Hollis blurted out.

Lydia nodded. "You really are an international politics professor," she said, and Hollis found herself blushing.

"You met on a mission?" Hollis asked.

"Why do you ask?"

The truthful answer was it sounded romantic. But Hollis just shrugged. "Curious, I guess."

"I've noticed. Yes … sort of. My father is from Ireland. Donegal. When I heard Liam's accent, I supposed it attracted me, reminded me of all the summers I spent here as a kid."

"You know Ireland well," Finn said.

"I know every inch of it." There was no mistaking the inference.

"So, Liam. How did he go missing?" Hollis thought it was better to get her talking about her fiancé than issuing vague threats that they had nowhere to hide.

Lydia nodded. "He's been working with Interpol on trying to up-root a counterfeit ring that seems to have based itself, at least in part, in Ireland. He went undercover about three months ago."

"Was Lahey part of that ring?" Hollis asked.

"I don't know. I'm not..." She sighed. "I'm not working on the same project. And if I go looking for Liam, it will set off bells that he's one of us. I'm hoping maybe his cover hasn't been blown. I'm hoping..." Her voice trailed off.

Finn reached into his wallet and pulled out the card that Lahey had given him. "Maybe this will help," he said, handing it over to Lydia. "That man who called himself Liam, he gave this to me last night. There isn't much on there. No name or anything, just a web address."

"And nothing much there," she said.

"Yeah," Finn looked confused for a moment, then nodded. "Well, I guess you saw it with the tracker. It's just one page, picture of a shovel, and an address. Druid Street, Galway. I thought it was odd because when Hollis and I were in the shop yesterday I overheard the manager talking about a package that had been misplaced. It's the same address of a package. The delivery man said it was being returned to sender, and should arrive back in Galway later today."

"Liam, or Patrick..." Hollis could feel the nervousness in her throat and tried to calm herself before starting again. "The man who was killed, he was in Eamon's shop yesterday. He seemed agitated. We didn't speak to him."

"You spoke to him at the theater, though," Lydia said.

A waiter appeared with more coffee.

"You need to tell me everything Patrick Lahey said to you."

"We talked about the Behan play," Finn said.

"He knew about it?"

Finn nodded.

Lydia leaned back and Hollis could practically see her thinking; an intense unfocused gaze and a slight smile that crept across her face. "You have to go there and see what the package has in it. If you get the seven-thirty train from Heuston Station, you'll be in Galway City by ten."

"We can't get any further involved," Finn said. "If you needed us to sit in a library and do research, I would stay until I found what could help...but chasing after missing spies, that's well outside our skill set."

"Your wife is a trained CIA agent."

"That was twenty years ago," he pointed out. "And she quit right after the academy."

"Yes," Hollis said, almost reflexively, "but I remember what I learned, and I have tried to keep myself ready for anything."

Finn glared at Hollis. "Theoretical danger is a far cry from actual bad guys with actual guns."

She conceded the point. A few minutes ago she was feeling lucky to be escaping unharmed, and she had to remember that. "I'm sorry, Lydia," she said. "I never became an agent precisely because I wanted a normal life."

Lydia's gaze hardened. "Let me put this another way then. I may not be able to shoot you here in this hotel, but I know where you live, and where you teach, and where you buy your groceries, and where you do pretty much everything in your boring little Midwestern college town. If something happens to Liam, I might not be able to find his killers and punish them, but I will be able to find you. And I will hold you responsible. So what do think about going to Galway?"

Finn took a sip of his coffee then glanced at Hollis with one of his *let's get out of here* looks, mainly reserved for the university-sponsored parties that were boring from invitation to good-night. It was usually up to Hollis to come up with a plausible, but gracious, excuse for the professor hosting the party. Now, as much as Hollis wanted to come up with the right thing to say, there was no gracious way she could find out of this situation.

Thirty

The train to Galway left Heuston Station exactly at seven thirty. Hollis remembered reading an article years earlier bemoaning Ireland's newfound efficiency during the country's boom days, an era of extraordinary economic growth that started in the mid-1990s. The author cited the trains leaving on time as an indication that the quirky Ireland of his youth had become just another capitalistic country, and was all the worse for it. As their train sped away, leaving Dublin behind, Hollis wondered if the man was happier when Ireland, like the US and the rest of Europe, fell off a cliff a decade later.

But looking around, it was clear just from the passengers, that Ireland had recovered from the worst of the 2008 crash. The train was nearly filled with men and women dressed in business clothes, along with vacationers from Ireland and abroad, and everyone seemed in a good mood.

"You keep yourself ready for anything," Finn said, with sarcasm that would be evident to a deaf man. "Why would you say that?"

"I don't think you've ever respected my skills. You think the yoga and martial arts are all about staying in shape for your benefit."

"Your *skills* have put us on a train to certain death."

"Oh come on," she said a little too loudly. The elderly woman in the seat across the aisle looked up from her knitting with a disapproving scowl. Hollis lowered her voice and tried to keep her annoyance in check. "She wasn't going to let us walk away no matter what I said. And if we stick together, we're not going to die."

Finn grunted.

"And by the way, that was a pretty stupid move you made at the hotel, standing between me and Lydia's gun. You could have gotten yourself killed."

"What was I supposed to do?"

"I don't know. It was incredibly brave and very sweet."

"I thought it was stupid."

"It was all three."

He shifted in his chair to face Hollis. "If we do get ourselves killed in this insane adventure, at least we'll go together."

Hollis leaned her head on his shoulder. "Just in case you live and I don't—"

"Which would only be right since you got us into this."

"Exactly. You have my permission to remarry."

"I couldn't be married to anyone but you," he said, kissing her head.

She looked up at him and they kissed lightly. That got a smile from the woman with the knitting. "You'd live alone the rest of your life?"

"I would. I'd probably sleep with some of the grad students, but I wouldn't let them spend the night."

She laughed. "Keep my picture on the nightstand, just to creep them out."

"Of course."

The train slowed, and then stopped at a station. Several people, including the knitter, got off, and several new people took their places. For a moment Hollis considered what might happen if she and Finn just got off the train, but she knew there was no point. As Lydia had made clear, she knew how to find them.

"Where's the address book?" Finn whispered.

She tapped the pocket of her purse. "Another question is, where is Lydia?" Hollis asked Finn. "I haven't seen her since she handed us the tickets."

"Maybe she's driving there, or taking another train. It might be smart not to be seen with us."

"But I bet we're not alone here."

Finn got up. "Maybe we should take a walk and see if anyone follows us."

They walked through several cars and, though Hollis checked every face she could, no one looked familiar. She did see a newspaper headline about Patrick Lahey's death at the Abbey Theatre. It read: COMEDY ENDS IN TRAGEDY. Clever, she thought, and a reminder to check what police have been saying about the death, and the American doctor who was at the scene.

At the dining car, Finn ordered two Cokes. "And a bag of potato chips."

"Chips?" said the confused man at the counter.

"Crisps," Finn corrected himself.

"I've got plain, dill pickle, vinegar, and my favorite, lamb vindaloo."

"How about a bag of plain and a bag of vinegar? They sound edible."

The man laughed. "Not an adventurer, are ya?"

"You'd be surprised." Finn paid the man, and he and Hollis found a table in the middle of the crowded car.

"Recognize anyone?" Hollis asked.

"Nope." He opened the plain bag and grabbed a handful of chips. "And I don't want to. Maybe we've got a few hours with no one chasing us."

A man in his twenties sat down across from Hollis, in the empty chair next to Finn. "Okay, mate? No other seats available."

Finn raised an eyebrow but he smiled. "Absolutely."

"Americans, are you? I love America. I was there once visiting a pack of cousins I have in Philadelphia." He ran his hands through the shaggy dark-brown hair that was getting in his eyes. When it was out of the way, Hollis could see he had bright blue eyes that lit up when he smiled.

"We're from Michigan," Finn told him.

"That's not close, is it?"

"About seven hundred miles away." Finn looked over at Hollis, who shrugged. There was no point in being wary of every friendly person, because in Ireland that would open the whole population to suspicion.

"It's only about two hundred and eighty kilometers across Ireland," the man said, "less than five hundred tip to toe. What's that in miles?"

"About a hundred and seventy miles across and three hundred down," Hollis answered.

"Well then, a few Irelands would fit between Philadelphia and Michigan, and that's not even halfway across the country, is it?"

Finn shook his head.

The man smiled. "We're small, but we've changed the world. You have a Starbucks in a lot of places, but show me a country without an Irish pub."

"And about twenty American presidents have Irish roots," Finn added.

"There ya go," the man said. "We're fighting above our weight, but that's always been our way. I'm Declan Murphy. I'm heading to Galway City. Where are you getting out?"

"The same," Hollis told him.

"On holiday?"

"Yes. We've been told that the west of Ireland is the place to get some quiet, and rest with our thoughts," she said, remembering the words of the taxi driver who drove them from the airport.

"Not in the city," Declan said. "It's mad. You'll have to get out to Connemara for some peace. Beautiful land too. Abandoned castles and forts and the like, if you're into that sort of thing."

"What's waiting for you in Galway?" Finn asked him.

"It's far enough from my parents to keep me from wanting to jump into the Irish Sea, but close enough to the Atlantic in case I change my mind."

Hollis laughed. It was a non-answer that was almost poetic.

"You could have gone anywhere on the west coast and had the same result," Finn pointed out.

"You're right there. But my parents won't pay for it unless I'm in school."

"Aren't you a little older than a typical university student?"

"I'm post-grad at NUI Galway. Trying to get my PhD in Psychology."

"Interested in unlocking the mysteries of the human mind?"

"Ah, not as complicated as that. Ireland's full of headers, so there's good money in it." He grabbed a few of the potato chips from the bag Finn had opened, and pointed across the aisle. "Like look at that gowl," he said about a man in a dark suit reading a copy of *The Irish Times*. "He keeps looking over here but when I catch his eye, he pops back under the paper."

Hollis spun around, chastising herself for one of the most unsubtle moves she'd ever made. As she did, the man in question outdid her in

155

transparency, practically ripping the paper as he struggled to hide behind it.

"What do you suppose he's on about?" Declan asked.

"Probably just likes to eavesdrop," Finn offered, though he glanced over at Hollis as he said it.

"We should talk louder then," Declan said. "Help him out." He laughed and grabbed another handful of chips. Then he stood up. "I'll get the next round," he said, and ordered two more bags of crisps from the man behind the counter. As he was waiting he leaned down to the man with the newspaper and said, loudly, "You want to join us?"

The man folded his paper, got up, and left the dining car. Hollis told herself that it was probably nothing. No spy or criminal would be that obvious, she assumed. But she scanned every face in the car, even giving their relaxed PhD friend a second look.

But all she got back was a wide, guileless smile.

Thirty-One

Hollis and Finn said goodbye to Declan outside the Galway railway station. Hollis found a pay phone and tried David again. Still no luck. It was only a few minutes' taxi ride to the hotel Lydia had told them about, just at the edge of the old town. Once they'd checked in, they stood in the room, staring at each other, unsure what to do.

"I think this whole plan is idiotic," Finn said. "It's worse than that. It's reckless."

"You're not wrong," Hollis admitted. "But I don't think we have a choice."

Sitting at Westbury in Dublin, it had seemed simple enough, especially as Lydia explained it. Hollis and Finn would go to the Druid Street address and wait for the package that was supposed to be delivered by three p.m. Lydia could hack into the delivery system and track the package, so she'd give them a good sense of when it would be delivered. If possible, they'd intercept it, though how they'd do that wasn't exactly clear. But if they couldn't, they'd wait to see who did get it and call the number Lydia had given them. Druid, she'd said, was in the old town section of Galway, a busy tourist area, and they'd fit right in.

"Do you think she's here, watching us?" Hollis asked.

"Well somebody is, don't you think? We haven't been alone since we landed in Ireland."

"If Lydia is watching us, we're in trouble if we don't go to Druid Street. And if someone else is watching us..."

"So, it's just a matter of who we want killing us," Finn said. He pulled the bullet out of his pocket to drive home his point.

"If it helps, I believe Lydia's trying to find the man she loves."

"It doesn't."

"And there's still the matter of your name possibly being linked to a criminal organization as the authenticator of a fake painting."

"I don't even authenticate paintings," he said. Then he tilted his head a little, a sure sign to Hollis that he was about to rethink his position. "Though I could, I suppose. I mean, I have written papers on how literature has inspired some of the most famous paintings in the world. Plus I do have a doctorate in art history."

"You're not making a great case for your innocence."

"Good point. Make me shut up if we're ever interrogated by Interpol."

As he spoke Hollis's phone pinged. The text said PACKAGE ARRIVES IN THIRTY. She showed the message to Finn.

Finn responded to the news by sitting on the bed. "Maybe we shouldn't go."

"We're hitting every pay phone we can find and David's still unreachable. I don't even know if he's getting our messages. I don't know if he's ..." She didn't finish the sentence. She didn't want to think about what could be keeping him from checking in. "So either we go now, or we're on our own to find a plan B."

Finn sighed, but it was more of a hostile exhale. "We don't have a plan B."

"Then I guess we go."

———

It was raining when they left the hotel and it only got worse as they turned onto High Street. In less than two days Hollis had gotten used to the fact that the rain wouldn't last long, and neither would the sunshine. It felt like a metaphor for the whole trip—neither good news nor bad seemed to last long enough to take advantage of it.

Unlike Dublin, with its pristine Georgian architecture and well-manicured squares, Galway—at least this part of Galway—looked carved from rock. Many of the buildings were a rough, light-brown stone and the pedestrian-only road was a smoother version of the same stone, cut into bricks. The streets wound in what seemed to be circles, with side streets curling off like branches on a particularly convoluted tree. Like Grafton Street in Dublin, High Street was filled with a mix of tourist shops and local stores; unlike Dublin, it made no concession to the tourists. It seemed to say, "I've outlived worse than you."

Which made sense. Before the train had even left Dublin, Finn had researched the city and found that the area where they were staying had been the only medieval city in the area, and a well-known one at that. Christopher Columbus had visited in 1477.

"So we're following in the footsteps of an explorer."

"Don't make this cool," he'd said, but he'd smiled a little. She could see that some small part of him was enjoying a world beyond books.

But now that they were actually in Galway, they weren't explorers; they were back to being spies. And ill-equipped ones at that. When they got lost, a woman, doing her best to be helpful, said Druid Street was just past the shop with wool sweaters in the window. But all it took was a few steps away from her to realize her advice was worthless. It seemed that, except for the pubs, every business was selling wool fisherman-style sweaters, and they all looked remarkably similar.

Street signs were sparingly used, and put high on the buildings, offering only sporadic guidance. They walked down the length of the street, then back again, and with each moment that ticked away, the knot in Hollis's stomach got tighter. When they turned left onto a small off-shoot of High Street, she gave up. It had been almost thirty minutes since they'd left the hotel, so the package was either delivered or about to be. A tall, gray-haired man with a long umbrella walked past her, and she put her hand out.

"I'm sorry," she said. "I'm late for an appointment on Druid Street. I can't find it."

His lips curled upward. "You're not as lost as you think."

"Is this Druid Street?" she guessed, blushing as she said it.

"Only for a short while."

She narrowed her eyes and took a breath. It was hard enough trying to find their way out of this mess, now she had to solve a riddle? "Is it changing names?" she asked.

He smiled and pointed toward the end of the block. "Druid is just these five buildings," he said. "So don't walk too far or you'll be finished with it."

As he walked off, clicking the bottom of his umbrella on the road, the sun came out. Hollis took it as a positive sign until Finn whispered in her ear, "So which one is the building we're watching? The address was Druid Street, Galway. There was no number."

The Irish, Hollis decided, were not fond of a straight answer in person or in postal addresses.

There was a tea shop on the corner, so Finn went inside for to-go cups while Hollis kept watch outside the shop. Getting tea was an excuse for them to stay at the corner, and in the meantime Hollis kept busy pretending to be looking at her phone. The smartphone was an amazing weapon of surveillance, she thought, providing the perfect excuse to just stand there seemingly busy. But out of the corner of her eye she saw a FedEx truck pull around the corner and stop. As it did, Finn walked out of the shop with two cups. He saw where she was looking and, without explaining himself, handed her both cups. He walked toward the truck with such confidence she wasn't sure if she should be amazed by it, or terrified. She decided on the latter.

The driver got out of the truck with a small package in his hand. He headed toward a three-story building on the end of the street, just as it bent into a new road.

She saw Finn reach the same building, and her heart stopped. "What's he going to say?" she asked no one. But Finn passed the driver without looking at him, and instead walked toward the door as if he were about to go inside. When the driver reached him, Finn turned and looked surprised. They chatted, though Hollis couldn't hear what they were saying. It seemed friendly. The driver handed him something. A pen. "Oh God," Hollis murmured, "he's signing for the package. He's actually doing it."

Then the door to the building opened. Hollis held her breath. Her hands felt hot, burning. She looked down and saw that she'd squeezed the paper cups so hard she'd broken them. The hot tea was now pouring over her fingers. She dropped the cups and took a few steps, then stopped. Would walking over there make it worse? What would she say?

A red-haired woman emerged from the building. She was holding something black. She was holding a gun. Or was it a gun? Hollis had a stray thought that if she screamed, it would divert attention and Finn could run.

But Finn didn't look like he wanted to run. He was still chatting with the driver. The FedEx man handed him the package. The woman looked over at Finn. He glanced toward her and smiled. She said something to him. His smile grew wider. He spoke to her. It all seemed friendly. But then she moved the hand holding the black thing and shook it. It opened wide as she passed the men. An umbrella. Hollis was so focused on Finn that she didn't notice the rain had started again. Hollis raised her cell phone up, trying to look like she was reading emails, but she snapped a few photos as the woman walked toward her. Then, once she was close, Hollis pretended to be texting, trying to look calm and disinterested. She was relieved that it seemed to work. The woman came toward her, then passed, without looking her way.

Just a moment later, Finn started walking back toward Hollis, the brown package tucked beneath his arm.

Thirty-Two

O nce Finn had the package it occurred to Hollis
that it could be a set-up, maybe a bomb. But Finn
nixed the idea.

"There's something hard in there, but it's small.
Most of the package is flexible," he said, "Like there's
papers inside. Maybe a fake Behan manuscript. Let's
get back to the room and open it."

"No. Let's go somewhere else. We can double
back later and go back to the hotel. If someone's following us, I don't want to lead them right to our
room."

"The people following us knew where we were
staying in Dublin. No one knows we're in Galway,
except Lydia."

"It would be pretty easy to trace our credit cards.
We had to use one to check into the hotel."

"Where's all the stuff spies are supposed to get? Fake IDs and credit cards, guns in the shape of pens, phones in our shoes, cones of silence ..."

Hollis laughed a little. "If we're Maxwell Smart and Agent 99, that makes Lydia an agent of Chaos."

"That sounds about right. We're supposed to call her now, aren't we?"

The answer was yes, obviously. That was the agreement they'd made. Lydia would know from tracking the package that it had been signed for. She was probably in Galway somewhere waiting for them to bring it to her. What neither Finn nor Hollis could figure out was whether they'd be safer once they turned the package over to her, or whether it would be the last choice they'd make.

"Maybe we take a moment and figure out what we do before we call anyone," Hollis suggested.

They both glanced back toward the building. There was no one walking on the little street, but it didn't mean there wasn't someone in a window somewhere.

"Okay," Finn said, "but I don't want to carry this around. We're taking too much of a risk." He was sounding like the same old Finn, but he was grinning from ear to ear. Hollis could tell that, despite his fear, Finn's obsessive need to understand everything had kicked into overdrive.

"Let's get out of here," she said. "We'll find a place to hang out."

They headed back toward High Street, and Finn took her hand. They walked through the maze of people and shops, street musicians and pub goers. Finn kept the package held tightly in one hand and he kept his other hand locked with Hollis's. She couldn't remember the last time they'd held hands this long. Normally, he'd grasp hers for a moment, squeeze, and let go. Kisses were mainly when they said goodnight, and sex ... Well. She hesitated to calculate how often that happened these days, and when it did, it was the paint-by-numbers routine of people so familiar with each other's bodies and moods they didn't need to fumble and experiment.

But now, wandering through the streets of Galway, Finn held tight to her hand, and when he glanced her way, he smiled. If not for the nagging feeling they were about to be killed, it would have been romantic.

Thirty-Three

There was a W.B. Yeats quote, "Being Irish, he had an abiding sense of tragedy that sustained him through temporary periods of joy." He thought of that while he watched Finn and Hollis walk down High Street with the package, looking happy and holding hands. Optimists, the Americans. Not the Irish, though. The Irish steeled themselves against the coming heartbreak, always aware that no matter how bright the day, it could still storm. It was the weather, his da used to say. It made fatalists of them all.

But Hollis and Finn were looking pleased with themselves. They'd beaten him to the package in a move that even he had to admit was a bit daring. But that was no matter. They were easy enough to find.

They'd been lovely on the train, sharing their crisps and chatting. They were as smart as their resumes suggested they would be, but kinder and friendlier than he'd expected.

He felt bad for them. He did, honestly.

Thirty-Four

Hollis had no idea where they were going and neither did Finn, it seemed. But after several minutes of
walking, he stopped at one of the countless shops
with the cream-colored, elaborately knit wool sweaters on display, and pointed to a picture of John Wayne
in the window.

"This is our safe haven," he said.

O'Maille's had a timelessness to it. The shop was
both modern, with abstract woven blankets and car-
digans, and steeped in tradition, with shawls and
tweed caps everywhere Hollis looked. And it was
covered floor to ceiling in every use for wool possible. When Finn asked about the photo of John
Wayne, the clerk explained that the shop had made
some of the costumes in 1952's *The Quiet Man*.

"We've seen it," Hollis said.

"Ah, ya have. It's a grand movie. Of course, Ireland was never like that. Not really. Though we do have pretty cottages, and women that are easy to love and hard to live with."

"We have those in the States too," Finn said.

Hollis ignored the male bonding and wandered the shop. There were jackets, scarves, ties, and the seemingly ubiquitous sweaters. She picked up a hand-woven brown and cream throw. The wool was soft and warm. She felt protected just holding it. "I'll take this," she said.

"I love how you keep taking time out from running for our lives to shop for souvenirs," Finn whispered to her.

"It's not just a souvenir." When the man rang up the purchase and put the blanket in a bag, Hollis took the package from Finn, placing it between the folds of the throw, hidden from view. "It should keep our other souvenir safe, at least for now."

"Okay, that was smart," he conceded. He took her hand again as they left the shop. "And it's a nice blanket, goes with the couch."

"I was thinking the same thing," she said. "You're in an awfully good mood under the circumstances."

"Am I?" he said. "I guess I like finding out I'm just as good at this spy thing as your ex-boyfriend."

Hollis leaned her head against his shoulder. "You're better."

"I don't think he sets the bar that high," he said, a slight blush creeping across his face. "Let's find somewhere we can sit down and figure out how to survive this."

They walked to a pub down the street from O'Maille's. Hollis hadn't seen anyone familiar (or anyone unfamiliar) paying too much attention. But it didn't make her feel any safer.

The pub was divided into several small rooms. The first was filled by a long bar, with only a few patrons sitting at it. The second had tables in it, though all but one were empty. The third had nothing in it, except for a stage and a sign that read, MUSIC NIGHTLY. It was past lunchtime, she realized, and before anyone would be heading out after work. A good time to notice someone following them. They walked back to the bar and asked for menus.

"Do you want a Guinness?" Hollis asked Finn.

"We should branch out, be a little daring."

"We should? What have you done with my husband?"

He rolled his eyes. "Is Rebel Red a good craft beer?" Finn asked the bartender, a tall, slight man with long blond hair tied back in a ponytail.

"It's good, yeah," the bartender said. "It's made by Franciscan monks in Cork. It's one of my favorites."

Finn looked over at Hollis, who nodded. How could they not try a beer made by monks? "We'll have two," Finn told him, "and I'll have the roast beef dinner."

"That comes with Brussels sprouts and mash," the bartender said.

"Sounds perfect."

"You don't like Brussels sprouts," Hollis said.

"I can't remember the last time I had them."

"You don't like them, so I don't cook them."

"I think I know what vegetables I like, Holly. I'm not useless." He handed his menu to the bartender. "I'm fine with the sprouts."

"I'll have the pasta primavera," Hollis said.

The bartender poured their beers. "Ye can sit down and I'll bring the food over when it's ready."

They choose a booth in the middle room of the pub, Hollis put the bag against the wall, in view but hard to reach unless someone was willing to make a scene, which she was hoping wasn't the case.

Finn leaned in. "Where's Peter Moodley?" he asked, his voice just above a whisper. "Don't you think it's weird he's not popping up unannounced?"

"And why isn't Lydia calling or texting to find out what happened about the package?"

"Do you think she's waiting for us at the hotel?"

"What if we don't go back there?" Hollis asked. "We could check in somewhere else and keep calling David."

"But our suitcases are back at the hotel with David's money in them," Finn reminded her. "We only have credit cards with our names on them. The two thousand euro you put in your purse this morning isn't going to be enough to buy us two plane tickets home. Eventually we'll have to go back to the room."

"Okay, second idea—we could open the package here. At least then we'd know what we were risking our lives for. And Lydia didn't say anything about us delivering the package unopened."

"I think that was implied, though. What if someone's watching us?"

He had a point. Hollis didn't have a third idea, so she took a swig of her beer. It was good; had a kind of caramel taste to it that she quite liked, but she was almost immediately lightheaded. The lack of sleep...the stress...the guns pointed at her—they were all beginning to take their toll. Her body longed to lie down and her mind to shut off.

"We're in the driver's seat with this package," Finn said. "As much as we can be, anyway. We just need to be careful about our moves."

She looked up at him. "I agree. Which is why I don't know what you were thinking walking over to that delivery guy. And what did that woman say to you?"

"What woman?"

"The woman who walked out of the building."

"Oh," he smiled. "I went over because that's the only way I could get the package. I thought worst case, I would at least be able to see the address and know it was the right one."

"But you passed the guy by as if you didn't notice him."

"Well, I couldn't just walk over and say, 'I think you have a package for Eamon Byrnes.' He'd want to see ID or something," Finn said. "I figured if I was casual about it, he wouldn't be suspicious. We sort of reached the door at the same time and I just said hello."

"You told him you were Eamon."

"Yeah. I fumbled with my keys for a moment as if I couldn't find the right one. Thankfully he didn't wait until I tried to use them. But I did see there was a small gold sign for the first floor that read, 'Eamon Byrnes Antiques. By Appointment Only,' so I knew I was in the right place. I said something about running late for a new client, and he gave me the package. I signed Eamon's name and here we are."

"And the woman. She wasn't maybe watching to see who got the package?"

"I don't think so. She said she'd just gotten her hair done and now the rain was going to ruin it. I told her she looked great."

Hollis tried to remember the woman as she walked passed. "She didn't just get her hair done," she said. "It was messy."

"I didn't notice that. Then again, I barely notice when I get my own hair cut."

A now-familiar panic was creeping back into Hollis's throat. "I'll bet she was watching you talk to the FedEx guy and came out to get a better look."

"Or she wasn't. Maybe she was just going somewhere. Maybe messy is a style in Galway."

"Maybe."

The bartender brought over their plates. Finn's plate was piled with roast beef and mashed potatoes, soaked in a dark gravy, with roasted green Brussels sprouts to one side. Hollis waited for Finn to taste his, but he just smiled.

"Looks good, doesn't it?" he asked.

"It does." Hollis could see peas and chopped carrots in her pasta, but when she took a bite there was something else. Something odd. It took a moment before she realized what it was. "There's a potato in my pasta primavera," she said.

Finn laughed. "You have to immerse yourself in the culture, and in Ireland, I guess that includes potatoes."

She took another bite. It was pretty good, she had to admit, as long as she didn't think about the carb overload.

Finn pierced a Brussels sprout with his fork and brought it to his mouth. He took a bite, then seemed to rethink it. He dropped the fork, grabbed his napkin, and quietly spit the vegetable into it.

Hollis tried not to gloat, but she was irrationally pleased to be right about Finn's preferences.

He put his fork on the meat and was about to cut, but he paused. "Before I eat the roast beef?" he asked.

"You love roast beef."

"Good."

Hollis took the sprouts from his plate and handed over several pieces of potato from her dish. She did her best to enjoy the meal, but she kept remembering the redheaded woman walking past her. Deep in her bones Hollis knew that she and Finn had made a terrible mistake.

"You know Sinn Fein," she said.

"The Irish political party?" Finn asked. "They helped bring about Irish independence in the 1920s. Still a major political party now. Any other quizzes, professor?"

"The name means, 'We Ourselves.' It's an Irish saying that means basically we'll determine our own fate."

"Are we starting a revolution?"

"I know that in the last few years, we've sort of been operating on parallel tracks, with your work and my work, and not really a lot that we shared."

"We still love each other." There was a defensive edge in his voice, as if he were waiting for her to explain that the problems in their marriage were his fault.

"Of course we do. But you can't pretend that we've needed each other for a very long time. But here, now, we do. Our lives literally depend on us being there for each other. We can't let anyone else decide for us what will happen. If we're going to have any shot at a fiftieth wedding anniversary, we back each other up, not let anything or anyone get between us. 'We Ourselves.' Promise."

"I made that promise a long time ago." He reached over to her plate and folded some of her pasta on his fork. "I'm not breaking it now."

Thirty-Five

When they couldn't delay any longer, Finn and Hollis walked back to their hotel. They'd discussed a dozen different possibilities, both aware that the missing agent had become the least of their worries. If they turned the package over to Lydia, she might be grateful, or she might kill them. She sounded genuinely concerned about finding the man, at least to Hollis, but what if she was just a good actor? Finn worried that Peter Moodley would arrest them both for working on behalf of TCT. Maybe it could be straightened out if Peter cared about the truth. If he wasn't an inside man for TCT. If he was even Interpol. It was a dizzying amount of *ifs*.

By the time they'd reached the hotel lobby, they'd agreed to a plan. They would carefully open the package in the room, take photos of the contents, and email them to David. It was beginning to feel like a long shot, but maybe he would respond with an answer on how to proceed. If he didn't, then they would rewrap the package, check out of their room, and leave it with the hotel clerk just before getting in a taxi to the train station. Then, and only then, would they call Lydia with the location of the package and a lie about their whereabouts. Once home they would find someone at the Justice Department or Interpol or the CIA, whoever would listen, and tell them everything they knew.

———

They took the elevator up to their floor and walked the quiet hallway to their door. At their room they both took a deep breath before Finn opened the door. In Dublin they'd gone through the same thing and found the place empty.

But not in Galway.

Everything looked as neat as before. A crisp white duvet still covered the double bed, with a deep merlot bed scarf neatly displayed at the edge. The framed photos of Galway still hung on the wall, straight and in place. A small table by the window still had nothing but the morning's paper on it, just where Finn had left it when they checked in. Their luggage was still on the luggage racks along the wall, untouched. The TV and lights were off, just as they had left them. Everything was normal.

But as soon as they walked into the room, they saw a jacket draped across the desk chair. A jacket that didn't belong to either of them.

Finn gripped Hollis's arm. She nodded. They started to back out of the room.

"There you are!" a man's voice boomed and the door to the bathroom opened. David walked out. "I've been waiting hours for you."

Hollis instinctively hid the O'Maille's bag behind her even as she felt a palpable wave of relief. "We've been trying to reach you."

"That's why I'm here. I got the messages and figured it was safer if I came in person."

———

While David raided the minibar, grabbing several bottles of Harp as well as two tiny bottles of Jameson's, Hollis tucked the bag behind the bed. David didn't seem to notice or care. Finn nodded as she did it, and she knew he was thinking the same as she was. There was plenty of time later to share what they'd found, once they were both sure it was the right move. After so long of being out of step, it felt good that she and Finn were working as a team.

David poured himself a whiskey and offered one to Finn, who drank it, and Hollis, who left hers untouched.

"Where have you been?" she asked.

"I'm sorry about that. It couldn't be helped."

"Couldn't someone have gotten word to us that you were on your way?"

"It wasn't safe."

Hollis had wanted to be calm and reasonable, but watching David help himself to some minibar peanuts as if nothing was wrong just made her angry. "We were out here on our own, in real danger."

"I know. I'm really very sorry. I had no idea it was going to turn out like this. I got word in D.C. that Eamon wasn't at the shop and then I lost track of you."

"I think that's the other way around," Finn said. "We called you so many times I lost count."

David grabbed the bottle opener off the table. It took several tries for him to get the cap off the beer. When he finally did, he closed his eyes and took a long drink. Even after he took the bottle from his lips, his eyes remained closed. Hollis could feel herself getting more alarmed with each passing second. She moved slightly to see him from behind. No gun in his waistband. She moved again, slowly, putting her hands on the chair that held his jacket. As discreetly as she could, she patted at it. Nothing there either. She looked at Finn, who wasn't taking his eyes off David.

"David?" Hollis said, as quietly and calmly as she could. "Please tell us what's going on."

"I'm not sure. Something is wrong. When I tried to get in touch with you, they banned me from the office, took my work cell … just froze me out. I was able to hack into a computer and hear your messages, but by then it wasn't safe to call. So I got on a plane."

"What are you saying?" Finn demanded. "Your bosses wanted us to be out here with no backup and people getting killed?"

"Someone got killed?" David nearly shouted. His hand shaking, he took another drink of the beer. "Who?"

"Answer our questions first," Hollis said. "Why would you be shut out of your office? You're the one who arranged this whole thing. You're our handler."

David's gaze lowered. He just stood there, silently.

"David?" Hollis tried again. "You're our handler, aren't you?"

"I was in over my head from the beginning. I wanted to get out from behind a desk, and I guess I overstepped. I … I didn't actually get a promotion. I sort of took that role on myself. I had read the article about how Finn discovered the Dickens manuscript was a fake, and when this thing came up, I figured, you know …" He looked at Hollis.

"Figured an old friend would help you out."

His shoulders slumped. Revealing his lie didn't seem to help, from what Hollis could see, it only weighed more heavily on him.

"I've applied for handler a number of times. I'm not getting promoted. You have to understand, the clock is ticking on my career," he said. "It's not like teaching with tenure and crusty old professors being practically a cliché. There's all this new technology, and spying is a young man's game. I'm just not keeping up. And there are budget cuts coming. People think there's an unlimited amount of money for the intelligence community, but that's just in the movies. Even the field guys have to fill out expense reports. It's not James Bond, you know."

"David…" Hollis tried to interrupt, to calm him down, but there was no stopping him.

"I'm in real danger of losing my job. And with my divorce taking half my assets…I mean…You have no idea. You guys have each other…"

"Don't." Hollis put up a hand. "This is the wrong audience if you're looking for sympathy."

He nodded. "I realize that. I'm just trying to explain. I needed a win. Something to show what I'm capable of."

"Does Interpol even know why we're here?"

David's gaze shifted to the floor once again. As it did, Hollis felt a woozy warmth move through her body—part embarrassment, part rage.

"But they must have approved of our being here. Where did the fifty thousand come from? And the money for the hotel and plane tickets?"

"I cashed in my 401k."

She didn't dare look at Finn but she could hear him grunting, and even though she couldn't see it, she knew his eye was twitching. David, for his part, was completely silent.

"So they think we're just trying to get our hands on the manuscript for some rich collector, or maybe we're working for TCT?" she said.

David shook his head. "You're both well-respected professors. You're not criminals."

"We know that, but you didn't tell them."

179

"I tried, but it all got complicated. I was suspended for going against protocol and they wouldn't listen to anything I said after that. I knew they were monitoring my calls, so I couldn't get in touch. I flew to Dublin right away, but you guys had left by then. Thank God you used your own credit cards or I would never have found you."

"That is good news," Finn said flatly.

"Why Galway?" David asked.

"Lydia Dempsey sent us," Hollis said.

"Insisted on it," Finn added. "At gunpoint. I don't understand why she didn't tell you we were here. I assume you're helping her find her fiancé, or did you lie to her too?"

David stared at Finn a moment. "Who's Lydia Dempsey?"

Thirty-Six

She's not working with you?" Finn asked. "She wasn't our contact in Dublin?"

"No."

"Who was it?"

"I guess it doesn't matter if I tell you now. The contact you were supposed to meet with was a man named Patrick Lahey."

"Patrick Lahey?" Hollis's head was spinning. "Gray hair, maybe sixty or so?"

"Yes."

"We'd heard he's either an artist or an art forger, depending on who's providing the bio."

"He's a bit of both. Did he ever show?"

"Not at Bewley's. He was at the theater, though," she said. "And when we talked to him, he didn't let on that he was our contact."

David looked confused and slightly alarmed, which did nothing to comfort Hollis. "The theater? Your messages said you were worried that you were in danger. You didn't say anything about going to the theater or talking to Lahey."

"We were trying to keep our messages vague."

"Okay," he said, but he didn't seem to really understand. "Why would you go for a night on the town if you were afraid?"

"There was someone who met us at Bewley's," Finn said. "Peter Moodley. You know him?"

"No. Who did he say he was?"

"He didn't. But he kind of put it in our heads that we were supposed to go to the Abbey Theatre that night. And that's where we ran into Lahey."

"Some man came up to you at Bewley's and told you to go to the Abbey Theatre. And you went?" David poured himself another drink.

Hollis wanted to tell him that the situation called for clear, sober heads, but she wasn't sure David would be a help either sober or drunk. "We wanted to talk to you first, but you didn't answer."

"No, you were busy trying to get a promotion," Finn said, his voice moving from annoyed to angry in just one syllable. "And the only way to do that, apparently, was to put two innocent people in harm's way."

"I know I should have been more honest with you, but all I did was send you to get some fake papers, using your expertise as cover. You were supposed to walk across the street, hand over the manuscript, and then go back to being small-town bookworms."

"Hey!" Hollis jumped in. "We would love to go back to being bookworms, but people are threatening our lives."

David looked about to escalate the argument but seemed to think better of it. He put his hands up in surrender. "You're right. This is my fault. I'll get you home. I'll get you out of this. Just walk me through everything that's happened."

Finn took a breath, then began telling David what Hollis immediately noticed was an abbreviated version of the events. Finn was a born storyteller, so he normally added in tiny details to bring life to the tale— from the look on a man's face to the temperature in the room. This time, though, he breezed through all of that, sticking to the facts and even then, he left out as much as he said.

He told David how he and Hollis had walked to Eamon's shop and engaged the shop's manager in conversation, but he didn't mention the part about how Hollis had gone into the shop's office and pocketed an address book. Finn said that they'd been followed by a woman they later found out was Lydia Dempsey and a man who called himself Peter Moodley, but he didn't tell David they'd almost been mugged on their way to Bewley's. He said that Lydia had insisted they go to Galway, but he didn't mention, or even glance toward, the O'Maille's bag with the hidden package waiting to be opened.

Finn spoke effortlessly and with complete sincerity. Had she not been with him, Hollis would have believed he was telling everything he knew.

When Finn was done, David asked, "What did Lahey say to you at the theater?"

Hollis watched Finn smile. It was the one he always gave her when he was about to lie. Not that David would have noticed, but years of marriage give away even the most subtle tells. Finn's lies to her were usually about how he'd be happy to clean the garage or talk about their relationship. The lie he was concocting was more important.

"We went up to him, and said we'd recognized him from the shop. I introduced myself, he told us he was Patrick Lahey, an artist who sometimes worked with Eamon. Then we talked about the play."

There was that smoothness again that made Finn such a captivating storyteller. She watched carefully, but David didn't react to anything Finn was telling him, and it made Hollis wonder if the name

Lahey had really given them—Liam Tierney—would have had a different effect. David had never told them the name of the missing agent, and now she was wondering if he even knew it. She wanted to blame David for manipulating her, but the truth was she'd done it herself.

"He didn't bring up the manuscript?" David asked.

"No," Finn said. "I did."

"You did?"

"Well, he asked why we were in Dublin. I figured whatever side he was on, he would know why, and if I lied it would be more suspicious."

"That makes sense." David smiled toward Hollis. "I think your husband makes a better spy than me."

She put effort into not rolling her eyes. At this point she would have thought anyone was a better agent than David. "I've never been more proud of him."

Finn blushed a little.

David looked embarrassed too, but he turned back to Finn. "What did he ask about the manuscript?"

"He didn't seem that interested."

David nodded. "And that was it? He didn't offer any information, any names of people connected to Eamon? Anything at all?"

Finn was running out of steam, Hollis could tell. He looked toward her, and she jumped into the conversation. "He told us Eamon had a shop in Galway. The Dublin shop was supposed to have been managed by his daughter, but it didn't work out."

"Okay. And then you saw the play, went home, and this Lydia Dempsey woman, what? Came to your hotel and forced you to come to Galway? Does she think the manuscript is here?" David finished his Harp, while Finn downed the whiskey Hollis had left untouched.

"There was something else. About Lahey," Finn said, as he placed the empty glass hard against the desk.

"What?"

"He's dead. Someone killed him during the play."

David sat down. "Who?"

"We got out of there. We didn't want to be the next victims," Hollis said.

"And you didn't see who did it?"

"No," she said. "But Lydia Dempsey was there, and so was Peter Moodley."

"So were about a hundred other people," Finn added. "Any one of them could have killed Lahey."

"So what do we do now?" David asked.

They were all silent for a moment. Then Hollis remembered her phone. "I took pictures," she said. "Maybe you'll recognize someone as being Interpol."

David took the cell and looked at the last photo she took first, of the redheaded woman Finn had spoken to. He shook his head. "No idea who that is," he said. Then he flipped backward, through Hollis's vacation photos of Dublin, to the photo she took of Peter Moodley when she and Finn stopped at the Duke Pub. David's face went pale.

"Does he look familiar?" Finn asked.

"This man's name is Peter Naidoo," David said.

Hollis let out a breath. "You know him? That's good. He's Interpol."

David put the phone down. "He used to be Interpol. Now he's dead."

Thirty-Seven

We just saw him yesterday," Finn said. "When did he die?"

"As I far as I know, he's been dead for about three years." David grabbed the last of the small bottles of whiskey from the minibar, poured himself another drink, and finished it in one gulp. Hollis started to worry that he'd be drunk before he could explain what was going on.

"What does that mean?" she asked. "He obviously didn't die three years ago."

David nodded. "Obviously." He grabbed the room service menu. "Have you eaten? I'm starved."

Before she could stop him, David ordered three entrees, several desserts, a pot of coffee, and a large bottle of whiskey.

"I need you to focus, David," Hollis said. "I need you to tell us what has you so spooked."

He sat in the corner chair. "Here's what I know about Naidoo—or Moodley, or whatever he's calling himself these days. He's about forty, comes from Cape Town, South Africa. He was a soldier of fortune around parts of Africa, then disappeared for several years. He showed up as a student at Cambridge about thirteen years ago. Joined MI6. He was a fixer."

"What does that mean?" Finn asked.

"He was in British Intelligence."

"I got that part," an exasperated Finn said. "What does it mean that he was a fixer?"

"He got rid of evidence, things that intelligence communities don't want people to know," Hollis explained.

"Like what?"

Hollis and David exchanged a glance.

"Like witnesses?" Finn asked, more loudly. "Like idiots who put themselves in the middle of an international crime ring and need to be gotten rid of?"

Hollis shook her head, but she didn't want to speak. David chimed in, "Like paperwork that could compromise identities."

Finn's shoulders relaxed. "Like the Behan manuscript."

"Yes."

"So he's not dangerous?"

"Well, I mean ..." David stumbled. "I suppose if the mission were sufficiently compromised ..."

"Fantastic!" Finn started pacing back and forth like a death row inmate getting his last exercise in the yard. "And I was worried about Peter ruining Hollis's and my careers, our good names being thrown in the mud, and both of us being locked in a prison as members of a secret criminal organization. That all seems so naïve now. Peter's a *fixer* working in intelligence who will murder us. And no one will ever know what happened."

Hollis just stood there. One of them had to stay calm. "David, you said he was dead."

"He was … or officially, he was. Three years ago he was on a mission in Bangkok. I don't know the details. It was inter-agency, like most Interpol missions. A CIA friend of mine was involved. Someone you knew, Hols … Brad Thomas."

"You told me Brad had quit the agency."

"I wanted to downplay the truth. I'm sorry, I thought it would scare you off if you knew. The truth is Brad went into the field and made something of a name for himself. He was the agent I wished I'd been. The agent you could have been."

That fantasy, she realized, was over. "I don't want to play games about what could have been. What happened, David?"

"I don't know, exactly. I just know that whatever happened on that mission, he never came home. They were part of a subgroup of Interpol, less police work, more undercover operations. They go by the name Blue."

"What does it stand for?"

"I don't know. I don't even know what they do. They're a splinter group, under the umbrella of Interpol, but I don't know exactly who they answer to. Brad and Peter were in Bangkok, something went wrong. They said it was a single-engine plane crash, bodies never recovered. Brad was a friend of mine, I couldn't just let it sit, so I went looking into it, a few key strokes here and there."

"You hacked into files?"

"It is my area of expertise. That's the first time I ever heard of Peter Naidoo. The word was, he died right alongside Brad."

"Except he didn't."

"I guess not."

Finn stopped pacing. "So what does that have to do with a missing agent in Ireland?"

"Maybe nothing." David looked at Hollis. "I really am sorry. I've put your lives in danger and we're no closer to finding the missing agent, and in less than thirty-six hours he's probably a dead man."

"My wife and I have been wondering about that," Finn said. "Why kill him Monday? If he's compromised, why are you sure he's not already dead?"

David rubbed his eyes. "We're not sure, we just... hope. Our agent was able to determine the identity of at least one member of TCT. We've been following him for several months. And we know that money from the sale of a forged painting—"

"The Francis Bacon painting," Finn said.

"How do you know about..." David's voice trailed off. "I guess it doesn't matter, but yes, money from that sale, we believe, is being divvied up between five individuals. One person we know about, and four others. We think that the money is currently in a bank account in the Seychelles. And we further believe that the faked Behan manuscript contains information about the account number and password, as well as the identities of at least one other member of the group. And, we think, information about our agent's whereabouts."

"That still doesn't explain Monday."

"I'm getting to that. TCT keeps money in accounts all over the world. In dollars, euros, pounds, yen; every currency you can imagine. It's very difficult to track. In fact, it's painstaking work that I've been involved with as well as many others. But it appears we've succeeded, at least with the individual we've identified. There's an account in Belize and another in Panama. That individual's money will go to one of those."

"Interesting choices," Finn said.

"They're all countries with very secretive banking laws," David said. "The sorts of places where money disappears from prying eyes. If we knew the account information for the bank in the Seychelles, we could stop the money from being transferred, but if we can't, Interpol will work with local authorities in Panama and Belize to freeze the accounts in the limited window we have, which is Monday. It's just one fifth of the money from the Bacon painting, but it's better than nothing. The thing is, we can hide our tracks for the Seychelles account, but once the money is transferred, if we freeze just those two accounts in Panama and Belize, it will be clear we're on to that specific sale. That will be signing our man's death warrant."

"So don't freeze them."

"That was discussed but disregarded. My bosses feel that if we do nothing, odds are the money will disappear again. A few clicks of a mouse are all it takes these days to move millions of dollars. And those millions are just the tip of the iceberg; it's hundreds of millions at this point. Maybe billions. If we're going to bring down TCT, we have to get the money."

"I thought they were just forgers and art thieves. How is it billions of dollars?" Hollis asked.

"They are just forgers and thieves, but they have a cause." He dismissed whatever their cause was with the wave of his hand. "It's just a way for some genius to consolidate international crime rings through the dark channels of the Internet, where it's much easier for them to sell, and much harder for us to identify them. Over the last few years, there've been a number of high-end art and jewel thefts. And on top of that, a lot of fakes—paintings, jewelry, even currency—flooding the international market. Art is the new oil. Screw with its value, make it impossible to know what's real and what isn't, and you've got the potential to destabilize countries."

"So, if we can find the manuscript before Monday, we might save the agent's life and have a bargaining chip with Peter Moodley." She sounded confident but if the stakes were this high, and the group this dangerous, she and Finn were in a mess that could follow them long after they left Ireland—assuming they left at all.

David looked exhausted and embarrassed. For a moment he just stared straight ahead then he looked over at Hollis and mouthed, "I'm sorry."

"If you're sorry," Hollis said, "then do something other than sit there getting drunk."

He nodded. "Okay, you're right. Show me this Lydia woman's picture. Maybe I can figure out how she's involved in all this."

"I didn't take it," Hollis admitted. "When I saw her first at Trinity I didn't think much about it, and there really wasn't a chance after that." Instead, Hollis described Lydia as best she could, hoping David would be able to identify her.

But he couldn't. "A petite brunette with a smart mouth and a red trench coat, who might be CIA."

"I know. It's not a lot to go on. But you didn't send her?"

"No. I sent Lahey."

Finn's jaw clenched so tight Hollis worried it might break off. "Did your bosses send her?"

"I guess it's possible." David looked defeated. "I've just blown my whole career thinking I could be a big man. I'm in so much trouble."

"*You're* in so much trouble?" Finn took a step forward, looking like he was ready to throw a punch. But before he could do anything, there was a knock on the door.

They all froze.

"It's probably room service," Hollis said and took a few steps for the door. But Finn grabbed her arm.

"They always say it's room service in the movies, and then a guy pulls out an AK-47," he said. "Let David get it. He ordered the food."

David got up slowly. Finn pushed Hollis into the bathroom and locked the door. She could hear the door to the room creak open. A man said, "Where shall I leave this sir?" David mumbled something. Then silence for several of the longest seconds Hollis could remember. Finally, "Thanks very much, Mr. Larsson. Have a lovely evening."

Finn whispered into Hollis's ear, "He signed my name to the bill?"

"I guess so," she whispered back. It probably shouldn't have mattered at that moment, but it was a little annoying that they were now paying, literally, for David's screw-ups.

The door to the room shut. A few more moments passed, then there was a knock on the bathroom door. Hollis opened the door to David, facing them with a nervous smile on his face.

"The food is here," he said. "But before we eat, there's something we should probably discuss."

Thirty-Eight

Finn and Hollis walked back into the main room. In the center was a room service table covered with a white tablecloth and practically bursting with food. It was impossible to see what was under the plate covers, but that didn't matter. Because standing behind the table, holding a gun in one hand and pouring herself a whiskey with the other, was Lydia Dempsey.

"She came in with the waiter," David said through a tight smile. "Your description of her was pretty good, Hols."

Lydia raised an eyebrow. "I thought you were going to call me when you picked up the package."

"We were." Hollis pointed toward David. "We got delayed."

"I can see that. It's one hell of a sob story he tells. His old buddy killed in Bangkok. Peter Naidoo returning from the dead..." She rolled her eyes. "The

193

one redeeming thing about having to listen to it was that Finn here seemed about as annoyed as I was. You, on the other hand, Hollis, were way too patient. Maybe you're still carrying a torch for David."

"How do you know what we said?" Hollis asked.

"I bugged the room while you were out this afternoon." She let out a dramatic sigh. "Amateurs. You didn't even bother to look." She reached under the base of a lamp and pulled out a small bug. Then she waved the gun toward David and motioned for him to sit on the bed, which he did. "We might as well eat. No sense in all of this going to waste. Finn, you can join David for the moment. Hollis, why don't you see what we've got?"

Finn sat next to David on the bed, his eye twitching and his jaw clenched. Hollis picked up the plate warmers one by one, revealing steak with mushrooms and baby potatoes, shepherd's pie, salmon, an apple pie, and chocolate cake. It was beautifully plated, but all Hollis could think was how much she wanted to throw up.

"Well, dig in," Lydia said.

"I'm not hungry," Hollis told her. "A big lunch."

"Then have some coffee. I'd like to be civilized. It's not often that I get to spend time with two renowned professors and whoever that is." She waved her gun in David's direction. "I'd like to have a conversation."

Hollis poured cups of coffee for David and Finn, and then one for herself. Lydia told her she'd stick with the whiskey. "That's too big a bottle to go to waste," she said, grabbing the Jameson's for another pour. "So you're some sad sack from tech support who wants to play spy, is that the story?" Lydia asked David.

"I'm not tech support," he said. "I'm a fully trained agent. My specialty is hunting down information online. I assume you're CIA."

"Assume what you like, Doug."

"David."

Lydia shrugged.

It didn't make sense. In Dublin she'd said that David had sent her. She knew his name. Hollis let out an involuntary snicker when she realized what had happened. "You bugged the room in Dublin too. You heard us talking. You heard us say David's name."

Lydia smiled. "Hollis Larsson, you get the most improved fake spy award."

David got up. Lydia pointed her gun at him, but he ignored her and made his way toward the food. It didn't seem like bravery, just a man grasping for even a modicum of self-respect. "I haven't eaten since I left D.C.," he said. "The food on the plane was awful." He took the plate with the steak, sat down at the desk, and started eating. "I should have ordered wine," he added, but it was more of a mumble than anything.

"You sent these two innocents after a missing agent?" Lydia asked him.

"I hear he's your fiancé."

"I'm deeply worried that something will go wrong and I'll never get him back."

"I'll bet you are," David said, his mouth full of potato.

"You've been tracking TCT?" she asked.

"For nearly two years now."

Finn put his coffee cup on the nightstand and gestured to Hollis to sit next to him. She was still standing near the food, next to the chair where Lydia had planted herself. Hollis knew Finn wanted her out of Lydia's way. The gun was now on her lap, seemingly forgotten while Lydia drank her third whiskey and taunted David. Finn waved his hand again, clearly wanting her to come to him. But Hollis didn't want to get out of the way. She wanted to wait until she had a moment, so she could...do something. Run, or grab Lydia's gun...or something. Ideas were flying through her head but they all seemed impractical or dangerous. And, even if she could come up with something that had a shot at succeeding, Hollis wasn't sure she could move. She tried to convey all

195

that in eye contact with Finn, but he just looked angrier and more afraid.

"What do you know about Monday?" Lydia asked David.

"Only that it's the day."

"You're certain?"

He shrugged. "Nothing is certain."

"Not unless someone finds that manuscript."

"Maybe we could help each other. My man in Dublin seems to have died, Eamon is missing, and I'm out of ideas."

"I need to find my fiancé."

"What's his name?" David asked.

Lydia smiled. "You don't know, do you? The manuscript will only get you so far. You need the name."

Hollis felt sick. David didn't even know that Liam Tierney was the name of the man they were risking their lives to save. She started going over a lecture in her head, one that she gave her own students every year, one she had memorized but clearly stopped listening to. That in politics, and often in life, we only seek out information that confirms what we already believe and disregard outcomes that don't suit our preferred narrative. Wars are fought, elections are lost, governments are toppled, all because objective data is ignored in favor of what *feels* true. She'd lectured her students over and over on the dangers of confirmation bias, and yet she'd ignored it herself. A chance for adventure had caused her to overlook the holes in David's story, and Finn's desire to make her happy had carried him along for the ride.

Lydia ignored David's question. "There's word about someone from inside the community helping TCT."

"Any idea who?" David asked.

"Not really. Is that what you're trying to figure out?"

"At the moment," he said, "I'm just trying to stay alive."

Lydia poured herself another drink. As she did she looked over at Hollis, as if she were just now remembering she was in the room. "By the way, where is my package?"

Finn and Hollis exchanged a quick glance. Hollis assumed he was thinking the same thing she was: could they get away with playing dumb, or would they have to hand over their one bargaining chip before they even knew what was inside?

Lydia seemed to pick up on the debate. "The only way I leave this room is with that package under my arm. So you can give it to me, or I can kill all three of you and search for it."

Hollis found the motivation she needed to move her legs. She walked to the other side of the room, to where she had left the O'Maille's bag, and lifted it onto the bed.

"I thought that was just a blanket you bought as a souvenir," David said. "I was pretty surprised that you took time out to shop."

"There's a package we picked up this afternoon. It's wrapped in the blanket," Hollis explained.

"Why didn't you tell me you had something?" he asked.

Finn got up. "I don't know why we should help you," he said. "Or you." He pointed toward Lydia.

"I'm the one with the gun," she reminded him.

Hollis unrolled the throw she and Finn had bought, and inside was the small package addressed to Eamon.

"Open it," Lydia directed.

Hollis carefully opened the box. For the first time it occurred to her the contents might be dangerous, or even terrifying. Kidnappers sent fingers and earlobes through the mail, didn't they?

But inside was just wadded up newspapers. Lydia and David moved closer, both at the opposite side of the bed from Hollis. Finn stayed behind them, near the desk.

"Is that it?" Lydia asked. "Just papers?"

Hollis felt around for something and found a hard lump. She took a deep breath and prepared for the worst. Then she unwrapped the newspaper around it. As she did, she noticed that a phrase on the paper was circled in pencil. She crinkled it as she moved it away and kept unwrapping until she found a white porcelain baby's rattle decorated with shamrocks.

"Looks like Belleek," Finn said, referring to the Northern Irish company known for its delicate pottery. "Seems impractical for a baby."

"I think it's just meant to be a keepsake," Hollis said. It was pretty, she thought, as she examined it more closely. Large for a baby's rattle, but there didn't seem to be anything that suggested it had been broken and repaired—or that it might hold something more pertinent to their situation hidden in the porcelain.

Lydia didn't bother with an examination. She grabbed the rattle and smashed it against the nightstand. There were bits of the delicate ceramic everywhere, but nothing else. She took the box and turned it over. A small card fell out. They all watched it float to the bed. David went to grab it, but Hollis got there first. Lydia cocked her gun and pointed it right at Hollis.

"Read it out loud," she said.

"'To Danu's first child. On your baptism at the parish nearest to Boston.'"

"Who is Danu?" David demanded.

"Eamon has a daughter," Hollis said, her eyes darting toward Finn. Did he remember that Eamon's daughter was named Siobhan? She was hoping if he did, he'd keep his mouth shut about it. But Finn seemed not to be listening.

"I'm done," he shouted.

Lydia and David turned to face Finn. The gun pointed inches from his face. "Not until I say you are," Lydia told him.

"Then shoot me or shut up."

Lydia looked amused, but Hollis was terrified. It wasn't like Finn to shout, but obviously he'd reached his breaking point. "He's cranky from too little sleep," she said.

It didn't help. Finn just got angrier. "I'm cranky from being pushed around and lied to and treated like some pawn in this ridiculous game. All of this nonsense for a baby's rattle. I'm calling for a bellhop to take our bags. Hollis and I are going home." He grabbed the room phone, and as he did, he knocked against David, throwing him momentarily off balance.

David fell against Lydia onto the bed, landing on top of her. He took the opportunity to attempt to get control. Hollis darted out of the way as the two began wrestling for the gun. She reached the room service table just as Lydia started getting the upper hand on David.

"Get off me, you moron!" Lydia shouted.

Finn grabbed the steak knife off David's plate and put it to Lydia's throat. "Drop the gun," he said.

She laughed and started to sit up. Finn pressed the knife into her just a little, drawing blood. Lydia looked almost as surprised as Finn did.

"Your carotid artery is right underneath this skin. If it's cut, you'll start to lose consciousness in about ten seconds. And you'll be dead in less than two minutes."

She stopped moving but she stared hard at Finn. "You're not a killer."

"I'm not a spy either, but I'm figuring out that you have to do whatever needs to be done." He nodded toward the gun. "Hands in the air. Slowly."

"Careful with that knife, Finn," Lydia said. "We're all on the same team."

As she moved her hand off the gun, David grabbed it, and stood up. "No, we're not. We don't even know who you are."

Finn moved back, but he held onto the knife. David pointed the gun directly at Lydia.

"Really?" she said. "Tell me, Tech Support, when's the last time you went to the firing range?"

She had a point. David's hands were shaking. Lydia shifted her weight on the bed, and it seemed to Hollis she was about to make a move.

Finn was gripping the knife, but she knew it was useless now. Lydia would never let him get close enough to use it, even if Finn could bring himself to stab her, which Hollis knew he couldn't.

And if Lydia got the gun ...

Hollis reached behind her to the bottle of whiskey. She hesitated but if she was going to do it, she had to do it quickly. She grabbed the bottle by the neck and, using all her strength, crashed it over Lydia's head.

Lydia turned toward Hollis and smiled. Then she started to get up. For a moment it looked like she was about to put her hands around Hollis's neck. But she only took one staggering step before crumbling to the floor.

Thirty-Nine

I s she unconscious?" David asked.

"For a couple of minutes, maybe more," Hollis said. "There's a lot of variables with a head injury."

David's breathing was heavy and he looked like he might collapse, but he nodded. "Then we should get out of here, get someplace safe so we can figure out where the missing manuscript might be."

"We can't just leave her here like this. She'll come after us," Finn said.

"Should we kill her?" David asked.

"No," Hollis and Finn responded in unison.

Hollis ran to the closet, grabbed the hotel robes, and pulled the belt from one of them. "Tie her hands," she told David.

David dropped the gun on the bed, knelt on the floor, and tied Lydia's hands behind her back.

"Double knot it," Finn told him. He grabbed a lamp, used the knife to cut the cord, then handed it to David. "Twist this around her ankles and the leg of the desk. It's not going to stop her but maybe it will slow her down."

David did as he was told. He looked so overwhelmed that Hollis couldn't help but wonder how he'd managed to stay in the agency all these years.

"Hollis is right," Finn said to David. "There's a lot that can happen when you hit someone over the head. Check to see if she's alive."

David turned Lydia on her back and leaned over her. "She's out cold, but she's still breathing."

"That's good," Finn said. As he spoke, he grabbed the gun off the bed and knocked it against David's head. David fell on top of Lydia, unconscious.

"What the hell did you do that for?" Hollis yelled.

"Do you trust him? Really trust him?"

"Yes. Of course … I don't know."

"Because if we go with him, we're trusting him with our lives. And so far, he hasn't been exactly thinking about our safety. 'We Ourselves,' remember?"

She stared at Finn, trying to make sense of everything that was happening, but there was no time. She didn't know if she trusted David, but she did trust Finn. She grabbed the belt from the other robe and threw it to him. "'We Ourselves.'"

As he tied David's hands, she grabbed the newspapers and card, stuffed them back in the box, and threw them in the bag with the blanket from O'Maille's.

"Check David's pockets," she said. "He said he rented a car. He must have keys."

"Good idea." Finn searched in the pockets and found the keys, a ticket for the hotel's parking lot, and his wallet. He grabbed Lydia's wallet as well.

"You're robbing them?"

"They've been tracing our credit cards, bugging our rooms. What if the euros are marked?" he asked. "Odds are their money is clean. And if we're going to get out of this, we'll need money."

It was a good point. She took the two thousand euros from her purse and returned it to the package that contained the rest of David's fifty thousand. Then she put the package back in her suitcase.

"Why don't you just leave it?" Finn asked.

"Marked or not, he might spend it to come after us. Take out your phone," she said as she grabbed hers from her purse.

"They're turned off."

"I think they can still trace us somehow. I'm not taking any chances."

Finn handed his over, and Hollis threw both phones under the bed.

Finn grabbed both suitcases while Hollis picked up her purse and the bag from O'Maille's. She let him out first, put the "Do Not Disturb" sign on the outside handle, and shut the door.

———

"Which car is it?" Finn asked as soon as they were in the parking lot.

"It's a gray Mazda," she said, pointing to the key fob. "The license number is on it. We just have to look at all the cars until we find the right license plate." Easier said than done, she thought. The lot was filled with gray cars, many of them Mazdas. How much time would it take for David or Lydia to wake up and come looking for them?

"There's a faster way." Finn pressed the alarm button on the key fob. Immediately there was a beeping sound from the next row, at the end. They ran toward the noise. As soon as they spotted it, Finn pressed the key again, and the noise stopped. "Let's hope no one comes to see what that was about."

"People stopped listening to car alarms years ago." At least she hoped they did.

They dumped their suitcases in the trunk and jumped into the car. Hollis had intended to sit in the passenger seat, but she found herself behind the wheel. "Oh crap, they drive on the other side," she said.

"So drive. It can't be that hard."

"And it's a stick shift."

"Hollis. Just drive!"

"Okay." She tried to catch her breath. "My dad taught me how to drive a stick when I was sixteen. He wanted me to have my grandpa's car for my birthday."

"That's the first bit of luck we've had since we got here."

"That was twenty-four years ago, Finn."

He put his hand on hers. "You've got an amazing memory. You're going to remember how to do this."

"Okay. Just remind me what I do first."

"I never learned."

"You never read a book about it? You've read books on everything."

"Clearly not everything," he said, his eyes locked on the parking lot door. "Holly, we really have to get out of here."

"Right." She put her feet on the brake and clutch, turned the car on, and shifted into reverse. "Fingers crossed." She moved her foot from the brake to the gas, and tapped. The car lurched backward. She nearly hit the wall, but she managed to get her foot on the brake in time. "Did I ever tell you my dad gave up after two lessons and bought me an automatic?"

"It's going to be fine." To her ears, though, he didn't sound very sure.

She tried again, putting the car in first, and moving her foot to the gas. She was a little steadier, she thought. The car moved forward slowly. When they reached the attendant, Finn took twenty euros out of Lydia's wallet and handed it over.

"Wow," he said in a half whisper as Hollis drove out of the lot.

"Surprised I haven't crashed yet?"

"No. Lydia's wallet. It must have a couple of thousand euros in it." He opened David's wallet and counted out the bills. "Probably five hundred, I think. Maybe we can use one of the credit cards to buy plane tickets for a flight to Michigan. It will throw them off the scent." He stuffed the money in his own wallet, and put the other two in the pocket of his jacket. "We can use cash to buy our real plane tickets to D.C. and find someone who can actually help us."

"Good plan. Lydia and David will probably figure we're dumb enough to use a credit card. We have been so far."

"Is it a plan? It feels like we're running blind. But you're the one with the covert training, so you must have an idea."

She reached over and took his hand. "I just want you to know something. I have no idea what we're doing."

Even in the dark car she could see his eyes crinkle at the corners. "I think that's what you said on our wedding night and that worked out fine."

She didn't want to, but she laughed. Then a car behind her beeped loudly, and she drove forward into the busy city streets of Galway. As she did, she noticed a car pass them in the opposite direction. When it drove into the brightly lit parking lot of the hotel, she was almost sure she saw Peter Moodley behind the wheel.

Forty

Hollis was done keeping things from Finn, so as she pulled onto the street and away from the hotel, she told him what she saw. She expected him to be upset, but he took the news calmly.

"Then we got out just in time," he said.

"You don't think he'll … get rid of David or Lydia, do you?"

"I'm not rooting for someone to die, but Lydia is dangerous, and whatever happens, David brought it on himself. It's time to admit you were wrong about Lydia looking for her missing fiancé."

"I don't know that I was wrong. There's something more personal, more desperate about her wanting to find him than either Peter or David."

"If I'm right that this isn't about some lost love, then you have to lose every argument we have for the next year."

"Deal. But I don't think I'm going to get in any arguments with you anymore. I've never seen you angry like you were in the hotel room."

He laughed. "Did I ever tell you I played Nathan Detroit in a high school production of *Guys and Dolls*?"

"No!"

"And I was one of the twelve angry men in summer stock right before college."

"You were acting back there?"

"I figured if I created a distraction, I could knock the gun out of Lydia's hands, or get David to do it," he said.

"That was taking a risk."

"We were running out of options. There was nothing of any help in that package we picked up."

"There might have been. The newspaper had something circled. I just glanced at it so I don't know what it was, but maybe the real message was in there."

"When we stop, we'll examine it." Finn looked out the window. "Where are we going anyway?"

It was a good question. They'd only been driving about ten minutes but were nearly at the outskirts of the city. Ahead of them was a highway, to the right a four-lane road. Hollis was beginning to feel comfortable behind the wheel, even if it was on the other side from what she was used to. It helped that they'd been on a main road most of the time, driving straight, not making any turns or hitting any roundabouts. Traffic was light, but it was early Saturday evening, not quite seven o'clock. The sun was still high up in the sky, reminding Hollis how far north Ireland is. And, thankfully, it wasn't raining.

But they couldn't drive around forever. They needed a destination.

"Isn't Shannon Airport on the west coast? Maybe we could get a flight from there," Finn said. But Hollis didn't want to get on a plane just yet. She had a hunch she wanted to test out first.

"I was thinking about the note with the baby rattle," she said. "The parish nearest Boston. Maybe there's a Boston in Ireland and the note is pointing us toward it."

"Maybe. And there's something else bugging me about that note. Danu's child. Danu is the Celtic Goddess of the Tuatha de Danann."

She tried to remember who that was but nothing came up. Mythology was more of Finn's interest than hers. She shrugged her shoulders at him.

"There's a lot of legends that surround them," he said, "but the main one is that they were the Irish race of Gods, who had perfected the use of magic. They were driven underground after a defeat by another group, and became a kind of fairy people who use magic."

"Like leprechauns?"

"Yeah. Danu's child could be a leprechaun." He laughed as he said it.

"We're supposed to take this seriously?"

"I don't know."

She looked down at the gas gauge—the tank was half full. "Let's stop at the next gas station."

"We're not out of gas."

"We don't want to run out on some country road in the middle of nowhere."

Finn looked skeptical but a minute later he pointed to a sign that read Petrol on the right side of the road. "Over there."

Instinctively, Hollis got into the right lane to turn. A car coming toward her slammed on the brakes.

"Eejit!" the driver yelled out his window.

All Hollis could do was smile apologetically and pull into the station.

"You drove into oncoming traffic," Finn said.

"I realize that now."

Once they were safely parked, Hollis took her hands off the wheel and saw that her hands were shaking. Finn got out and pumped the gas, so Hollis went into the mini-mart attached to the station. She smiled at the cashier as she walked in, but he barely took notice. He was reading a magazine with the kind of disinterest that only someone in their twenties can pull off. Same the world over, she thought. With a hipster beard and unkept brown hair that curled at odd angles, he could be one of her students at Bradford who barely noticed her, either.

Hollis wandered the aisles, picking up two bottles of water, a package of Jacob's digestive biscuits, and a bottle of Tylenol. Her hands were still shaking and her heart still pounding, and now her head had joined in the fun. She brought all of her items to the counter, just as a man in his sixties entered the shop.

"Hiya, Jimmy," the man said to the cashier.

"How are things, Sean?"

"Same everywhere."

Hollis smiled at the man's response. "Lovely evening," Hollis said to the cashier.

"That'll be eleven thirty-five."

Hollis took out her debit card. "Oh, wait. I need my husband to pay for this. He's got the cash."

"We take plastic."

"Not this one." She went to the store's window and waved to Finn, who was leaning against the car. When he saw her, he waved back. She waved more frantically.

"You alright?" the clerk said.

"Yes, fine." She gestured more wildly, and Finn finally took the hint and started walking toward her.

"You need something?" Finn asked as he entered the shop.

She held up her debit card. "Cash."

"Right." Finn reached into his wallet and pulled out a twenty-euro bill for the clerk. "Do you have a map of Ireland? We're trying to get to Shannon Airport."

"Yeah, sure, but your phone will have better directions."

"We don't have phones," Finn said.

"Or a GPS gadget. A lot of rentals have them."

"Not ours."

"Right. I thought the Irish were struggling to keep up with America. I guess it's the other way around." The man looked behind the counter for a map. "I'll show you how to get there."

"How do you get to Boston?" Hollis asked. "The Boston in Ireland. If there's a Boston in Ireland."

"There might be," the cashier said. "There's a lot of places in Ireland."

"There is. But ya can't get there from here." The older man approached the counter, balancing a cup of coffee with the paper and a small roll.

Finn laughed. "You can get anywhere from anywhere, can't you?"

"Where's there a village called Boston?" Jimmy, the cashier, asked the older man.

"By the Burren." Sean turned to Hollis. "Do ya have family in Boston?"

"No, just..." Hollis stumbled. "Looking for interesting places."

"The Burren is interesting, alright. Enjoying your visit?"

Hollis smiled. "I've never had a trip quite like this."

"Then you're doing it right," he said, smiling back. "There's a lot of nice places to see in that part of the country, by the Burren. You should go to the Cliffs of Moher..."

Hollis could see that the man was settling in for a long chat, while Finn was looking nervous. "You said there's a Boston. How do we get there?"

"You can't keep on the way you're going," Sean told him. "You have to turn back the other way if it's the coast road ya want. You'll have a nice view while you drive, if you're not in a hurry."

"These two don't want to take the coast road," Jimmy, the cashier, said. "Do you, missus?"

"I don't know," Hollis confessed. "Why wouldn't we want the coast road?"

"How long ya been driving in Ireland?"

"About twenty minutes."

Both men laughed. "So it's the M6 you're after," Jimmy said. "And from there the N18. I'll show you on the map."

Jimmy pulled out a map of Ireland's west coast and traced the route with his finger. "Simple enough, if ya turn back and go Dominick Street to Bridge Street…"

"There'll be loads of traffic," Sean told him. "You can get Market Street from here and that'll take ya right to Abbeygate."

"Ah, you're mad," Jimmy said. "Listen to me, now. Turn back and go to Dominick Street…"

Finn took the map while the two men continued to discuss which street would be a better choice. "I'm sure we'll be okay," he said, dropping another ten euros on the counter.

But Hollis wasn't so sure. A car had pulled up next to theirs, and a familiar face emerged from the driver's seat, looking angry and out of patience.

Forty-One

The area around the pumps was lit up, framing Lydia Dempsey like an actor on stage. She looked angry, and while one hand was on the pump, putting gas into a small white car, the other was rubbing the back of her head, right where the bottle had hit her. Hollis took a little pleasure in that.

There was no sign of David or Peter. Whatever had happened in the hotel, only Lydia seemed to be on their trail. Hollis grabbed Finn's arm and pointed out the window.

"Any chance we can go out the back?" Finn asked Jimmy.

"Isn't your car out front?"

"It's a scavenger hunt," Hollis said. "One of the other competitors is outside and we don't want her to know what we've found out."

Jimmy smiled at Hollis in a way that suggested he wasn't buying a word of her story. "What's this about, really?"

Finn reached into his wallet and took out five twenty-euro bills. "Does it matter?"

Jimmy took the cash. "Not to me."

Hollis could see Lydia walking toward the door of the convenience store. "We have to go now."

"You can go out the employee entrance in back and wait around the corner until she's gone," Jimmy said.

"And you won't tell her we were here?" Hollis asked.

"There's nothing to tell."

Sean waved toward Hollis. "Come on, now. I'll show you."

Hollis followed Sean toward the back of the store with Finn close behind. The employee door stuck a little and Sean had to give it a good pull. Hollis tried to stay calm, but she knew Lydia had been ready to kill them before Finn had put a knife to her throat and Hollis had hit her with a whiskey bottle. She was hardly going to be in a more understanding mood now.

The door finally gave, and Sean let Hollis and Finn go ahead of him. She could hear the bell of the front door tinkle just as Sean closed the door, shutting them off from the store.

"The exit is there," Sean said. "Leave it to Jimmy and me to keep her talking and give you a good head start."

Hollis gave the man a quick hug. "Thank you for helping us. You don't even know who we are."

"Are you dangerous criminals?"

"No," Finn said. "We're spies trying to stay one step ahead of an international ring of art thieves."

Sean laughed. "I knew it had to be something like that."

Finn took out his wallet, pulling out another stack of euros, but Sean waved him off. "We're a nation of rebels," he said. "And we all have to stick together. Be safe, whatever you're doing."

———

Finn went out the back door first and motioned for Hollis. She crept behind him. They were undetectable by the trash cans in back, and on the windowless wall to the side. But when they turned the corner to the front of the station, all Hollis could see was the floor-to-ceiling windows and the brightly lit pumps. Their car was at the station nearest the street, with another set of pumps between it and the store, but it was barely any cover.

"How did she find us anyway?" Finn whispered as they stood at the corner, neither seemingly ready to step out in view.

"Maybe it's a coincidence?" But even as she said it she didn't believe it. "The wallet. I bet she put a tracking device in her own wallet."

"That woman is paranoid."

"She has to be."

Finn took Lydia and David's wallets out of his jacket pocket and threw them both as far as he could toward the back of the gas station. "What if she knows the car?"

"I don't think she knew who David was until he showed up at the hotel. She wouldn't have been watching his car."

"Let's hope so. We walk fast, but not run," Finn suggested. "If we don't look like we're trying to get away, maybe she won't notice."

They each took a deep breath and Finn started walking. Hollis followed him, making a few quick glances toward the store. She could see Lydia with her back to the front, and Sean behind her. Jimmy was ringing her up slowly, chatting and smiling. She must want to strangle them for delaying her, Hollis thought, and then was slightly nervous that she might.

They reached the car and got in. Hollis's hands were shaking, but she got the key in the ignition. "This isn't the time to make a mistake with the clutch," she said out loud.

"You won't." Finn took her hand and kissed it lightly. "You're a trained spy. Top of your class. You know what you're doing."

She nodded, slipped the car into first, and much to her amazement, drove away from the station without hitting anything.

Forty-Two

We get off the highway at the next exit," Finn said
after about forty minutes of driving.

"And then what?"

Finn studied the map for a moment. "It looks
like small roads after that."

Ireland looked like anywhere from the highway
and she'd almost forgotten they'd traveled thousands
of miles from home. But once they took the exit,
Hollis was reminded of how different a place Ireland
really was from her little college town in Michigan.

The road narrowed to two lanes as they entered a
small village. A little stone bridge went over a stream
on the main street. Shops built from concrete and
covered in painted plaster lined each side of the road.
The buildings were colorful, with variations from a

pale yellow to bright blue and deep red. But as they left the village one color stood out—green.

When they drove up a hill, they could see a dozen or more small fields stretching out in front of them. Each patch of grass seemed to have its own shade, from the deepest hunter to a bright kelly green, with purple and white wildflowers adding their color to the mix. Zigzagging through the fields were neatly piled stones fitted together to create fences. Beyond adding a craggy splendor, the fences held in flocks of sheep, who for their part seemed disinterested in escaping. They grazed the deep grass, fat and wooly, looking content. A farmer in faded jeans and rain boots leaned against the stone fence, one hand around a cigarette, the other petting his border collie. It looked to Hollis as though she'd walked into a postcard. Even the air smelled different; an earthy, slightly sweet scent surrounded them that felt both ancient and timeless. Beyond the fields the sun was surrendering to evening and Hollis had a slight moment of panic that the scene would disappear in front of her, as if they'd happened upon a magic they weren't supposed to have seen.

She slowed the car to take it in, and could see that Finn, too, was overwhelmed with the beauty of it. It was unlike Dublin or Galway, unlike anywhere she'd ever been, Hollis thought.

"Almost worth all the trouble we've been through to see this," Finn said. Then he added, "Almost" again.

"It's getting dark. Maybe we should find some place to spend the night. Drive the rest of the way to Boston in the morning. If we're going to look for a leprechaun at a church, we can't do it at night."

"Let's get closer. It can't be much longer anyway," Finn said, glancing down at the map. "A few towns over. I think we make a right at the next road, the one coming up."

"What road?" All Hollis could see was a break in the stone fence.

"There," he said, pointing to the break.

Hollis took a right onto what seemed more like a suggestion of a road than an actual one. The grass gave way to gravel after a few feet, but the road was so narrow there was barely room for the car. A few inches to the left or right would mean scratching up against the stone fence, or a tree branch digging into the car's paint job. It didn't help that just then a large drop of water fell onto the windshield. More drops followed until it was a soft and steady rain.

She drove slowly. "How long are we on this?"

Finn looked at the map. "It looks like it comes to a fork and we go left."

Her shoulders tensed. She really had no idea what she was doing. No idea if Interpol had put them on their most wanted list. No idea if they had escaped Lydia or Peter, if Lydia had let David live. No idea what they were looking for by chasing down the clues from the note, or if it would save the life of the missing agent, or keep them both from being labeled members of the TCT. No idea, even, if they were trespassing on someone's land as they drove the tiny road. It would be helpful to be sure of something. And as the thought popped in her head, she realized there was one thing—Finn. He'd done what he'd once promised to do—been by her side for better or worse for the whole of their marriage. Like the flowers she planted every spring and the classes she taught every fall, he was a constant in her life. She'd forgotten the pleasures of certainty.

"Why are you smiling?" His voice was suspicious.

"Just happy," she admitted.

"You really are nuts if running from people who want to kill us makes you happy."

"You make me happy."

"Oh."

She could see his shoulders relax. He leaned back and settled into his seat, a slight smile on his face matching hers.

The sun was sinking lower and the rain showed no sign of letting up. Hollis stared ahead, looking for the fork in the road that would hopefully get them on a main street with more room and a road sign. But after several minutes of driving they still hadn't seen the fork, and straight ahead was a hill. As they got nearer to the hill, she saw another reason to worry. A car was coming toward them.

"What do we do now?" she practically shouted. There was no way they'd both fit.

The other car was going almost as slowly as Hollis, but it was still coming.

"Should you stop?" Finn asked.

"What good would that do? We're still going to be trying to occupy the same space at the same time, and if I remember my physics classes, that's not really an option."

"One of you can back up."

"It isn't going to be me."

But just a few feet from their car, the other driver pulled into a tiny dent on the side of the road, giving Hollis just enough room to pass.

"That wasn't so bad," Finn said. "I knew they'd have to have a system for this kind of thing."

She bit her lip and kept moving forward. The Irish have a system, she thought, of indirect answers and charming riddles, and always having time to chat. I just need to relax and understand their way of doing things and everything will be fine. After all, she thought, it's two Americans and a South African that have put our lives in danger. So far the Irish have been nothing but kind.

A minute or so later, when she saw a dark van coming toward her, Hollis drove slow and steady, waiting for it to pull over. But it kept coming. She glanced to both sides but couldn't find anywhere to get out of the way. "He knows what he's doing, right?" she said more to herself than Finn.

"Doesn't look like it. He's going kind of fast."

"It looks like he's actually speeding up." She couldn't see the person in the driver's seat, with the rain and the darkness. All she could see was the van getting closer and closer.

"I think you're right, and he's only about twenty feet from us."

And then it was ten feet, and then five.

"He's coming straight for us," Finn shouted.

Hollis saw what she hoped was a chance to avoid a head on collision—a small break in the stone fence on a field to her left. She turned the wheel sharply and stepped on the gas.

Forty-Three

The car came to a stop in the field. Hollis and Finn looked back at the road, where the dark van had paused.

"That was on purpose," Finn said.

"If it was, what do we do now? Get out and run?"

"Can you drive?"

Hollis tried the car. The engine sputtered but didn't catch. She tried again but the sputtering was even weaker this time. She wanted to try a third time, and a fourth, but she knew enough to see there wasn't any point. The car wasn't going anywhere. "I think I hit a stone or something when I turned."

The lights on the van shut off. Hollis heard a door open. She shut off the lights of the car, leaving them all in complete darkness.

"Do we have anything we can use as a weapon?" Finn didn't wait for an answer, he started rifling through the glove box, coming up with only the renter's agreement and a box of Kleenex. "What did you do with Lydia's gun?"

"I didn't do anything with it. You were the one using it to hit David over the head. Didn't you bring it?"

"I dropped it on the bed, then I got distracted when we were talking about David's money being marked. I figured you would grab the gun."

"Why do you always put the responsibility on me to remember things?" she asked. "This is exactly like that time we went to Florida, and you were mad I didn't bring the book you were reading."

"I don't think this is *exactly* like that time."

If they were home, this would be the moment when she walked out of whatever room they were in before a spat turned into a full argument. That wasn't an option now.

"Maybe if we can get to the suitcases there's something in there?" But even as she said it, Hollis knew there was nothing in them that would be a decent weapon. All they could do was lock the doors and keep their eyes peeled on the back window, looking for any sign of the van's driver.

"Is he coming toward us?" Finn asked.

"I can't tell. Are we sure it's a he?"

"No. But Lydia had a small white car, not a black van. We saw it at the gas station."

"And I saw Peter's car when he drove into the parking lot at the hotel. It wasn't a van, either."

"And we're in David's car," Finn added. "So that's everybody, right?"

"Is it?"

They listened, but there was nothing except the wind. But this wasn't just a light breeze, or even the noise of rustling trees or grass as a storm is about to brew. It was a wail that felt almost like someone howling in the first, awful moments of grief. Hollis shuddered.

There was no light coming from the back, no figure coming into view. But from the other direction, a pair of dim lights appeared, then got closer. Hollis watched out the front as the lights moved steadily toward them while Finn kept his eyes on the darkness at the back.

"I think it's a truck," she said.

"Is that good news or bad?"

"I wish I knew."

The truck pulled close to the car. A figure jumped out of the driver's seat and headed toward them, backlit by the headlights of the truck. As he got closer, Hollis could see that it was a middle-aged man in tan pants, rain boots, and a dark wool sweater. He stopped just feet from where they were parked and looked beyond the car to something that had caught his eye.

"What's he doing?" Hollis whispered.

Finn just shrugged. He grabbed Hollis's hand and held it tight.

The man knocked on the driver's-side window and Hollis jumped. "You alright there?" he asked.

Finn and Hollis glanced at each other, and both nodded. If it was trouble, a car window wouldn't be enough to keep them from it, and if it was help, they had just caught a break. Finn rolled down his window.

"We've had an accident," Finn said.

"I can see that. Come in so, and get out of the rain."

They got out of the car, both looking back to the road. There was no one there and no van.

"There was someone coming toward us going very fast," Hollis explained. "There was nowhere to pull over."

"The black van. I thought he was coming to help, but when he saw me he drove away."

"Did you see what he looked like? Are you sure it was a he?" Finn asked.

The man shook his head. He leaned down and looked under the car. "I think you'll need work on this, but it's too late to know anything tonight. We'll know in the morning well enough. I'll drive ya to Bridie Walsh's Bed and Breakfast. She's likely to have a room and a cup a tea." The wind picked up again and the man looked around him. "A banshee wind."

"What's that mean?" Hollis asked.

"The story goes that the banshee howls to warn someone that death is coming for them." He smiled. "If you believe such things."

"Do you?"

He shrugged. "I do not. But no harm in saying an extra prayer tonight, I suppose," he said with a laugh. "But don't worry yourself, the banshee doesn't bother with tourists. At least, I don't think she does."

Hollis smiled, but the cold wind seemed to be surrounding her and whispering into her ear. The one small comfort was that if she was within earshot of the haunting sound, then so was the person in the black van. "I'm sorry about your fence," Hollis said as she wrapped her sweater tightly around her. "We'll pay for any damage."

The man just smiled. He walked over to the pile of stones and began putting them in place like a reverse Jenga, fitting stone on stone. Finn walked over to help, and between the two of them the fence was repaired in minutes.

"My son is an Inspector with the guards ... the police," the man said. "Bright lad, ambitious. But he comes home for a visit and he turns into a teenager again. He took this section down to move sheep to the field across the road. Too lazy to put it back correctly."

"You just take it apart and make a gate? And then put it back together?" Finn asked.

"Sure, and it's as easy as that. And lucky too, I'm guessing. It gave you a chance to get out of the way of that drunkard."

"How do you know he was drunk?"

"What else could he be? He was hardly trying to kill ye on purpose."

Finn and Hollis both nodded, but to Hollis it seemed impossible that the person driving the van had anything else in mind but killing them. But knowing that didn't answer the question of who it was, or why he wanted them dead.

Forty-Four

The man, who introduced himself as Martin Doherty, helped Finn and Hollis load their luggage onto his truck and drove them back toward the village they'd gone through earlier.

"It's not far," he told them. "Just under the bridge, across the river from the castle."

The bed-and-breakfast was almost as he described, at the foot of a small bridge, across a stream from the ruins of what had once been a modest castle. The home was two stories, all stone, with small white flowers climbing vines on both sides of a dark red door. It looked solid, as though it had been there for ages. And more than that, it seemed half hidden away. As she stepped out of the car, Hollis felt safe for the first time in days. No one would look for them here.

Martin had said that the owner, Bridie Walsh, had just celebrated her eightieth birthday and was closing up the place with plans to sell. That was why, he said, she'd be sure to have an available room.

"I hope we're not intruding," Hollis said.

"Nonsense. Come in now," Bridie said, showing them all inside a parlor.

It was a larger room than Hollis had expected, with floral upholstery on a long couch and two overstuffed armchairs. Lace curtains framed the windows, and a dozen different oil paintings depicting scenes of the Irish countryside dotted the walls. In the corner was a large wooden desk in a dark mahogany stain, and on it was a flat screen TV with *Moone Boy* playing quietly.

Bridie switched off the television and told them all to sit. "I'll put the kettle on," she said.

There was a small fire going, with the same slightly sweet smokiness Hollis had smelled earlier as they'd passed through town. When she went to investigate the wood, Martin grabbed a brick from a bucket. Close up it looked like a rectangular clump of dirt.

"Turf," he said, as he threw it on to the fire. "We've been burning it for thousands of years."

"It's an intoxicating scent," she said.

"It's as Irish as a good craic."

Hollis perked up at that word again. Before she left Ireland, she was determined to have some craic, whatever it was.

Bridie came in with a tray. "It's only tea and biscuits. I'm afraid I've nothing much else, though I'll make sure you have something for your breakfast."

"I believe this is what we owe you for the room," Finn said as he took out money from his wallet.

"But your car's broken down," she said. "That'll be a frightful expense."

Finn pressed the cash into her hand. "We're just grateful you're opening up for us."

She put the money in the pocket of her cardigan. "Eat up now. You must be starving with the hunger."

Hollis was suddenly aware of being very hungry, and after they'd finished the tea, Martin offered to take them next door to a pub that was still serving dinner. As they left, Bridie gave Hollis a key.

"This way you can come in when you like," she said. "I don't stay up as late as I did when I was as young as you."

"I'm forty," Hollis told her. "And Finn is about to be."

"As I said, young and in love." Bridie held Hollis's hand for a moment. "You got an awful scare today, but you look like you've come through it. You need a nice evening out to put yourself right."

"That's exactly what I need," Hollis admitted.

———

When they stepped into the Black Sheep, Hollis felt they'd found a dream of what an Irish pub should be. Old and dark with low-beamed ceilings and long wooden tables. The bar ran almost the length of the space, and there was a fireplace and the sweet scent of turf burning in it. They found seats at the end of the bar near the fire, and Hollis was almost hypnotized by the heat and light coming off the crackling flame. The chill in the air, the on-again, off-again rain, and the events of the last few days had made her anxious for comfort wherever she could find it.

Finn ordered three pints of Guinness, and, at the bartender's suggestion, three orders of chicken curry over rice. When they arrived, there was a side of chips, which made Hollis smile.

"It's not a meal without a potato," Martin said when she caught his eye. He picked up his Guinness. "*Slainte!*"

Word spread through the pub that a man had died just an hour before. "A neighbor of mine," Martin said. "Ninety-four last week."

Behind him, a man with a fiddle began playing a slow, sad tune, something Hollis recognized as a traditional Irish folk song. A few tables over, another man started singing. The pub quieted to listen to them. The man sang of leaving Ireland the way someone might weep at the final goodbye with their one true love. It was sweet and haunting and heartbreaking all at once.

"To Seamus Pierce," a man said, and raised his glass. "*Ar dheis Dé go raibh a anam.*"

"May his soul be in God's right hand," Martin explained.

"That's a beautiful song," Hollis said. "A reminder of how many Irish had left their country behind over the centuries, never to return home."

"Ah, and now there's another one left Ireland for good, poor Seamus. Heaven's alright a place, I suppose, but it's not the west country."

Hollis thought of the moaning wind that had wrapped around them in Martin's field, the sad cry of the banshee's wind warning of death. A warning that, she felt relieved, hadn't been for them, and then she felt guilty for being relieved.

After the first song, the fiddler changed to something more lively, and someone with a tin whistle joined in, and another with a guitar. Finn put his hand on Hollis's waist. She could feel the tension leaving their bodies as they let the music wash over them.

When they'd finished eating, Martin ordered a round of drinks. "Where were you headed when you got knocked off the road?"

"Boston," Finn told him. "It's not far from here is it?"

"Just a town or two over," he said. "What's in Boston for you?"

"We're trying to look into something for a friend. All we know is we have to find a church near Boston."

"There's more than one," Martin said.

"Our friend said it was the parish closest to Boston," Hollis explained.

Martin sighed. "He didn't give you a name of the place?"

She shook her head.

He turned toward a man sitting a few stools down. "Pat," he said. "What's the parish closest to Boston?"

The man, who looked like Barry Fitzgerald reincarnated, got off the stool and brought his drink closer to them. "What's this you're after?"

Finn explained that he and Hollis were doing an errand for a friend. Though his explanation sounded vague, Pat seemed to accept it, filling in the blanks for himself.

"An American friend looking for his roots?" the man asked.

"Something like that," Finn told him.

"It must be Our Lady of Saints church, just down the road from the town. But it's a funny thing the way your friend put it. My mother was from the Aran Islands, and I sometimes heard people on the islands say that they were the closest part of Ireland to America, and their little church was the parish closest to Boston. But of course they meant your Boston, in Massachusetts."

Hollis felt her face flush. "Inishmore is one of the Aran Islands, isn't it?"

"It 'tis."

She turned to Finn. "Our friend from the Abbey Theatre was from Inishmore. That can't be a coincidence. And he also said that he and Eamon grew up together. It would make sense that if Eamon were looking to keep something safe, he might bring it home."

"You want to keep going with this, even after today?" he asked.

"I want answers. And I don't trust David to keep us safe, or save our reputations, do you?"

Finn didn't answer. Instead he turned to Martin and Pat. "I think it's my turn for a round."

"I won't turn it down," Pat said.

He settled into a chair next to Martin and they were soon joined by a couple from the village, and another woman named Eileen Sheehan, a retired teacher. Finn and Pat got into a passionate discussion of Irish literature, and a friendly competition as each man vied to find the more obscure writers to quote. Hollis and Eileen exchanged the worst excuses they'd heard from students over the years, discovering that American and Irish teenagers were equally ridiculous in the lengths they went to avoid homework. As the evening wore on, more people joined their group, the musicians started up again, and another round of Guinness was ordered by someone. Strangers treated them both like long-lost members of the family, and she felt as if she were.

"I've been wanting to ask someone," Hollis said to Martin. "We keep hearing about good craic. We want to have some, but we don't know what it is."

He laughed and pointed around the room. "This. A laugh, a grand time with friends, a bit of fun. That's a good craic. You must have something like it at home."

She looked across the small, crowded pub that had welcomed and warmed Finn and her. "Not like this."

Forty-Five

Martin told them the pub closed at eleven thirty, but when the time came, instead of kicking people out, the bartender locked the door, then went back to pouring drinks. She pointed it out to Finn and Pat.

"The pub is closed," Pat explained. "We like to keep the rules while breaking them. And when you're having fun, you don't let the clock tell you it's over."

For the first time since they'd arrived in Ireland, something made perfect sense. Hollis took her turn at ordering a round while Pat tried to stump Finn.

"'But I who have written this story, or rather this fable, give no credence to the various incidents related in it,'" Pat quoted. "'For some things in it are the deceptions of demons, other poetic figments; some are probable, others improbable; while still others are intended for the delectation of foolish men.' Tell me who that is, if you can."

Finn cocked his head, seeming to struggle. A man behind him gave two to one odds he wouldn't know the answer. Then Finn smiled. "It's from an epic poem about a war that started when the Queen of Connacht tried to steal a bull."

"What's it called? Extra points for the Irish name," Pat said.

"It's called 'The Cattle Raid of Cooley.'" Finn blushed. "Couldn't even begin to tell you the name in Irish, let alone pronounce it, but I'm pretty sure it dates back to the twelfth century."

"Well done. Even if you didn't get Tain Bo Cuailange, you still deserve a drink."

Around him, the bar applauded and Finn blushed even more.

An hour later, Hollis and Finn finished their final drinks for the night and left the half dozen or so stragglers with promises to return the next time they were in Ireland. Martin had fallen asleep at a table, but Pat and Finn exchanged email addresses, and Eileen gave Hollis a long hug and promised to friend her on Facebook.

"I feel like we've just left a family reunion," Finn said as they walked into the street.

She grabbed his hand and pulled him toward her. "Have I ever told you how glad I am that you're my family?" She kissed him, first playfully and then with a desire she hadn't felt in a long time.

"Come with me," he said, pulling her toward the small bridge that was in the opposite direction of the bed-and-breakfast.

She went without protesting, though she did wonder if he wasn't feeling the longing for her that she was for him. He led her across the bridge to a low stone wall that separated the castle ruins from the street.

"I'll help you climb over," he said.

"What are we doing?"

"We're storming a castle."

She put her foot on one of the stones that jutted out and pushed herself to the top of the wall. Finn followed, and they jumped the few feet to the other side.

Once in the grounds, they walked across the grass to the center of the castle, now just a few walls of varying heights. Its ruin made it all the more romantic, Hollis thought. She sat on the grass and leaned against one of the stone walls, looking up at the stars. There were a few drops of rain and a slight chill in the air, but she no longer minded.

Finn sat next to her and wrapped his arms around her. "'How many loved your moments of glad grace. And loved your beauty with love false or true. But one man loved the pilgrim soul in you. And loved the sorrows of your changing face.'" He kissed her forehead. "That's Yeats."

"That's beautiful. You love my changing face?"

"I love you. The whole package."

"Even the part that got you into this mess."

"Even that part. And we'll get out of it. Somehow."

She leaned her head onto his shoulder and kissed his neck while he recited poetry to her in the grassy ruins of an Irish castle.

Forty-Six

When she woke up the next morning, Hollis had a headache and a smile on her face. Finn was draped across her, snoring the way he did when he'd had too much to drink. He seemed dead to the world, but when she moved his arm, he woke up.

"What time is it?" Finn asked

"Seven thirty."

"Let's stay in bed all day."

"We can't. Bridie is making breakfast for us. And we have to come up with a plan."

Finn rolled over onto his back. "Right. A plan. For a moment there, I actually forgot about the various people trying to kill us."

"What are we going to do about the car?" Hollis asked as she pulled on enough clothes to make her decent for the trip down the hall to the bathroom.

"I met the local mechanic last night. Eddie ... Something. He said he'd tow the car to his garage this morning. We can stop there on our way out of town and see if it's fixed."

"I found out last night that we can catch a ferry to Inishmore. There's one that leaves from a town called Doolin that's about a half hour from here. And there's another one from Rosseveal, but that's back the other way and more than an hour's drive."

"Doolin it is," Finn got out of bed, grabbed Hollis by the waist, and kissed her.

———

Twenty minutes later, they went down the stairs to breakfast. Bridie was putting a large pot of tea on the table, which was set with three mugs.

"I'm so glad you'll be joining us," Hollis said.

"Oh that's not for me, dear. I have bad news and good news for you. Eddie rang from the garage this morning. He said it would be a few days before he can get the part he needs to fix your car. He said that seeing it's a rental, the smart move is to ring the rental agency's office in Galway and have them come for it."

"Can we get a bus?" Finn asked. "We're headed to Doolin."

"That's the good news. Just after you went out last night, a friend of yours arrived to help. I didn't know you knew anyone in Ireland, being visitors, but there ya go. I'll just get breakfast for the three of you, and you'll be in Doolin by midmorning."

She hurried back into the kitchen. Hollis felt a lump in her stomach, and one look at Finn made it clear he had one too.

"How?" Finn whispered. "No credit cards, no phones. How could someone trace us?"

"Could someone have followed us?"

"The man in the dark van yesterday. He must have."

236

"And he's here now?"

Finn got up from the table. "Let's get out of here."

"Our passports are upstairs."

He grunted. "We leave them. We'll figure that part out later. You don't want to run into our 'friend' in the hall. For right now, we'll walk to a bus stop, or hitch a ride, or something."

But just as Finn spoke, a shadow crossed the threshold to the breakfast room. "I hope I'm not late for breakfast," a familiar voice rang out.

And then Peter Moodley entered the room.

"We haven't started eating yet," Hollis said, trying to keep her voice strong and steady despite her growing fear. "In fact, we were both thinking we'd lie down for a while longer. Too much to drink last night."

"It's easy to do that when the beer is flowing and the company is good." Peter put his hand on Finn's shoulder. "But there's no better cure for a hangover than an Irish fry-up." He took a few steps in front of him, giving Finn no choice but to move back toward his seat. "It'll give us strength for the day."

"Do we need strength for it?" Finn asked, as Peter practically pushed him in his chair.

Peter just smiled. He walked to his chair, and his jacket opened slightly. Hollis could see the holster, and Peter caught her looking. "It's a Walther PPK."

"You carry the same gun as James Bond."

"Yes, but mine's a better caliber. A .380."

"That's the same as a 9mm, isn't it?"

"You know your guns."

He closed his jacket over the holster just as Bridie came in the room with a tray loaded down by three large plates. "Enjoy your breakfast," she said. "If you need seconds, I've got more in the kitchen. You won't leave hungry."

She was right. Hollis looked down at the fried egg, with a yolk that when punctured ran into the bacon. She assumed it was bacon, it looked more like long strips of ham, and tasted perfectly salted. The sausages were thick and long, but lighter in taste than American sausages. And that was only half the plate. The rest was filled with baked beans, a fried tomato, and a round black disc. Hollis poked at it.

"It's a pork sausage," Peter said. "It's really quite good. They call it blood pudding."

"They make it with pig's blood?"

"A little."

Hollis put her fork down and reached for a piece of soda bread instead, slathering it with the soft, creamy butter Bridie had put out.

"Not going to try it?"

"I don't think so."

"You surprise me, Dr. Larsson. I wouldn't have expected you to be put off by a little blood."

Hollis glanced over at Finn, who was pouring himself a second cup of tea. He looked relaxed. He was so good at seeming at ease, she thought with envy. But she noticed he'd glanced over at the door. He was making a plan, she assumed, but she had no idea what it was. Their usual couple's ESP wasn't designed for this situation.

"You left your hotel in quite a hurry," Peter said.

"We were trying to get away from someone who wanted to kill us," Finn answered.

Peter raised an eyebrow. "Not me. I just want to put you in prison."

"We didn't do anything illegal," Finn said. "We were helping Interpol."

"Assuming Blue answers to the bosses at Interpol," Hollis added.

"Blue?" Peter almost smiled.

"The group within the agency. More covert operations, less traditional police work. David explained it to us."

"Who is David?"

"The man you found in our room," Hollis said. "There was a woman too."

Peter shook his head slowly, as if he wasn't sure whether to believe them. "The room was empty when I arrived. Messy, with enough food to feed an army, but there wasn't anyone in it."

Now it was Hollis's turn not to be sure. "Would you tell us if you did find David, or would you just get rid of him and clean up the mess he left?"

"That sounds terrifying," Peter said. "And no, I wouldn't tell you. So well done you, Professor."

"We're not thieves," Finn said. "We're teachers."

"Which is the perfect cover for thieves," Peter told him. "And at the level TCT steals, I wouldn't call you thieves anyway. I'd call you economic terrorists, bent on upending financial markets and plunging the world into a deep depression. And I imagine your own government would call you traitors." He took a bite of his sausage. "But if you tell me where the money is—and, just as important, where the agent is—maybe you won't be put in some off shore detention center while various governments fight over who gets first crack at you. That could take years. It would be a shame to celebrate your fiftieth anniversary hundreds of miles apart, unaware if the other was even alive."

If he was attempting to scare her to her toes, it was working. But Hollis was determined not to show it. "We don't know where either of them are," she said. "But we did hear you were dead. Something happened in Bangkok?"

Peter looked startled, then sad, but only for a moment. He was very good at controlling himself, Hollis realized, but she'd gotten to him.

"You heard wrong."

"And you've heard wrong about us. We're just trying to help David."

"The friend you left for dead in a hotel room? That sounds very helpful."

She gave up. There was no point in trying to explain, it just sounded crazy. They were being bounced from one threat to another, and no one seemed to care that they had gotten themselves in this deep. If David had disappeared, or had been made to disappear, their last chance at an explanation might have gone with him.

Hollis ate the rest of her breakfast in silence, as did Finn. When Bridie would come in to check on them, it was Peter who chatted with her, while Hollis silently asked herself over and over, *How did he find us?*

Finn was right about not using credit cards. They hadn't touched them since they left the hotel in Galway. Nor had they used the Internet or GPS. And Peter couldn't have followed their car. He was entering the hotel as they were leaving. He could have seen them, she supposed. After all, they saw him. But he was already in the lane to enter the garage, with no way to turn around. He would have had to go into the garage and pay to come out again, and by then they were already on their way. And even if he'd managed it, if he'd been following that closely, why wait until breakfast? Why not grab them in the gas station, or when they were stuck in Martin's field? There was something else, she was convinced of it, something they'd missed that had brought Peter straight toward them.

She and Finn kept eating, kept delaying, until they'd cleaned their plates, which made Bridie smile. "Does my heart good to see my cooking so admired," she said. "And I'm glad to see you've got a friend to help you sort out the trouble with your car."

Finn got up from the table, finishing the last of his tea while he did. "Hollis and I need to finish packing before we go."

Peter got up with him, blocking his exit from the room. "That was wonderful, Bridie. Exactly what we needed. But I think Hollis can finish packing on her own. Why don't we go outside, Finn?"

Hollis glanced toward Finn. That had been his plan. If they went upstairs together, they could somehow escape from the second-story window of their room by the trellis. But separated, there was no chance.

"I'll be right back," she said.

"Take your time," Peter answered. "I won't let Finn out of my sight until you return." He patted his coat at the spot his gun was hidden.

Hollis held Finn's hand tightly, then left him behind to go upstairs.

Forty-Seven

Hollis went inside the room, where Finn had already packed the suitcases. The room looked the same as when they'd left it thirty minutes before. But then they were rekindling their romance, and even excited about figuring out the latest clue. It was frightening how quickly things kept changing. There had to be a way to get ahead of everyone, and stay ahead. Instead of going back downstairs quickly, Hollis sat on the bed and went through her case. She reopened the package that had once contained the rattle and looked for the circled words in the newspaper. It was from a story on a car thief that seemed to have nothing in common with the situation at hand. The cop's quote, "Confession is good for the soul," was the phrase she'd seen circled.

"That doesn't help much, does it," she said to herself.

She took out the papers and the note about Danu's child, and left them in the nightstand drawer. She emptied her purse, found the address book and her Bradford ID, and added them to the pile. She scribbled a note on the back of the receipt from O'Maille's. *Taken by a man named Peter Moodley, potential killer of Lahey in Abbey Theatre. Need help.*

She quickly went through her purse. She'd begun to wonder if maybe Peter had put a tracking device in it, but there was nothing she didn't recognize. She ran her hand against the lining, even emptied the coins from her wallet. Nothing. She wanted to go piece by piece through the luggage but they would be waiting downstairs, and Peter didn't seem the patient type, no matter how pleasantly he chatted with Bridie.

She put the items back into her purse, and was about to grab the suitcases when it struck her. It hadn't been *her* purse that Peter touched. It had been the one David gave them to hold the manuscript. She threw her case on the bed, zipped it open, and ran her hands through that handbag. Inside she found a round, metal disc no larger than a quarter. She hadn't kept up on tracking devices in her years since training, but she knew it had to be one. It certainly wasn't something of hers.

She threw the green purse on the bed, re-zipped her luggage, and went downstairs. Getting rid of it now wouldn't help them much unless they could get rid of Peter too, but one problem at a time, she told herself.

———

Neither Peter nor Finn were downstairs. Bridie appeared from the kitchen to say goodbye, and to let her know the men had gone out the front gate to Peter's car.

"Thanks for everything," she told Bridie.

"I'm sorry about the car, dear. Here's hoping your next trip to Ireland won't be as eventful."

"You don't know the half of it," she said. "Will you do me a favor?"

"Anything dear."

"After we've gone, can you call Martin and tell him we left him something in the nightstand drawer in the bedroom? Tell him it's a gift for his son."

"A gift for Martin's son? You've made all kinds of friends in Ireland, haven't you?"

Hollis attempted a smile.

"Are you all right?" Bridie asked.

She wanted to tell Bridie that she wasn't. That Peter wasn't a friend, but either a man intent on locking them up for a crime they didn't commit, or one with a plan to kill them. But telling Bridie now, with Peter just outside, would put her life in danger too.

"I'm fine. Just let Martin's son know about what's upstairs."

Hollis walked outside and closed the door behind her, rolling the cases down the pathway. She could see in the daylight that pink roses lined the path from the house to the gate, and at another time she would have loved to stop and enjoy them. She could even see the castle ruins across the bridge. In daylight it was a stone turret, with a few half walls around it. The stone fence they'd climbed the night before was crumbling in places. It was as romantic as it had been then, but looking at it now, it was almost impossible to believe she'd felt so relaxed and happy just a few hours earlier.

Her eyes moved from the castle to the street. Parked just in front of the bed and breakfast, was a dark van. *The* dark van that had run them off the road. Standing at the back of it in front of an open door, were Peter and Finn, talking to a third man. He had his back to her, but there was something vaguely familiar about him. Finn caught her eye and mouthed, *"Run,"* but she shook her head. She wasn't going anywhere without him. Had Peter been the driver of the van to run them off the road? Was the man they were talking to his accomplice? Every time she thought things were bad, they seemed to get worse.

She took one step closer when she heard a voice behind her. "Those cases are heavy. You should let me take them."

She turned and saw Declan Murphy, the young man from the train. "What are you ..." Her voice was feeble and she couldn't finish the sentence.

"You and Finn really do get around, don't you? I've had an awful time keeping up with you."

"What do you want?"

He smiled. In his hand she saw something. A syringe. Before she could react, she felt the sting of a needle in her neck, and the sensation of collapsing into his arms.

Forty-Eight

Hollis banged her head against the inside wall of the van. She felt woozy and her entire body ached. It took almost more energy than she had to open her eyes, but when she did she was relieved to see Finn across from her.

He looked better than she felt. He was sitting with his knees bent and his hands on the floor of the van, steadying himself against the constant movement. Their two suitcases were jammed against a spare tire, which kept them from moving, but Hollis's purse was sliding up and back. She put her foot out and caught the strap, pulling the bag toward her. There were no windows in the back, but there was light coming from the windshield, enough for her to see Finn give her a small, comforting smile.

"What's going on?" she whispered.

"They're driving us somewhere."

"*They* who?" She turned her head and felt a sharp pain in the center of her forehead. She longed for the simplicity of her hangover from the morning. At least it had been the prize of a night's fun. The reward this time was the outline of two hazy figures in the front of the van. She knew Declan Murphy must be one of them, but she could only see the back of the man in the driver's seat. "Who is…" It was hard to get the words out. She leaned her head against the wall of the van, which she immediately regretted when they hit a bump in the road. She wanted to move to Finn's arms, but she didn't have the energy. Everything felt like a struggle, as if she were weighted down with chains. But when she looked at her hands and feet, there was nothing holding her. Just the effect of the drug she'd been given, and she had no idea how long that would last.

"It's Keiran," Finn said, keeping his voice in the same low whisper that Hollis had used.

"From the shop?"

It made sense. He'd been in on the whole thing from the beginning, but they'd been too giddy with what they thought was a safe adventure to pay attention. She turned her head back to Finn, and for the first time realized they were alone in the back. "Where's Peter?"

"Down an embankment about three miles back. They pulled over once we were out of town, grabbed him out of the van, and rolled him down a hill."

"He let them?"

"He didn't have much say in the matter. He was out cold."

"They didn't kill him though?" she asked.

"I don't think so. I didn't hear any shots, and I don't think the tranquilizer was strong enough to kill. Yours wasn't."

"What do they want?"

247

"I don't know. They just walked up to us when Peter and I were standing outside. I recognized them both, but I didn't know what side they were on. For all I knew they were with Peter. Or Interpol trying to stop Peter.

"I don't think they're Interpol."

"Probably not, considering our circumstances. But I didn't know. And before I could do anything, they'd stabbed you and Peter with syringes full of tranquilizer and threw you both in the back of the van."

"Why not you?" she asked.

"Kieran said they'd only brought two syringes. One for each of us. I guess they hadn't planned on our running into Peter. Kieran said that he watched you drop kick that guy who tried to steal your purse, so he figured you were more of a threat than me." He frowned as he said it.

"What's wrong?"

"It's a bit emasculating."

She wanted to laugh that Finn was hurt no one had drugged him, but her face was sore, and it would only make him feel worse. "I'm glad you were awake. It makes me feel better to know you were watching over me."

"They knew I wouldn't put up a fuss if you were in danger, so I just got into the van."

"How long was I out?"

"About fifteen minutes." Finn glanced toward the front. "There's something else you should know."

"Worse than we've been kidnapped?"

"I don't know. It's something that happened before they showed up. When we went outside, Peter lit a cigarette, asked me if I wanted one. I said I did."

"You gave up smoking years ago."

"It seemed like a good moment to start up again."

248

"You promised me you would never have another cigarette. It was your fifth-anniversary present to me."

Finn gritted his teeth. "Do you really think the long-term effects of nicotine are our biggest problem right now?"

She bit her lip. "Fine. You had a cigarette. What happened then?"

"Peter said something odd. He said he'd been confused about us at the beginning, but once we came to the west of Ireland he figured it out."

"About David."

"Not about David," Finn said, his voice so low that Hollis could barely hear him. He glanced again toward the men in front, then leaned toward Hollis. "He asked me if I was going to go back to being a small-town college professor or if the allure of being the agent was too much to give up. He didn't say 'an' agent, as in, I like working undercover. He said, 'the' agent."

"He thinks you're the missing Interpol agent?"

"I've been thinking. Maybe Liam Tierney isn't missing. Maybe he's not even Interpol."

"Then who is he?" Hollis asked.

Finn shrugged, then the van came to a sudden stop.

Forty-Nine

You all right back there?" Declan called out.

"What do you want with us?" Hollis asked him.

"Ah now, don't be cross with me. Just enjoy yourselves a bit. Hard to see the scenery from the cheap seats, I know, but it's a grand part of the country we're in. The Burren, it's called. Do you know much about it?"

"Not really."

"Well, then we'll get out and stretch our legs a bit. You can see for yourself."

"Is that what this is, Declan?" she asked. "A guided tour of Ireland's countryside?"

"If ya like," he said. Then he turned up the radio, blasting the Cranberries.

Finn reached forward and grabbed Hollis's hand.

"Can we run?" she whispered to him.

He shook his head. "They have guns."

"We're not tied up. Maybe they don't know what they're doing. Maybe if we rush them, catch them by surprise ..."

"We can try," Finn said, but he didn't sound optimistic.

Hollis and Finn turned to face the doors, moving to a crouch so they'd be ready to jump if the opportunity arose. The van doors opened, and Declan was standing outside, smiling, holding an assault rifle pointed at Hollis.

"I understand you're the one with the black belt," he said. "I have to keep my eyes on you then."

As they stepped out, Hollis looked around at the landscape. It was quite unlike anything she'd seen in Ireland. There was still emerald green grass, but it was straining to break through the gray rock. There were odd flowers, varieties she hadn't seen in the rest of the country. And she could see the Atlantic Ocean in the distance, angrily crashing against the stone as if it stood in the way of the sea reclaiming this strange terrain.

"You both would know who Oliver Cromwell was," Declan said, "The devil himself in the form of an Englishman. He sent one of his generals here in 1650 or thereabouts, when he was terrorizing good, decent people. The man said of the Burren, 'There isn't a tree to hang a man, water to drown a man, nor soil to bury a man.' Seems a good place for a nice quiet chat, don't you think?"

Hollis shuddered, as much from his words as from the cold. She regretted the light cotton sweater she had on over her t-shirt, and choosing light tan pants and flat shoes. She hadn't dressed for a rocky terrain, or for a kidnapping. She wrapped her arms tight across her chest and noticed Finn doing the same.

"It's a bit cold today," Declan said, looking up at the dark sky. "That's the thing about Irish springs—you can't count on a nice day. Not like Australia. Or America."

"So you really did visit cousins in Philly," Hollis said. "And now Australia too."

"I've been a lot of places, Hollis."

"That's a lot of travel for a grad student in psychology."

He laughed. "It was only a small lie. In my own way I'm quite an expert on people. I knew you two had the bit between your teeth. Couldn't just leave well enough alone, and see where it landed ya."

"We don't actually know anything," Finn said. "We don't even know who you are."

"Don't ya?"

Kieran came to the back of the van holding a handgun that he waved around. It was clear to Hollis by the way he held it that Kieran knew nothing about guns. It should have been reassuring, but Hollis knew that it just made him more dangerous.

"That's enough chatter," Kieran said. "Let's take them inside."

Keiran led the way, wearing a black backpack that seemed heavy for his frame. They walked on weathered limestone, uneven and, at times, slippery. Hollis had no idea where they were headed and nothing in the landscape offered any clues. She felt as if she were on another planet, one that was both barren and full of life. It was eerie, but breathtaking.

"It's an odd place," Declan said as he walked behind them. "There's plants here that you only ever see in the Arctic, and other plants that are native to the Mediterranean. Here they grow side by side. They don't know why, the scientists. They don't even know how they got here. That's why I like this place. It's beautiful chaos."

"Is that what you're trying to create, Declan, beautiful chaos?" Finn asked. "Or should I call you Liam?"

"Nice try, Professor," he said.

"So Keiran is Liam?"

"Wrong again. You can look all you want but you won't find Liam Tierney."

Keiran stopped in front of a cave, put down his backpack, and looked around. "Too dark a day for tourists this far out," he said. "I guess we got lucky." He pushed Finn toward the entrance to the cave, but Finn resisted until Declan moved his gun just inches from Hollis's nose.

"There won't be a bit left of her lovely face if you force me to shoot," he told Finn.

Reluctantly, Finn ducked his head and entered the cave with Keiran close behind. Hollis tried to follow, but Declan held up his hand to stop her.

"You're not separating us, and if you try, you will have to shoot me. I won't leave him any other way," Hollis said.

"I'm not going to shoot you and I'm not going to separate you, so there's no need to scold me. I'm terrified enough of Americans as it is."

"You're terrified of Americans?"

"Well, you're all so confident. There's not a one of you that slouches. You walk around like you own the earth, which I suppose you very nearly do. And you smile. All of you Americans. Always smiling. It's overwhelming for a country boy like me."

"I thought you were from Dublin."

Declan looked to the sky briefly, a slight smile on his face. "My ma always said if you don't have a good memory, you better tell the truth. I suppose I should have listened to her."

Hollis tried looking behind Declan toward the entrance to the cave, but he was nearly a half foot taller than her and the cave was dark. All she could do was wait and listen. But she couldn't hear anything. No shouting, no gun shots. The silence, she hoped, was a good thing.

"I don't know what side of this craziness you're on," she said, "but we really are just two college professors from Michigan who thought we were helping to find a missing agent named Liam Tierney."

He scratched his head, then sighed. Then he sighed again. "Where's the manuscript?"

"I don't know."

"Where's Eamon?"

"I don't know that either."

"What do you know?"

She didn't know how to answer that, because the simple truth was that she wasn't sure about anything. Peter was either going to throw Finn and her in jail, kill them, or he was dead on the side of the road. David could be searching for them, or Lydia could have killed him and hidden his body. Liam Tierney could be an agent in trouble, or dead, or he might be the person standing in front of her. But one thing was certain: Declan wasn't going to let her see Finn until she answered his question.

"I know there's a woman named Lydia Dempsey who believes the man she loves is in trouble, and she'll do just about anything to save him."

Much to her surprise, his smile disappeared and he seemed almost wistful. "What makes you think I know Lydia Dempsey?"

"She showed me a picture of the man she said she loved. I couldn't see the man's face, but he had a birthmark on his palm. When you held up your hand to stop me from walking into the cave, I saw the same birthmark on your palm."

He seemed impressed. "I think *love* might be a strong word, as it turns out. Let's call it a mutually beneficial relationship."

"So you are Liam Tierney."

"There is no Liam Tierney. Not yet, anyway."

"Does Lydia know that? Is she in on this, or did you lie to her? I have kind of a bet with my husband about it."

"She told me things she shouldn't have, and I told her things I shouldn't have," he said.

"Is she CIA or TCT?"

"You can't be both?"

"I suppose you can be. You used to be Irish Military Intelligence."

He took a deep breath. "I seem to have lost the advantage that having a very large gun is supposed to give me. Let's get back to what you know about where the manuscript is."

"The one with the account number that leads to millions of dollars."

"There ya go, Dr. Larsson. You found your way to the subject at hand."

"Why are you looking for it? I thought you wrote it."

"Eamon Byrnes wrote it." Declan grunted in a way that was very similar to Finn. Maybe she just had that effect on men, she thought, exasperated them. If that was the case, she would wait and say nothing. It usually worked with her husband. Declan snorted a little and looked up toward the sky. "Mother of God," he whispered. Either it was a prayer or a curse, Hollis couldn't tell. Then he looked directly at Hollis. "Eamon is the agent."

That made no sense. David would have known, she started to tell herself, then decided to add it to the list of things David should have known. "An Interpol agent?"

"The agent for TCT who set up the sale. The rest of us only have a piece of the puzzle; Eamon's the one who knows the whole deal."

"That's the agent everyone has been looking for?"

"Who did you think?"

"Our handler told us something else ..."

"Peter Moodley? I've not met the man but I hear he's one of the best Interpol has. Always about getting the truth, always trying to do the right thing. I'm surprised he sent you without knowing who you were after."

"He didn't send us. A man named David Agnelli did."

"Who's that?"

The drugs she'd been given were still lingering, leaving her aching to sit down. But they were in competition with the adrenalin that jumped into high gear every time someone stuck a gun in her face. "It's a really long story. And I have a feeling it doesn't end well."

Declan stared at her a long while, then lowered his gun. "Cheer up, Hollis. If your husband is telling the same thing to Kieran, everything might work out."

There was nothing menacing in his eyes, just the same cheerful expression he'd had on the train to Galway, eating crisps and smiling. But she'd been wrong a lot this last week—wrong about David's competence, and if Declan was telling the truth, wrong about Peter Moodley's intentions. She wanted to believe that somehow she and Finn would get out of this alive if they kept calm and stayed together. Of all the things she'd been wrong about, she hoped she was right about that.

"Finn will be telling Keiran the same thing," she said, "because if we really were master spies, we wouldn't be in this mess in the first place."

As if on cue, Kieran walked out of the cave. "Bring her in."

Fifty

Hollis followed Kieran inside the cave, with Declan just steps behind. The temperature dropped about ten degrees, but that wasn't what made Hollis shiver. There was no sign of Finn.

Kieran kept walking, and Hollis tried to keep up, which wasn't easy. While he was wearing hiking boots, Hollis wore flats that slipped on the limestone rock with nearly every step. She'd never been in a cave before and it was more colorful than she had expected—the rock ranged from almost ivory to gold, with flecks of a rusty brown. It was also narrower than she would have liked. She felt, perhaps irrationally, like every breath was a struggle.

After a few yards, Kieran turned a corner, and seemed to disappear.

Hollis turned to Declan. "Where's Finn?"

"Just keep going, Hollis."

As she turned the corner, to Hollis's relief, she saw that Finn was alive. He was sitting on the ground, his wrists and ankles bound with duct tape, but otherwise he was unharmed. He let out a breath it seemed he'd been holding for a while, and smiled. She mouthed, "I love you," and he nodded.

"Sit down anywhere," Declan directed her. "Sorry there's nowhere comfortable."

Hollis ran over to Finn, sitting as close to him as she could, and circling his right arm with her hands. She wanted to touch him, to make sure he was okay, but she also knew if she tugged a little, it could loosen the tape. There was little chance they could escape with two guns pointed at them, but that didn't mean they shouldn't try.

Kieran grabbed the duct tape from his backpack and walked to where Hollis was sitting. But as he did, a bird flew into the cave, right past him and landed on a rock above where Hollis and Finn were sitting. It was black with a white belly and blue-black wings, quite pretty to Hollis's eyes. It didn't look like a particularly aggressive bird, but it stopped Kieran in his tracks.

"Get it out of here," he shouted to Declan.

"It's just a magpie. It'll do you no harm."

"It's bad luck."

"That's an old *piseog*."

"Get it out of here," Kieran said again.

Declan rolled his eyes, took off his jacket, and waved it at the bird, which flew farther into the cave.

"You sent it in the wrong direction," Kieran yelled.

"There's an exit that way, a few meters down. Maybe he'll find it."

"You better hope so."

"If you're going to fall for every stupid superstition, you've no business in our line of work." Declan's voice was tense, but steady. A man not easily rattled, thought Hollis. He would be the one to reason with—assuming reason mattered at this point. Declan pulled Kieran to one side and seemed to be counseling him, something the shop manager didn't appear to enjoy.

"What did you tell Kieran?" Hollis whispered to Finn.

"That there was fifty thousand euros in our suitcases, and he could have it all if he let us go. He said that kind of money wasn't worth the walk down the hill." He glanced toward the men, then lowered his voice even more. "I was thinking, though, that if Peter is okay, he'll find us. He must have put a tracker in our luggage, that's the only way he could have kept on our trail. I'm willing to risk prison if it gets us out of here."

Hollis felt herself going suddenly pale. "He did use a tracker. He put it in the green purse. I realized that in the bedroom at the bed-and-breakfast, so I left the purse there. Even if he is okay, I don't think he'll be able to find us now."

Finn leaned his shoulder onto hers. "Then we'll get out of this ourselves. Your years of martial arts training and knowledge of weaponry, and my almost total recall of Irish literature. It's a winning combination."

She laughed a little. "Did you remember reading anything in the classics about how to disarm two criminals and escape from a cave?"

"Didn't come up a lot in the works of James Joyce."

Declan grabbed the duct tape from Kieran. "Go see what you can find," he directed him. Kieran gave one last icy stare at Hollis and Finn, then left the cave. Declan knelt in front of Hollis. "Put your hands out."

She did as directed, keeping her elbows close together. Somewhere in the back of her mind she recalled her CIA training about getting out of restraints. The closer her elbows were, the easier it would be to use her arms to pull the tape apart. She realized that Declan must have known the same trick, because he smiled when she did it. But he didn't adjust her arms. Instead, he wrapped her wrists with about half the tape that covered Finn's wrists. He put even less effort into taping her ankles together. She could feel a looseness in the wrap even as he was finishing.

Then he slowly patted her down, going through her pockets but finding nothing. He did the same with Finn. He pulled out Finn's wallet and smiled when he saw all the cash.

"If I'd known teaching paid this well, I'd have worked harder at my lessons," he said, then put the wallet back in Finn's pocket.

"You and Kieran are working together? I should have seen that," Hollis said.

"We're not working together so much as I've taken on an apprentice. And you *should* have seen it, Hollis. You bumped right into me on Grafton Street. I was following you, texting Kieran about you. I thought you used to be a spy or something. You didn't even recognize me when I got on the train."

She bit her lip. She remembered bumping into a polite man who was busy texting, but she never really looked at his face. "I was excited to be in Dublin."

"Well, it's a grand city, so you're forgiven."

"So you're TCT," Finn said.

"What do you know about it?" Declan asked.

"That it's a dangerous criminal organization that was involved in the sale of a fake Francis Bacon painting for a hundred and twenty-five million dollars. The real painting is out there somewhere. Aren't you worried it will surface?"

"Do you know what a free port is?"

"There are places in some countries around the world that allow rich people to store valuables … art and antiquities, to avoid paying taxes on them in their home country."

"Priceless things that should be in a museum for the whole world to enjoy, but they sit in crates. The real Bacon is in a free port in Zurich, and the fake"—he laughed—"is headed to a free port in Monaco. I could make a dozen more, and odds are they'd sit in warehouses all over the world, never seen, never enjoyed, and none of the eejits who bought the work would ever be the wiser."

"You can't make a dozen more," Hollis said. "You killed Patrick Lahey, and he was the forger, wasn't he?"

Declan looked startled by the accusation. "I didn't kill him. How do I know you didn't kill him? You were sitting right behind him at the theater."

"You were there?"

"And you didn't notice, Hollis. You need to work on that. But never mind, I had my own troubles. I was trying to give Lydia the slip. Woman scorned and all that."

"We didn't kill him," Finn said. "We're not working for TCT, which you obviously know. And in case you're wondering, we're not Interpol."

"I'm not wondering, actually. It's a terrible shame. Patrick was a good man." Hollis thought she heard a catch in Declan's throat. He swallowed hard. "He was a true believer in the cause."

"What cause? Getting rich?" Finn asked.

Declan sat on a small rock and faced them. "'Was the earth made to preserve a few covetous, proud men to live at ease, and for them to bag and barn up the treasures of the earth from others, that these may beg and starve in a fruitful land,'" he said, "'or was it made to preserve all her children?'"

Hollis paused. She knew that line from somewhere, a class she'd taken in grad school on failed political movements. "That's Gerrard Winstanley," she finally remembered.

Finn pumped his bounded wrists. "That's it. The shovel on Lahey's card. It was a symbol of your organization. You're a new incarnation of the Diggers."

"An homage, really," Declan said, smiling. He leaned in. "They believed that resources were in the hands of too few men, resources that were left unused or squandered needlessly, while the rest of us had to share what was left over. And it may be almost four hundred years ago, but that was one Englishman who knew what he was talking about."

"So the money you'll get from the forged painting, the hundred and twenty-five million, you're going to share with the world?" Finn asked.

Declan shrugged. "The point isn't the money, it's the disruption. It's the devaluation of items rich people collect."

"TCT, the common treasury," Hollis blurted out. "Wasn't that what Winstanley called the land? Something that belonged to everyone."

"Yes, and that's what art is. That's what antiquities are. They don't belong in free ports, making the rich richer and depriving the rest of us of their beauty. They belong to all of us. But tech billionaires, and oil billionaires, and the well-connected of the world—they buy art and rare books and priceless objects like they're stocks in a company, and then squirrel them away. They don't even hang them on their own walls in their own homes, where at least a special few might enjoy them. They don't care about the work, they only care about the money."

"So you're donating the money to a museum to help them compete at auction?" Finn said, a smirk on his face. He was baiting Declan into defending his stand. Finn loved a good intellectual argument, Hollis knew, but maybe this wasn't the time.

Declan stood up. She could see that he was getting animated, and there was no telling how passionate he would get about his cause, especially when his motives were challenged and weapons were involved. Kieran had still not returned from wherever he'd gone, so Declan couldn't be putting on a show for him. Hollis's already slim hopes that he was undercover for Interpol were coming to an end.

"We don't care what you do with the money," Hollis jumped in. "Finn doesn't mean anything by what he said. He gets argumentative sometimes for the sake of it. He actually said something similar to what you said when he first heard the painting had sold privately without anyone being able to even see it."

Declan looked at her, his face in a scowl. Then he turned to Finn. "There's an Irish saying you'll like Finn. 'If you want praise, die. If you want blame, marry.' You already have one. Be careful you don't try for both."

Fifty-One

Kieran walked back into the cave, shaking his head.

"Stay put," Declan said. He grabbed Kieran's arm and pulled him several yards away from Hollis and Finn.

Hollis watched as the two men whispered. She couldn't hear them, but she could see that neither looked pleased. Finally Declan let out a sigh, and it set Kieran off. He waved his gun at him and came stomping back toward Hollis and Finn. He pointed the gun at Finn's head but his eyes were on Hollis.

"What did you take from the back room of the shop?"

"I don't know what you're talking about."

He pressed the gun into Finn's head. "You want to try again?"

"Don't lie, Hollis," Declan said. "I was on the stairs at the shop, hiding when you came in. I nearly fell down at one point. I couldn't see what you were doing, but you had a go at the desk, that much I could tell."

"An address book," she said. She kept her eyes locked with Finn, trying to look hopeful and strong, but her tear ducts betrayed her. A drop of salty water ran down her cheek. "I don't have it anymore. I gave it to the police. Indirectly. I gave it to a friend to hand over to his son, who's an inspector with the Garda."

"What did the address book have in it?" Declan asked.

"The names of authors. I just skimmed it. The only one I remember is Brendan Behan."

"Did it have any clues about the manuscript?"

"No. I swear. It didn't."

Kieran pressed the gun even harder, and Finn closed his eyes. Hollis screamed.

"Take the gun away," Declan said.

Kieran hesitated, but after a moment he bent his elbow, pointing the gun toward the ceiling.

"None of your friends—Peter or that David fellow   have the man uscript?" Declan asked.

Finn shook his head. "They're looking for it, the same as you. Maybe Eamon sold it to someone else."

"He wouldn't have done that. And Patrick Lahey didn't say anything to you about Eamon?"

"No. He just told us he sold things to Eamon from time to time. That they'd grown up together. Nothing that will get you what you want."

Declan took a deep breath, seeming to consider something. Then he turned to Kieran. "They don't seem to be as much help as we hoped. *Cad a dheanaimid leo?*"

Kieran gave Hollis an icy stare. *"Againn a mharu iad."*

The magpie came back into the room, flying circles overhead. Declan tried to swat it away, but Kieran raised his gun and shot it. The bird dropped to the ground in a thud as Hollis's ears rang. Her wide eyes met Finn's equally distressed gaze.

"Well, that certainly showed him," Declan said with a laugh. Kieran scowled and walked out of the cave.

"Killing us doesn't get you that manuscript," Hollis said to Declan. "It only complicates your life."

"Hollis, dear, my life is far more complicated than you know. I doubt two dead Americans would make it any worse."

"Two innocent Americans," Finn pointed out. "Kieran obviously searched through our stuff and didn't find the manuscript. That's why he came back so frustrated. You know in your heart, Declan, that Hollis and I are telling the truth."

Declan said nothing, only turned his head in the direction Kieran had walked. "Ssh, now."

Hollis strained to hear what he was listening to, and eventually she did. It was the sound of a car.

"Don't go anywhere," Declan told Hollis and Finn with a wink. "Be back in a jiff." He walked off toward the entrance, disappearing around the corner.

As soon as Declan was out of sight, Hollis began working at the tape, opening her elbows as wide as she could to stretch the tape and then banging the space between her wrists on the sharpest rock she could reach. "We have to get out of here. I don't know what Declan said when they were talking in Gaelic, but Keiran said something about killing us."

"How do you know?" Finn asked.

"*Mharu* is Irish for 'kill.' I looked up some words that might come in handy if something went wrong."

"When?"

266

"Before we left home."

"You thought knowing the Irish word for *kill* would come in handy?"

"Well, it did, didn't it?" The tape on her wrists gave way and she immediately began helping Finn with his. While Declan had gone easy binding her, Kieran hadn't done the same favor for Finn.

"Take the tape off of your feet and see if there's anything in the backpack that we can use to cut this stuff off me," Finn said, keeping his eyes peeled in the direction Declan and Kieran had walked.

She ripped the tape off her ankles quickly and rushed to the backpack, rifling through an odd assortment of tools, a bulletproof vest, a bottle of whiskey, and what looked like the scope of a sniper rifle. "I think he's prepared for a standoff with the police," she said. "Or something worse."

"We'll tell someone when we're safe. But right now you really need to find something to cut this tape off me."

Hollis kept looking until she found a pocket knife. She ran back to Finn, cutting the tape off his wrists and ankles as quickly as she could. They could hear talking outside the cave, a woman's voice. Finn grabbed Hollis's hand and led her in the other direction, deeper into the cave.

Fifty-Two

The farther they walked, the more slippery the rock became. Hollis held on to Finn's hand, and with the other, she braced herself against the wall.

"Declan said there was another exit," Finn said. "I think he was saying that for our benefit. The way he wrapped the duct tape around you, he was looking for a chance to let us go."

"You think he actually might be Interpol? I'd all but eliminated that possibility."

"I think you were right to. If he were Interpol, why wouldn't he tell us when Kieran left the cave? I think he's TCT. He sounded like he meant what he said about Winstanley."

"An honorable thief?"

"Let's hope so."

Hollis could see a stream of light just around a bend. The walls were getting closer and the ceiling lower, so any escape wasn't coming soon enough for her. They walked toward the exit, and as they did, Hollis could hear people talking.

Finn peered out.

"What are you seeing?" Hollis asked.

"Nothing. They're at the entrance, and there's a bend in the cave, so we're around the corner."

He took a step outside and Hollis joined him. The light almost hurt her eyes. They'd only been inside the cave for about an hour, but it was enough to make her grateful for fresh air and daylight, even on a day that threatened to storm.

She could see the dark van parked down the hill, and next to it a tan car. Not the same car Lydia was driving, Hollis remembered, so whoever the female voice was, it likely wasn't her.

"Is hotwiring a car one of the many skills you never mentioned to me?" Finn asked.

"I'm afraid not. What are the odds there are keys left in the ignition?"

"Probably slim. We could make a run for it."

"Run where? It's miles of gray rock and the ocean."

Finn leaned down, resting his chin on Hollis's head. "We can't just stand here. They'll be walking back into the cave any second, and whatever kind of a gentleman Declan might be, I don't think Kieran would be of the same mind."

He was right. He was often right. She realized she should tell him that more often. And she would—once they were home and safe in front of their TV, back to their lives. But for now they needed action, and she knew he was asking her, in his own way, to make the choice for them.

She took a few steps forward, toward where she still heard the voices. If she knew who the woman was, maybe that would help her make a plan. As the cave curved, she saw the back of Kieran's legs. Next to that was the bottom half of a woman in tight black jeans and hiking boots. She couldn't see Declan, but she could hear him.

"Look," he said, "we're as in the dark as you are and we're running out of time."

"I don't care about the money anymore," she said. "I want to find my da. He isn't picking up his mobile. He isn't at the place in Galway. If the two of you have done something to him..."

"We haven't. I swear it."

"But you have the Americans?" she asked. "They have to know where the manuscript is. There were supposed to be clues in it."

"And they have the package, you're sure?" Kieran asked.

"I am."

Kieran spun around to face Declan and practically spit the words in his face. "I told you they knew more than they said."

"Wait," Declan's voice was getting louder too. "Just wait a minute before you go back in. We need to think."

"This is all my fault," she said, and started crying.

"Let's bring her into the cave," Kieran said, "before she brings too much attention."

"No." Declan's voice was strong. "What we need to say has to be said in private. Our guests aren't going anywhere. Let's just take a walk and all calm down."

"I didn't come all this way for a morning stroll," Kieran said.

"Okay then, Kieran. If you want Siobhan and me to make all the decisions without you, then go back in the cave. We'll be there in a few minutes."

Hollis could hear Kieran grunt. Siobhan. Eamon's daughter was somehow mixed in to this mess. Hollis waved toward Finn and he came up behind her. They watched as the others moved away from them. Hollis stepped out of hiding and saw the back of the woman, with long, red, messy hair. She knew immediately, even without seeing her face, that she was the one Finn had spoken to when he picked up the package.

Finn and Hollis made their way down the hill as quickly as they could. Finn kept checking back to see if any of the others had noticed them, but Hollis didn't want to look. She decided she'd prefer to get shot in the back of the head rather than watch the bullet come at her.

When they got to the van, Hollis did turn around and look up toward the cave. There was no sign of Declan or the others, at least for now. Finn checked the van for keys and came back empty-handed. Hollis looked in the back for anything they could use as a weapon—a tire iron or even an umbrella—but she didn't have any more luck than Finn. Finn had been right about Kieran going through their suitcases. They'd been opened and the contents thrown around the van. The fifty thousand euros was stacked in a corner, ready to be packed up again in a hurry. A pretty sure sign to Hollis that despite his bragging, the money was worth the walk to Kieran. She took a pair of gym shoes from her case and changed from her flats. Easier to run in, she thought. Then she grabbed her purse and went to the other car, where Finn had gone looking for keys.

"Nothing," he said. "It's even locked. It's nice to know that international criminals still worry about getting their cars stolen."

"I don't think she's a pro. I think she got herself into some kind of trouble that dragged her father into this." Hollis looked around. "Let's just walk. Keiran said something about a bad day for tourists to come this far. So there must be tourists somewhere. Burren's a national park. Maybe there's a visitor's center."

They took one last look back and saw nothing, then walked straight ahead, out of the sightline of the cave, as quickly as they could.

Fifty-Three

After about a half mile, they saw a sign for parking a kilometer ahead. Finn wrapped his arms around the pole, declaring he'd take a selfie with it if he still had his phone.

"You hate selfies," Hollis reminded him.

"I love everything that screams of civilization and safety and help."

"Then in another kilometer, you'll be doing back-flips."

Even for someone used to running marathons, the walk toward the visitor's center was almost longer than Hollis could stand. It wasn't the distance, or the rocky terrain; it was the expectation that, at any min-ute, a hail of gunfire would put holes into her and the man she loved.

Finn had started smiling as they got farther from the black van, but Hollis didn't dare get her hopes up until she saw a large one-story building and a sign that read Car Park. There were several tour buses in the parking lot, and a group of about a dozen people milling about.

"If you're heading to the Cliffs, you need to take the blue bus over there," a man in a red jacket said to the crowd, pointing toward a bus parked off to his right. "The center bus, that's headed to Lisdoonvana and Lahinch. And the yellow one on the left, that's for Doolin."

Several people began walking toward the buses, while others stayed behind taking photos and chatting. The man directing them looked resigned to it, as someone used to dealing with tourists would need to be. Hollis and Finn walked into the building and found themselves in a souvenir shop, crowded with at least thirty people all picking though racks of t-shirts, shelves of mugs, and other mementos.

"I know you had to leave the blanket and the earrings behind, so if you want to pick up a keychain or snow globe, now's the time," Finn said.

"You want something to remember the trip by?"

He laughed. Just the sound of it relaxed Hollis. They were safe, almost safe. All they needed was to find someone who could phone the police before Kieran and the others found them.

"Did you get separated from the tour?" A short, sixty-ish woman with a blond bob and a Texas accent looked up at Hollis.

"Why?"

"You have that stain, honey, on your pants. You'll have to wash that before you go home if you're going to get it out."

Hollis looked down at her tan pants, which now had a brown streak down the side. "I must have gotten it from the cave's wall," she said more to Finn than the woman.

"That's a shame. But it was really beautiful, wasn't it?" the woman continued.

."The cave?" Hollis looked up and saw posters on the wall showing images from inside a cave that was clearly larger and better lit than the one she and Finn had just escaped from. The poster read *Ailwee Cave*. "Yes, it's lovely."

"You better get your souvenirs quickly. The bus leaves in a few minutes." The woman grabbed a bottle of perfume made from the flowers found in the Burren and hurried off to the cashier.

"Trouble," Finn whispered to Hollis and pointed through the large window to the road they'd just walked up.

It was Siobhan and Kieran, and Kieran was looking angrier than he had in the cave.

"Where's Declan?" she wondered.

"Obviously he wasn't able to stop them. Which means they may have his gun."

"If they come in here, all these people are in danger."

"If we go out there, we're the ones in danger."

Hollis pulled Finn farther back into the store. She grabbed a book on the Burren, a tweed cap, and a cream wool sweater.

"I was kidding about the key chain," Finn said.

"Give me some cash."

He took out his wallet and gave her hundreds of euros—half the cash he still had from Lydia and David. "In case we get separated," he said, as he pressed the bills in her hand. "Tell me this is part of a plan and not some weird compulsion of yours to buy souvenirs every time we risk our lives."

"Wait here." After she paid for the items, she pulled the tags off the cap and gave it to Finn. "This will make you look like a real tourist." She put the sweater on and moved them both toward the exit, staying as much with the crowd as possible.

The man in the red jacket came through the swinging door. "Buses are leaving in one minute. Everybody needs to be headed toward the

274

right bus. So if you can wrap up your purchases now, the drivers are already inside."

Hollis moved the souvenir bag up toward her face, and she and Finn went outside the door next to a family of five. She tried to stay calm, to not look toward Keiran or draw attention to herself, but the crowd they were with was walking slowly, still taking photos. She wanted to scream for them to hurry. She tried to remember what pants or shoes Keiran and Siobhan had been wearing, to see if they were among the people around her. She didn't dare look up at the faces. It would be too easy to make eye contact, and then it was all over. But she found she couldn't remember how either of them had been dressed. So she just kept walking, her arm linked with Finn's, and kept an eye out for the bus.

It was probably only fifty feet between the door and the bus on the left, but it seemed as though they would never arrive. When it was finally her turn to step into the bus, she took one quick look back. Thankfully, she saw only tourists. She and Finn found seats at the back, sinking as low as they could, and waited as the bus filled up with happy, mainly American, tourists, laughing about their adventure in the caves.

"This bus goes to Doolin," Finn whispered. "And if I remember what you said yesterday, Doolin has a ferry to Inishmore."

"We don't have to take it. We just have to get out of here."

"These people all know who we are and where we live. There's only one way to put this all behind us. We're finding that stupid manuscript and getting our lives back."

The door to the bus closed. Hollis looked out the window and saw Kieran and Siobhan walking into the visitor's center. But standing in the parking lot alone was Declan Murphy, Kieran's backpack at his feet. He saw Hollis through the bus window and winked.

Fifty-Four

Declan watched the bus pull away with Finn and Hollis on it, doing their best to hide from view. Good for them, he thought, though he had made it as easy as he could.

They were no good to him dead, not until he had the manuscript. It hadn't been among their belongings, nor were the clues Eamon had sent in the package.

But they knew what the clues were; they knew where it would lead. And bless them, they seemed determined to stay on the trail. All he had to do was follow them until he got what he wanted.

Whatever happened after that, as his auntie always said, was in the Lord's hands.

Fifty-Five

The bus drove down a steep hill that seemed destined to end in the ocean. It took a sharp turn just before it could have gone off the cliff, then sped down a narrow road that had the hill on one side and death on the other.

"Lovely view, the coast road," someone said.

The one thing that had gone right on this day, Hollis said to Finn, was that she wasn't at the wheel. She silently thanked the men at the gas station who had suggested the inland route.

"You think Declan and the others could drive here faster?" she asked.

"I guess we'll find out soon enough."

When they pulled into Doolin, Finn and Hollis followed the others off the bus and looked around, but there was no one waiting for them.

"Where's the ferry to Inishmore?" Finn asked a man coming out of a shop.

"Just down the road there." He looked at them, up and down, with a barely contained laugh. "Aren't you a couple of plastic paddies. Enjoying your holiday?"

"We are, thanks." Finn took off his tweed cap and threw it in the souvenir bag.

"What did he mean?" Hollis asked as they walked away.

"I think he meant we looked like idiots."

Hollis pulled her sweater tighter. "I don't care. This sweater is warm against the wind."

———

Doolin was a pretty little town, with a main street that was just on one side of the road, its back to the Atlantic. The buildings were colorful, made from the same concrete and painted plaster that had begun to feel "Irish" to Hollis. There was music playing from a speaker attached to a chocolate shop and a sign in the window of the pub next door that called Doolin the home of "traditional music." It would have been nice, she thought, to spend the day wandering in and out of the stores and tea shops on the street. It would be nicer still to know for sure that one of the many people who seemed to want them dead or in prison wasn't going to pop up unannounced, gun in hand.

They walked down the street, feeling the wind on their faces. Though the clouds were moving inland, the sky still threatened to storm, so it was difficult to figure out the time. Hollis had stopped wearing a watch when she became addicted to her cell phone. It was an odd feeling not to check emails and news updates, but she could manage without them. Not knowing the time, though, made her feel lost. She grabbed Finn's wrist and pulled it toward her. To her amazement, it wasn't even ten thirty in the morning yet. How had they gone through so much in just a few hours?

"You can get a lot accomplished if you get up early enough," she said.

"If you call getting kidnapped an accomplishment."

"Tell me we're not crazy."

They'd discussed it again and again on the bus, whispering and speaking in code as much as possible. Their passports were sitting in the van, so leaving the country was out of the question. They could walk into a police station, but their story barely seemed plausible to them, and they were living it. Assuming they were believed, all it would take was one phone call about two Americans claiming to have been kidnapped, and everyone they were running from would know exactly where to find them. No, she thought, they had made a plan on the ride to Doolin and they were going to stick to it.

Finn squeezed Hollis's hand. "You're sure that Declan saw you on the bus?"

"Yes. Which means he saw the bus was going to Doolin."

"But he's not here. And there were three buses all leaving at the same time. Maybe he thinks we picked that one at random."

"Maybe. Or he knows where Eamon grew up and put two and two together."

Neither seemed to have an answer for any of it. So they kept moving toward the pier.

They walked longer than they expected. They stayed on high alert, jumping at the loud squawks of seagulls flying overhead, and looking for enemies in the wild grasses and stone fences that stood between them and the water. It took at least fifteen minutes before they reached the pier. But at least the ferry was waiting, and people were starting to board.

There was just a small ticket office and a covered waiting area, which several dozen people were already crowding under. Around the corner from the line for tickets, Hollis spotted a pay phone. "Last chance to change our minds."

Finn grabbed some coins from his pocket. "You get the tickets and I'll call Bridie and tell her where we're going. Hopefully Martin's son has everything you left for him and she'll tell us that the cavalry is coming."

"Who is the cavalry? Peter ... David ... Lydia? So far the only person who's tried to help us is Declan, and he's a criminal."

"We can trust Bridie and Martin. And we'll have to trust Martin's son. There has to be someone who wants to do the right thing. Besides us." He kissed her forehead. "Get return tickets. I'm feeling optimistic."

Hollis watched Finn head toward the phone, then reluctantly let him out of sight as she moved toward the ticket line. There were only three sailings to Inishmore, the next one leaving in just ten minutes. Plenty of time for Kieran to show up ready to shoot, if Declan told them where she and Finn were going. But he had let them escape, even helped them ... so perhaps he wouldn't tell Kieran. There was no point in being sure, or even almost sure. Everything they'd encountered in Ireland, good and bad, had been a surprise.

In the last forty-eight hours they'd had guns pointed at them, a man killed in front of them, mysterious packages to pick up, and kidnappers to escape from. In a rare moment of seeming normality, Hollis wanted to take stock of it all, work out the puzzle of baby rattles and leprechauns and fake Behan manuscripts, but her head was spinning. She felt nervous and excited, dreading whatever came next, and filled with the kind of anticipation that was normally reserved for a kid about to open his Christmas presents. This must be what a real covert op feels like every day, she thought, no longer envious of it, but also—to her surprise after all they'd been through—not exactly unhappy about the feeling, either.

The woman ahead of her was taking her time buying tickets, asking questions about seasickness and what snacks were for sale on board, an odd combination of concerns, at least to Hollis. While she waited, she grabbed a free map of the island, with the major sights, including three churches, all highlighted. She scanned the map trying to find clues in a church name or a street, but there was nothing she could see.

Finally, she reached the counter. "Two returns to Inishmore."

As the man printed up the tickets, a group of British children ran by, laughing and chasing each other. Their father looked like he was doing his best to corral them, and failing. One of the kids bumped against Hollis.

"I'm sorry," the father said to her.

"It's fine." She glanced up with an understanding smile, which quickly melted into panic. Out of the corner of her eye, she saw a red coat.

She grabbed the tickets and walked quickly to the pay phone.

"No, that's okay," Finn said into the phone. "Yes, we're fine. Thanks. Thanks for everything, Bridie ... Yes, if we come back that way, we'll absolutely stop in."

When he hung up, he looked concerned. "You going to tell me something bad," Hollis said.

"Peter showed up at Bridie's about a half hour after we all left, so he must have woken up from the drug and walked back. She said he looked fine, not hurt, just annoyed. He told her that he lost track of us. Martin and his son had just taken the stuff out of the drawer. Since Peter was supposed to be a friend of ours, they showed him everything."

"What did he do?"

"It was a mess. Your note said Peter was Patrick Lahey's killer and he'd kidnapped us. Martin's son tried to arrest him, and there was a lot of shouting. Peter flashed a badge, but they didn't believe him. Then he wrote down a license plate number and told them to track it. And while they were calling for backup, he disappeared."

"He must have seen the license plate on the black van before he was drugged."

"So if he's able to track it, he'll be on Declan and Kieran's trail," Finn said. "And even if he's not, I told Bridie that the police should be on the lookout for them."

"Did you tell her we were going to Doolin?"

"No. I want to keep word from getting back to Peter. Maybe he is Interpol, but I didn't like his threats this morning. Unless we can prove our innocence, I'm not sure he'll be on our side."

"I'm not sure he will be even then. Remember David and Lydia had said something in the hotel room about an inside man at Interpol."

"Good point."

"And speaking of Lydia."

"What about her?" Finn asked.

"I think she's here. I saw a red trench coat."

"That can't be unusual. You used to have a red coat."

"It's her. I didn't see her face, but I just know it's her."

A line was forming to board the ferry, while a few others hurried to buy tickets. "At least there's a crowd here," Finn said. "We'll be safe in the middle of all these people."

"I'm sure that's what Patrick Lahey thought the night he went to the Abbey Theatre."

Fifty-Six

The ferry wasn't sold out, but there were plenty of both tourists and locals taking advantage of a quick trip between mainland Ireland and the cluster of small islands that were about fifteen miles off-shore. Hollis and Finn went downstairs to a large seating area. Finn bought some Cokes and candy—"to keep their energy up"—while Hollis walked outside to look around.

Inis Mor, as it was spelled in Irish, was the largest of the three islands that made up the Aran Islands, according to the map, but it was still only about five miles long and less than two miles across. There were only about eight hundred fifty people living on it, and only one main town—Kilronan. It would be easy, Hollis hoped, to find someone who knew Patrick Lahey and Eamon Byrnes. And easier still to find the parish closest to Boston.

As the boat pulled out of Doolin's harbor, Hollis watched the beautiful cluster of painted buildings disappear from view until all she could see was the Atlantic Ocean, the seagulls, and a sky that seemed finally to have shaken the clouds.

"Let's try to find Eamon first," Finn said, when he joined her. "If he can just tell us where the manuscript is, we won't have to go chasing around the village on some high-stakes scavenger hunt."

"You really think he's hiding out there?"

"It makes sense. If you're scared, you go home."

"But why didn't his daughter think of that? She clearly looked for him in Galway, and she said he wasn't picking up the phone. Why wouldn't he tell her where he is?"

"I don't know. Maybe he's hiding from her."

It was a thought that made Hollis a little sad. She knew almost nothing about Eamon except that he was somehow mixed up in TCT. And what Kieran had said at the shop. Eamon was a widower with no close family after his daughter had moved to Australia. The place Declan had said he'd visited. There were close ties between nearly everyone she'd encountered in TCT. Patrick and Eamon grew up together, Kieran worked for Eamon, and Siobhan was his daughter. Far from being a vast international organization, it seemed to be a family affair. Though nothing yet explained how Declan fit into it.

"We should look around," Finn said to her, tossing his empty Coke can into a recycling bin. "I'd rather find Lydia than have her find us."

"And what will we do then?"

"I'm hoping something will come to us in the moment." He grabbed her hand. "Unless you think it's better to look for a place to hide until we dock."

It was a subtle change, but Hollis was charmed by it. Finn, the problem solver, the man in charge, was happy to be co-captain.

"We should confront her," Hollis suggested. "Find out what side she's working on. There was something between her and Declan—I win that bet, by the way. And he seemed to confirm she was CIA, just like she said. But he didn't rule out that she was also TCT."

"Declan could have used their pillow talk to further his cause and now she wants revenge," Finn suggested.

"Then let's help her get it. Lydia seems a bit unhinged, but I'd rather have her on our side than against us."

Finn nodded. "All eyes out for a red coat," he said, as he opened the glass door and ducked to avoid hitting his head on the lintel.

———

Inside the main downstairs compartment there were rows of benches, most of which were more than half full. Lydia wasn't sitting on any of them, so Hollis and Finn walked through to the other side and up the stairs to the seating area above.

The strong wind hit them as soon as they were outside. The ferry was going full speed, and even though the water was calm, the ride was bumpy. Hollis now understood why the woman at the ticket office was concerned about seasickness.

They walked through the crowds, looking in opposite directions. The deal was that the first person to spot Lydia would squeeze the other's hand. But they made it through the entire area without either using the signal.

"There's a spot up front, sort of wedged between the captain's area and the front of the boat," Hollis said. "That's the only place left."

They walked back through the seating area, toward the captain's bridge. There was just enough space on either side for one person to walk through. They went right, moving slowly, each holding onto the railing that kept them from falling overboard, while also trying to hold on to each other. But after a few steps, Finn let go of Hollis's hand to steady himself against the wall of the bridge. Then a few more steps, and he stopped suddenly.

"Red coat," he whispered.

"Then let's go talk to her."

"No." He moved back, forcing Hollis to do the same, until they were both back in the seating area.

"I thought we said we would…"

"She's not alone."

A chime interrupted Finn, and as they were standing next to the bridge, it was almost deafening. A voice came on loud speaker. "This is your captain. We'll be pulling into Kilronan in five minutes. It gets a bit uneven as we dock, so please sit for the remainder of the ride, and until we're safely stopped. There's nothing in Inishmore so exciting you need to risk your life to be first off the boat."

Those people milling about began sitting. Out of the corner of her eye, Hollis saw a figure emerge from the front of the boat, so she grabbed Finn's arm and moved him back to the tight space they'd been in—between the bridge and the railing.

She put one hand on the wall and gripped the railing with the other. The boat rocked back and forth as it slowed and turned toward the pier. Finn was behind her, his hands in the same position as hers. But his height presented more of a problem. He squatted slightly to move his center of gravity lower, and lessen his chances of going over. Water splashed onto the railing. Hollis wrapped her fingers tighter, but the wet railing was no longer easy to grip.

The only good news was it gave them both a good view of the main compartment while keeping them mostly hidden. And it allowed Hollis to see what Finn had meant. Siobhan and Kieran had walked back and taken seats on one of the benches. Lydia moved past them, sitting one row behind as if she hadn't just been chatting with them moments before. Lydia seemed calm. But in front of her, Kieran had one hand inside his jacket, as if he were hiding a weapon and ready to use it at any second.

Fifty-Seven

The ferry lurched forward, and Hollis almost lost her grip. Then it turned, stopped, and moved forward again. With each movement, Hollis did her best to stay upright. Behind her, Finn seemed to struggle even more.

"We need to move toward the seats," he said.

"If we do, Kieran will see us." She nodded toward the shore, just feet from where they were standing. "It can't be more than a minute until we're docked. Just hang on."

"If I throw up on you ..."

"I won't take it personally."

But the ferry stopped a second time. And this time, its engines turned off. Finn leaned against Hollis and rested his head on her back.

Siobhan and Kieran were among the first to get up and head toward the exit. People crowded behind them. Hollis searched for any other face she might recognize, but no one stood out. She started to move but Finn grabbed her arm.

"Wait. Watch Lydia."

Lydia was one of the few left seated.

They stayed in place waiting for Lydia to move so they could follow her, but she seemed in no hurry. Finally, when they were sure that Kieran and Siobhan had disembarked along with most of the others, Hollis and Finn came out of their hiding space.

"Hey there," Hollis said.

Lydia looked up. If she was surprised, she didn't show it.

"Following us?" Finn asked.

"Not you. Not anymore."

"Siobhan then. How did you know to look for her?"

"You said Eamon had a daughter, so I tracked her down. Found her this morning and followed her here. Then surprise! I ran into my two favorite completely innocent professors who told me they wanted nothing more than to return to their boring lives. And yet, here you are, still on the chase."

"Where did you pick up her trail?" Hollis asked.

"At a national park."

"The Burren," Hollis said. "If you were there this morning, you watched Kieran and Declan put guns to our heads and did nothing to help us."

Lydia stood up. "I have other priorities."

"I guess Declan isn't the man you thought he was," Finn added. "Or maybe he is."

She walked over to Finn, standing close. Her small frame was dwarfed by his height, but still she looked undaunted. "In Dublin you were both skittish, like two kittens cowering at a piece of string. But

289

not anymore. Now you're more certain, more angry. I like it. It makes me realize that you're actually a very attractive man."

Finn blushed.

"Don't worry, I don't chase after married men."

"Good to know you have your limits," he said.

She laughed and turned toward Hollis. "But don't think I won't get back at you for hitting me over the head with that bottle. Waste of good whiskey."

"I believed you when you said you were in love with the man in that photo," Hollis said.

Lydia's eyes softened. "I believed it when I took the photo. It was the day I told him about a stash of paintings I'd come across in my work, belonging to a man being held on an indefinite detainment in the Middle East. I thought Liam ..." She grimaced. "... *Declan* might be interested to know one of the paintings was done by an Irishman."

"Francis Bacon."

She nodded. "And then suddenly the painting, or a reasonable facsimile, shows up in a private sale. Just the sort of thing to raise eyebrows in my world and get some very unhappy fingers pointed at me at Langley. But luckily for me, I wasn't the only one who shared information. We'd run into Patrick Lahey one night at a pub, and Declan told me Patrick was a painter. Once the fake Bacon turned up, I started to put the pieces together. Finding the money from the sale would go a long way to restoring full faith in me. And turning Declan in—that would go a long way toward making me feel a little less of a fool."

"You killed Lahey because he wouldn't tell you where Declan was," Hollis said, taking a guess.

The softness in her eyes disappeared, and Lydia gave Hollis a long, cold stare. "You really have no idea how much of a boys' club my world is. It's hard for women to rise to the top, and then to get conned ..."

"He seemed a bit wistful about you. I wouldn't say it was entirely a con."

She tilted her head and smiled. "Well, that will give him something to think about when he's in solitary." Then she turned and walked toward the exit. "I didn't kill Lahey. But don't think I won't kill you both if you get in my way again."

They watched her get off the ferry, then waited as people came up from down below to disembark.

Hollis and Finn were nearly the last off the boat. By the time they stood on solid ground, most of the crowd had moved beyond the pier, including Lydia and the two she was following. It was tempting to just stay at the pier and let all of them fight it out. But then they would never know the truth.

Finn pointed out a rack of bicycles for rent. "Where to first?"

"We don't know where we're going," Hollis reminded him. "But maybe we can find out." She walked over to a man standing near the pier, drinking from a water bottle and checking his cell phone. "Do you know Eamon Byrnes?" she asked the man.

"I do, yeah, but he's not around much these days," the man said. "Do you know him?"

"We're trying to find his house."

"It's not far. Get in now, I'll take ya."

"Get in?"

He pointed to a dark red pony cart, with room for four passengers in the back and a driver up front. The horse was a beautiful soft white, with dark brown spots and an ivory mane, and the cart had an old-fashioned charm to it.

"You take tourists around the island?"

"I do, yeah."

"I know it's not the usual route, but we're happy to pay you for your time."

He waved her off. *"Sásta cuidiú,"* he said. "Happy to help a friend of poor Eamon."

Finn and Hollis took their places on the cart, and their driver said a few words to the horse, who gave a grunting acknowledgement before taking the steps to the main road. As hard as it was to imagine that they were running from killers, on the trail of a missing criminal and a forged play, it was stunning to realize they were doing it at a slow trot. A car and several bicyclists passed them, and Hollis knew that Lydia and the others would be there far ahead of them. But for just that moment, she didn't care. She was awed by the stark beauty of the landscape. It shared the west of Ireland's love of stone fences and cows, but it seemed isolated and lonely, on its own against the harsh Atlantic.

Their driver tipped his hat to every pedestrian and shouted, *"Maidin mhaith,"* as he passed. He told them his name was Tim Collins, and he'd been raised on Inishmore, and was now raising his children here. He looked either thirty or a hundred. It was hard to tell. His face was weathered and deeply tan, making the wrinkles around his deep green eyes more prominent, and highlighting a bright smile.

"We speak Irish here," he told them. "The English never bothered to conquer us so, like a portion of the west country, we've kept the language as our own."

"It's a hard language to learn," Finn said.

"It is, yeah. But that makes it all the more special. They learn it in school all over the country, but they don't speak it after that. Shame too."

But Declan and Keiran both did, Hollis remembered. Maybe Declan had ties to the island, or at least the west country. She was tempted to ask if he knew Declan Murphy or Kieran O'Malley, but what if he did and he tipped them off? She went a safer route. "How well do you know Eamon?" she asked.

"Ah, you know everyone well on the islands. Hard not to. Eamon's a good man, even with his troubles."

"I know his wife died. And of course his daughter, Siobhan ..." She left the sentence unfinished, hoping it would prompt Tim to finish the thought.

"That was sad, all right. Drugs are a terrible thing. Getting her right again nearly put Eamon in the poorhouse. He had a lot of nice things he sold at a big shop in Galway, then he had to move to a small space off the main drag, from what I heard, just to stay afloat. What she didn't steal to buy her drugs, he sold to pay for her treatment."

"But she's better now ..."

"I think she is, yeah. In Australia, last I heard."

"When's the last time you saw Eamon?"

"Long time ago now. I didn't think he came home anymore. He rented out the place after Nora died, and left it to his neighbor, Mary Kelly, to manage for him. Siobhan used to come out here with some less-than-desirable friends, and I guess seeing the place just broke his heart. Shame too. It's been in his family for as long as anyone can remember." He pulled on the reins, and the horse came to a stop. "That's it there, though that's not Eamon's car out front."

They said their goodbyes after Tim gave them his cell number in case they needed him again. Then Hollis and Finn waited until he'd turned back toward the main road before they walked toward the cottage.

It was almost a movie set, Hollis thought. The stones that made up the walls were painted a crisp white and it was topped with a thatched roof. There were flower boxes at every window and roses on the pathway. And right in the center was an emerald green door bearing a sign that read Cead Mile Failte. She had spent enough time in Irish bars to know that meant "A Hundred Thousand Welcomes," though she doubted Eamon would feel that way today.

But it was hard to spend much time looking at the cottage, because the view of the Atlantic was extraordinary. Eamon's cottage was only twenty or so yards from the edge of a cliff. No beach, no soft slope leading gently into the water—just a sheer drop to the ocean and nothing but the special emptiness of clear blue water and gray sky ahead. It was as though Eamon lived at the end of the world. Even though she knew that at her back was a road and a town and ferries and jet planes and everything the modern world can offer, Hollis felt she had stepped into an alternate reality. Ireland, she'd been learning, held onto its identity with the fierceness of a mother protecting her child. Even as it embraced all the realities of conventional modern life, it found a way to be separate, to be eccentric, wild, and free. There was a lesson in there, she decided, on how she would live from here forward.

Assuming, that is, she did live.

"There's no movement in the house," Finn said, stirring her from her thoughts. "There's lace curtains in the window so I can barely see in, but there doesn't seem to be anyone there."

"But Tim said that isn't Eamon's car. Somebody must be here."

"There's only one way to find out."

They moved toward the door to the cottage as quietly as they could. Finn mouthed, "One, two, three," then pushed down on the latch that held the door shut. It wasn't locked. He opened it slowly, stopping when a creak announced their arrival. But there was no turning back now. He opened the door completely and they walked inside.

There were two armchairs facing the fire, and the man she recognized from his photo as Eamon Byrnes was sitting in one of them. Even though there was nothing burning, the faint smell of turf hung in the air. But there was another scent, far less pleasant, and Hollis knew it immediately. The smell of death, coming from Eamon's body.

But Eamon hadn't been alone in the cottage, and now neither were they. Standing over Eamon's body was a familiar face, and one they weren't sure if they should be happy to see.

Fifty-Eight

I didn't kill him," David said. "I just got here."

She was no forensic expert, but even Hollis knew that a body didn't begin to smell minutes after death. Eamon, by the look of him, had been dead for days.

"How did he die?" Finn asked.

David pointed to a bullet wound at the back of Eamon's head.

"So he let someone into his cottage, sat down by the fire, and they shot him," Hollis said.

"Someone he knew," Finn added.

"Must have been." Hollis walked around the body looking for anything that might point out who that was. She saw a bruising across his cheek, as if he'd been hit, and a burn on his hand. There was a set of fireplace tools on the hearth, but the poker wasn't with the others. It was laying on the ground as if it had been thrown there. "I think someone was trying to get information out of Eamon, and either got what he was looking for and killed him, or gave up trying and killed him anyway."

David took a step back from the body, until he was almost across the room. It seemed odd to Hollis, almost as if he expected torture to be contagious. "And whoever that was," he said, "has the manuscript."

"Unless he didn't keep it here," Finn said.

"So where is it?" David asked.

She looked at him. He didn't seem in bad shape, considering that he'd been knocked out and left with Lydia, but he did seem scared. "How do you even know to be here?"

"When I woke up..." He glanced over at Finn. "Thanks by the way, you could have killed me."

"Obviously I didn't."

"When you woke up," Hollis reminded him to finish his thought.

"Lydia was kicking me off her, and you two were gone. You'd stolen my car, and Lydia wasn't exactly in a team building mood, so I was on my own. I called the rental agency. They told me it had been in an accident, so I tracked you down to a small village near Boston. That's when it hit me what you were doing. But I also saw Peter there, and then you guys got thrown into a van..."

"You let that happen?" Finn roared.

"What could I have done? No one at Justice is taking my calls. I had no idea where you were being taken, but you were with Peter Naidoo, or Moodley, or whatever he's going by. I figured he could handle himself."

"You told us he got rid of people!"

"I told you that was maybe what he did. Look, I'm a tech guy. You want me to chase down criminals—"

"No, *you* want *us* to chase down criminals," Hollis pointed out. "And maybe get killed doing it."

"Well, you didn't, because here you are."

"Which brings me back to my original question. How are *you* here?"

"When you left in the van, I went to a pub next door and starting asking people about the parish nearest Boston, and this man said you'd asked the same thing the night before. He told me it could mean Inishmore," he said. "So here I am."

"You didn't call the Garda?" Hollis asked.

"I'm sorry."

"You are the worst intelligence officer in the world."

"You don't think I'm aware of that? But if we find the manuscript…"

Finn let out a laugh. "Not with you, we're not."

David glanced over at Eamon's body. "But there's still a missing agent and there's only a few hours left."

"Eamon is the agent," Hollis said, nearly at a shout. "Not Interpol. A criminal agent who put together the sale of the fake Bacon. And obviously we're a little late to save him."

David stared at her. "But…"

"Somebody played you, David. Who was it?"

He looked like he was about to pass out. He stumbled backward into the oversized chair that matched Eamon's. "But the fake Behan manuscript exists?"

"Apparently."

"And it's on Inishmore?"

"That's what we think."

"Then there's still a chance to save my career." He got up. "And if you're not going to help me, then I'll do it on my own."

Hollis looked over at Finn, who didn't move to stop David from leaving the cottage. She heard his car start up and the wheels turn from the grass to the gravel. It had never been much of a competition between Finn and David all those years ago, but she was never more certain that she'd made the right choice.

"Good riddance," she murmured. As she spoke, she saw Finn smile.

It seemed creepy to Hollis to search a dead man's house, especially with his body sitting there, but they did it anyway. Hollis took the living room, which had few objects in it aside from the chairs, a desk, a bookcase, and a photograph of Eamon with the same woman, his wife she assumed, that Hollis had seen in the photo at the shop in Dublin. Finn went through the bedrooms. Both came up empty.

Hollis was already in the kitchen when Finn finished up in the rest of the house. "There's nothing in the drawers or wardrobe."

"Makes sense. If he rents it out, he wants to keep it impersonal," Hollis said. "The only things in here are biscuits and tea. Maybe there was something and David found it."

Finn scoffed at the idea. "If he had, he wouldn't have been bent over Eamon's body."

Finn and Hollis started opening cabinets, finding nothing but a few white dishes, a teapot, and some pretty blue and white serving bowls. Hollis started at the first cabinet, searching it again.

"I already looked there," Finn said.

"I know, but once we finish in here, there's only one place left to look."

Finn shook his head. "I'm not touching him. I don't care if he has a signed first edition of *Ulysses* in his jacket pocket."

"Well, I'm not doing it."

They stared at each other for a minute, each waiting for the other to budge, the way they usually acted when it was time to go through the tax receipts. Each hoping the other would give up first. She usually lasted longer than Finn, but this time neither moved.

"It's not going to be here," Finn said. "Why go to all the trouble of mailing a package to Kieran in Dublin with cryptic clues if he was going to keep the manuscript on him?"

"Or someone killed him and took it."

"So either it was here and the killer has it, or it was never here."

"He's been dead for days. If the killer had it, whatever information it contains would already be in play."

"So what then?"

"When you want to hide something from me, where do you put it?" she asked.

"I don't hide things from you, Holly."

There was no time for this. "Okay, but when you bought that Bears jersey at an auction after telling me you weren't going to bid on it, you put it on the top shelf in the basement behind the Christmas decorations, because you know I can't reach that box without your help."

He froze. "Then how did you know I put it there?"

She stared at him, and he put his hands up in defeat. "You're saying Eamon would put it somewhere he knew only he would look."

"Yes."

"Where?"

That stumped them both until Hollis thought of something and went back into the living room. "The whole house is impersonal. The knickknacks are the sort you'd find at any high-end souvenir store, nothing that looks part of a collection. The paperbacks in the bookcase are in a dozen languages, clearly left by people who've rented the cottage. They're not Eamon's, not books he's loved and kept." She paused and pointed toward one object. "But he has a framed photograph, just one. That's the sort of thing only he would pay attention to."

She took the photo out of the frame. In the back was an Irish passport with Eamon's photo, but the name under his picture was Liam Tierney. "So I guess we found him," she said. "Declan was telling the truth about Eamon being the agent."

"But Declan also said we'd never find Liam Tierney."

"Maybe that's because he killed him. Except that doesn't make sense, either. If he killed him, why not kill us?" she asked. "I don't see a phone to call the police, and I'm not patting Eamon down to see if he has a cell."

"I have a better idea." Finn took out the map of Inishmore Hollis had gotten at the ticket booth and spread it out on the desk. "There are three churches. If it's the one nearest Boston, it has to be the church closest to the west side of the island, near the water."

There were two that fit the criteria, St. Joseph's and St. Michael's. Neither one stood out as the obvious choice, but St. Michael's was closer to Eamon's home, so they decided on that one.

"We call the police from there and let them know about Eamon, and then look around the church for clues."

"At least we know our only competition for the manuscript is Lydia," Finn said. "If Siobhan and Kieran find it first, she'll take it from them. And David will probably drive around in circles with no idea where to go next. Peter and Declan weren't on the ferry and there's not another one for hours, so I think we can stop watching for them."

"Not necessarily," Hollis said. She put her finger on a small advertisement in the corner of the map. *Helicopter Rides between Doolin and Inishmore. Available for Charter.*

Finn refolded the map. "Then I guess we have to hurry."

Fifty-Nine

Finn found two bicycles, not in the best of shape, leaning against the back wall of Eamon's house. It had been a long time since Hollis sat on a bike, and while the peddling came back to her easily enough, she'd forgotten how tiring it could be. Cycling required an entirely different set of muscles than marathons, and the seat wasn't exactly padded for comfort.

She didn't have the energy to enjoy the beautiful green fields on either side, or the cows grazing the hill on the right. But as long as she kept her focus on their destination, she knew she'd be okay.

Finn was riding up ahead and seemed to be doing better than she was. After about ten minutes of peddling she realized she was in danger of losing him. She called out to him to slow down, and he turned.

"What?" he yelled.

Ping.

Something hit the rock wall on the left side of the road near Finn.

Ping.

Another sound, another rock exploded.

"Finn!" Hollis yelled out. "Down."

Then the ping felt more like a slam, as the back wheel of her bicycle was hit and the frame pushed her to the ground. She moved the bike off her and jumped over the rock wall. She ducked just in time to miss being hit by a bullet.

Finn was crouched down about ten feet from her. She crawled toward him. Rocks exploding on top of her as she moved.

"Must be Kieran," Finn said when she got to his side.

"He's got to be up on the hill," Hollis said, looking around. There wasn't much to cover them, aside from the wall, and that was only about three feet high. If the shooter started moving closer, they were dead where they sat. "I don't think we can make it to the church."

"What about there?" Finn pointed toward what looked like an abandoned house. The same painted stone as Eamon's but a dirty white, and the thatched roof was completely missing. It wasn't much, but it was better than waiting for the shooter to find them.

Keeping as low as possible, they ran toward the building. There were two more shots, then silence. Once they were behind the house's crumbling wall, they peered out, looking for evidence of Kieran or whoever it was coming closer. But there was nothing.

"Do you think he gave up?" Finn asked.

"I hope so. Maybe he was just trying to scare us."

"Mission accomplished." Finn looked back at her. "The church is just up ahead, maybe five minutes if we run. If we stick to the fields, as far from the road as possible, we'll probably be out of shooting range."

"*Probably* out of shooting range? And that's okay with you?"

"It has to be."

"Lydia was right."

"About what?"

"You've changed in the last few days."

"Oh." He looked out toward the road once more. "I thought you meant the other thing."

"You being good-looking?" Hollis laughed. "She was right about that too."

Finn grabbed her hand. "The whole package. Dangerous and hot. You're a lucky woman."

"Why don't you wait until people stop shooting at me before you declare me lucky?"

"Fair enough." He took a breath. "Ready?"

"Why not?"

They took off running, staying as far from the road as possible. There were no more shots, and no sign of anyone following them. But it was still the longest five minutes Hollis had ever run, and when she saw the church up ahead, she let out an almost accidental, "Thank God."

———

St. Michael's Catholic Church had a view of the ocean that rivaled Eamon's. Hollis wondered if it awed the residents of the island the way it did her, or whether they'd gotten so used to it that it served as little more than a backdrop to their lives. It was hard to imagine getting blasé about the extraordinary beauty of the rough shore, but then again, it had only taken a few days to get used to running from killers.

A small churchyard appeared to be beautifully tended, and stood almost as a warning between the church and the water. All the graves had flowers on them and the headstones were clean and straight. Hollis noticed that families all seemed to be buried together, and she wandered until she found the one that interested her—*Nora Byrne, Loving*

Wife and Mother. In a few days, Eamon's body would be buried along-side hers, Hollis reminded herself, and it seemed a peaceful place to be. But it also made her feel more than a little guilty for having left him there alone, while she and Finn, David, and who knew how many others trespassed in the house that had been in his family for generations.

She walked away from the grave toward Finn, who was studying the architecture of the church. It was simple, unpainted stone, allowing it to blend effortlessly with the landscape. And it was small, built in a rectangular shape with small juts out that probably resembled a cross from the air. It had the look of exactly what it was: a country church on the edge of the Atlantic.

Hollis and Finn opened the arched wooden door. In their focus on following Eamon's clues, they'd forgotten that it was Sunday. They walked into the noon mass just as the priest stepped to the lectern for his homily.

"I've just a few announcements before we get to today's scripture," the priest was saying.

Hollis and Finn stepped into the last pew and sat down, nodding hello to an elderly couple who shared the row. It must have been their regular pew, Hollis figured, because there was a little gold plaque attached to the row in front of them that read *O'Connor Family*. She had no idea if she and Finn had broken with tradition by sitting in a pew with someone else's name on it, but the elderly couple didn't seem to mind.

The church was simply decorated and even smaller than it looked from the outside. It might hold a hundred people if every seat was taken, but on this Sunday only about thirty churchgoers were in attendance. But it was, age-wise, a diverse group. There were older people, a few teenagers, and several families trying to keep young ones from escaping and running down the aisle. And sitting next to several of the pews, clearly on their best behavior, were a handful of dogs.

They looked to be regular churchgoers because when the congregation stood, they stood, and when the congregation sat, they sat.

What there wasn't, was any sign of Interpol agents, or TCT criminals, or anyone who might fall into both camps. For a moment, Hollis was pleased that they'd been the ones to figure out the first clue, but then it occurred to her that the others might all be at one of the other two churches on Inishmore, already finding the fake Behan manuscript and whatever secrets it held.

"As you all know, Noirin Flaherty had a birthday on Tuesday, though she's suggested rather strongly I not announce her age," the priest said. "If you were born before her, you already know it, and if you were born after her, well, it's none of your business." The priest was about fifty, with a strong head of salt-and-pepper hair and a ruddy complexion that came, no doubt, from exposure to the sea air. If she looked only at his mouth, he seemed to be taking his job very seriously, but there was a laugh in his eyes that made clear he was only having some fun. "And, of course, I did perform the wedding ceremony yesterday for Joseph Mc-Donough and Margaret O'Donnell. They had a lovely reception at the Aran Islands Hotel, with a DJ and everything. I had a couple of fast ones, and did a few spins on the floor, before coming back here to prepare for today's mass. They've gone off on their honeymoon to Spain and have threatened to make us all look at hundreds of holiday snaps upon their return, so we've been warned."

Hollis bit her lip to stop from laughing. She was Catholic, but more the wedding and funerals type, and Finn had been raised Lutheran. Neither had sat through a mass since their wedding, and never one as entertaining as this.

"We're not alone," Finn whispered to her, motioning to a side door where Lydia entered the church, taking a seat in a pew halfway to the altar. Hollis scanned the backs of everyone's heads again, just as she had when they first entered the tiny church. But Siobhan wasn't there. Nor was Keiran or Declan. If Lydia was following someone, she'd found new prey.

There was a noise at the back of the church as the door just behind them opened, then closed. Hollis slowly turned her head to the side, trying to be as subtle as possible. Peter Moodley was standing at the back door, staring at the back of Lydia's head.

Maybe she'd gotten it wrong. Maybe Lydia was now the one being followed and Peter had a new target in his sights.

Sixty

They all stayed where they were, waiting through the presentation of the gifts, the communion, and the hymns. Finally the priest stood and motioned for the congregation to stand as well. Hollis watched Lydia rise to her feet, prayer book in hand.

"Mass is ended," the priest said. "But before we go, there's a hurling match on at three, if you're looking for something to do today."

Hollis and Finn both started laughing, as much from the exhaustion and stress that had built up inside of them as the charming and completely off-topic words of the priest. When she could control herself, Hollis leaned over to the elderly woman beside her. "I'm sorry. I didn't mean to laugh."

"Nonsense. You enjoyed yourself. Isn't that lovely."

"Is he like this every week?"

"No, he's just here for a few weeks. Father Pat is in Chicago visiting family."

"What's his name?"

"Father Tom. I don't know his surname, but isn't he handsome?"

Her husband leaned over. "This one likes a bit of eye candy with her prayers."

Hollis laughed again, this time louder. Finn shushed her, but she couldn't help herself. At any moment someone was likely to arrest her, or shoot her, or both. She might as well get her giggles in while she could.

They waited in the pew until the church emptied out. Father Tom had positioned himself at the door, chatting with everyone while they left. It soon became apparent that if they waited for everyone to be finished with their goodbyes, it could be after dark before anyone had a chance to search the church.

Confession is good for the soul, Hollis recited to herself while she waited, trying to refocus on the task at hand. As she watched Peter, she saw that he wasn't watching Lydia now, but instead was fixed on the confessional box just to the left of her pew. Peter must have decided the confessional box was the place Eamon had been pointing to in his circled words. It made sense. What didn't make sense was Eamon hiding a manuscript in a tiny room that was, presumably, used frequently by dozens of people.

Peter moved toward the box. As he did, Lydia turned and watched him. She wasn't even trying to hide what she was doing, so Hollis decided that they might as well all take a look.

"You nearly got me arrested for kidnapping," Peter said as they approached. His voice was low and his tone respectful, which Hollis realized had everything to do with their location, and not his affection for them.

308

"Then you know how it feels to be innocent of a crime and have no one believe you," Finn answered.

"You haven't proven you're innocent."

"In my country," Finn said, "you're innocent until proven guilty."

"We're not in your country, Finn."

Hollis cleared her throat. "Actually, Ireland has the same language in their constitution, so it applies here as well."

Peter looked at her, first annoyed then amused. "You two are just a fountain of information, aren't you? Do you want to tell me what the note meant, or the newspaper clipping with the words circled about confession?"

"Yes, I'm all ears." Lydia had moved behind them.

"Is Peter who you're following now?" Hollis asked.

"Why?"

Finn stepped toward her. "Because Kieran was shooting at us about an hour ago. And you were tracking him and Siobhan, so you must have seen it."

"Are you suggesting I would stand around doing nothing while criminals shot at semi-innocent professors? Honestly Peter, I don't know where they get these ideas."

"Civilians," Peter agreed. "They tend to be very sensitive."

"But you also happen to be wrong about my tracking Kieran and Siobhan," Lydia said. "They weren't able to bring me to ..." She glanced toward Peter. "To the person I'm looking for, so as soon as I saw Peter, I figured I'd follow him. There's word that he's gone full Delta Force on this."

"That's a bit dramatic, Lydia," Peter said. "I sent Garda to the location of the black van that had taken us this morning."

"Because you knew we'd been kidnapped," Hollis said.

"Or because you had your friends help you with a getaway," Peter suggested.

Hollis rolled her eyes. "But you didn't find anyone?"

Peter shook his head. "Just the van."

"So no troops on Inishmore?" Finn asked.

"Two local guards. And I think you're going to be disappointed when your story about being shot at doesn't hold up." He walked to the back of the church and opened the door wide. Outside, Father Tom was chatting with a young uniformed officer standing beside a police car. "Can you open the rear door and show who we've got?" Peter called out.

"Sure thing," the officer said, opening up the door and pulling a handcuffed Kieran from the car. "You want to talk to him?"

"No thanks. Where's the other one?"

"Had to go to the toilet."

"Alone?"

"No, sir. With Garda O'Brien. But it's okay either way. I've arrested Siobhan many times, and she's never given me any trouble."

"How comforting. We'll be right out. You can put him back in the car." Peter turned toward Finn and Hollis. "They've been in custody since they walked off the boat. Care to change your story?"

"If Kieran O'Malley isn't the one shooting at us," Hollis said to Finn, "then who?" As she asked the question it occurred to her that two likely suspects were standing right next to them. "I think I need to sit down."

She was about to sit in the same pew they'd been in for mass, but Finn took her elbow. "I think you'd feel safer away from the door," he said, though it didn't make much sense to Hollis. He walked her to the other side of the small church and motioned for her to sit in a pew across from the confessional. If the point of going to the other side of the church was to get away from two potential killers, it hadn't worked.

Lydia and Peter followed them and watched while Hollis and Finn huddled in the pew.

"Are you having some kind of a breakdown?" Lydia asked.

"Just for the moment," Finn answered her. "We're not professionals, remember. You heard everything our friend David said in the hotel room. You can tell Peter we're not involved in TCT."

"I don't know what you're involved in," she said. "And I don't care. I just want the manuscript."

Peter turned to her. "Why does the CIA want the manuscript? It's a police matter."

"Then why are you here?"

"Interpol," he said. "It's right in the name. International police."

"You're MI6. And rumor has it you've gone to work for Blue."

"Have I?"

While Peter and Lydia bickered, Finn pointed to a little gold plaque, like the one for the O'Connor Family. Only this one read *The Kelly Family of Inis Mór.*

"This row has the best view of the confessional," Finn whispered to her. "I wondered if that's what Eamon was pointing to."

"The Kelly Family." Hollis searched her brain for any mention of that name.

"But I've been looking," Finn continued. "And I can't see anything leprechaun, so I don't know where this leads."

"I'll bet Siobhan knows. The package was meant for Kieran, and I think that he was going to share it with her. The clues Eamon left, they're things that would make sense to her."

"Well, I don't think she's going to tell us," he said. "So we'll have to figure out the next best thing."

"If your wife is dead and your daughter is away in Australia, who would you talk to? Who's the next person you might be closest to?" Hollis didn't know Eamon enough to know the answer, but their cart driver,

Tim Collins, did. And he'd mentioned one name, Hollis remembered. A woman named ... Mary Kelly.

She knelt down and made the sign of the cross. Finn followed her lead. "We have to get out of here without bringing them with us," she whispered to him. "We need a distraction."

Sixty-One

Finn stood up. "I want to talk to Siobhan." His voice was loud, insistent.

"I don't think that's a good idea, mate." Peter put his hand up to stop him, but Finn just laughed and went out the side door.

"Where's he going?"

"He just told you," Hollis said.

Peter and Lydia went out the front, to the police car with Keiran and Siobhan inside, the church door shutting behind him in the rush. Hollis stayed put. Finn came back in the side door. "Let's go that way," he said, pointing to the altar.

They ran to the back of the altar and found a door to the church office. They closed it behind them and waited, but Peter hadn't returned.

"Is it really this easy to get away from spies?" Finn asked.

"Not to put a damper on your excitement, but we haven't gotten away yet. And we have no idea where Mary Kelly lives."

Finn swept his hand across the room. "She's got to be a member of this parish, or there wouldn't be a family plaque. And if she's a member, there's a record here."

"We're going to rifle through church records?"

"You have a better idea?"

She thought for a moment. "No. I wish I did, but no. If the priest catches us, you're going to have to come up with a story."

"Didn't you hear him? There's a hurling match on this afternoon. He's not coming in here to do paperwork."

Just in case Finn was wrong, they moved quickly. Finn looked in files for anyone with the surname Kelly, while Hollis checked the Rolodex on the desk.

"Found it!" Finn called out, pulling a file from the cabinet. "Mary Kelly buried her husband last year. Michael Kelly."

"I'm sorry to hear that."

"You'll be even sorrier when I tell you there's no address. People on the island probably just know where everyone lives. But there is a phone number. Should we call?"

"And say what? Your friend Eamon is dead and we're trying to track down the clues he left. Oh, and one more question. You don't happen to be a leprechaun, do you?"

"I wasn't going to ask her that," Finn said. "It would have been obvious if we saw her in person and she had a little green hat."

Hollis laughed, despite herself. "Peter is going to find us here any minute. Let's just call her and make something up."

Finn picked up the receiver from the church's phone and handed it to her. "Good luck."

Hollis shook her head, but she took the receiver anyway. And she congratulated herself on not arguing about it. She tried to calm herself down while the phone rang. But as it continued to ring with no answer, she just got more panicked.

Finally a female voice, small and quiet, answered the phone. "Hello?"

"Mrs. Kelly? Mary Kelly?" Hollis struggled for something to say before it came to her. "I'm interested in renting Eamon's cottage. He said that if I came to Inishmore I should talk to you about it."

"Yes, that's right dear. When would you like to rent it?"

"Now. If possible. Can I come to your home and discuss it?"

"I suppose. Now I must warn you I haven't got anything baked fresh for tea."

Hollis smiled at the concern over strangers. "I wouldn't expect a fuss. We've given you no notice. I just need to know where you live."

"You can ask anyone in town and they'll direct you."

The Irish indirectness. Hollis tried again. "Why don't you get me started? I'm at St. Michael's Church."

"Then you're just down the road. Go through the churchyard, and follow the road south..."

"Toward Eamon's?"

"Yes. You'll have no trouble spotting it. It's a little white house with roses in front and a red door. About a quarter mile from the church. I'll put the kettle on."

Finn was gesturing wildly for Hollis to hang up, and when she did, he pulled her to her feet, leaned into her ear, and said, "Go out the window to the side. I think Peter is coming back to find us."

She pulled the window up and climbed out, with Finn close behind. Luckily they were on the side by the churchyard, so they ducked low and moved quickly south. Hollis concentrated on her footing and on figuring out how far a quarter mile would be on the winding road, and how to distinguish Mary's house from all the other white cottages with roses and red doors.

Sixty-Two

Excuse me," Hollis said to a woman walking down the road.

"I can't help you now," she said. "I'm praying."

"Oh, sorry." She looked at Finn, who didn't seem to have an idea of what to do next either. But they'd been walking for about five minutes at a fast pace, which Hollis figured should put them at the quarter-mile mark. But there wasn't a house in sight.

Finn slowed his pace to match the praying woman's. "I have no idea where Mary Kelly's house is," he said loudly. "I don't want to be late for tea."

The woman stopped. "Is it Mary Kelly you're after? She's just down that lane, there." She pointed to a path nearly overgrown with hedges. "Are you family?"

"No, just on holiday looking to rent the Byrnes place."

She looked them over. "That'll be nice for you. A nice quiet place away from the violence of big-city life in America."

"We come from a small town," Finn corrected her.

"It's fine." Hollis grabbed his arm. "You're absolutely right. In fact, we're looking forward to the quiet. Sorry for interrupting your prayers." Once the woman had walked far enough up the road, Hollis turned to Finn. "Why do you always have to be right?"

"I don't *have* to be right. I just often am."

She hugged him.

"What's that about?" he asked.

"I would strangle you for being so argumentative, but there's already enough people trying to kill us. Let's go."

"When they stop trying to kill us, I want to reopen this discussion, because I'm not argumentative."

She laughed. "And you're going to hammer the point until I agree with you."

He paused for a moment, then clearly understood she was mocking him. He shrugged. "Exactly."

———

Mary's house, like Eamon's, faced the ocean, though it was farther back. Hollis realized they must have passed it running from the sniper, whoever that was, to the church. If they'd known to look for it, they could have saved themselves a step.

A small, fragile woman opened the door. "Is it yourselves?"

"I suppose so," Hollis answered. "We called about Eamon's cottage."

"Then come in so, and get out of the cold air." Mary ushered them into a small, beautifully decorated room with a soft blue couch and two armchairs. There was a fire burning and the now-familiar scent of turf filled the air. "You were at mass, were you?" she asked.

"Yes, Father Tom..."

She let out a laugh. "He's a good soul. Loves his hurling. I always enjoy when he comes to the islands. I was sorry to miss him today."

Without explaining her absence or anything else, she disappeared from the room, leaving Finn and Hollis alone.

"What do we ask her?" Hollis said.

"Maybe we just look around and see if we find something." Finn was already moving about the room, lifting vases and figurines off their shelves, looking for clues. But Hollis was drawn to something else. The walls were covered in paintings—ballerinas that looked like a Degas she'd seen in the Art Institute of Chicago. A Monet, Picasso, Chagall...

Mary reappeared in the doorway, holding a large worn silver tray with three cups of tea and four different kinds of biscuits. "Those are my brother's," she said when she saw Hollis looking at the paintings. "When he was training, he copied the masters to learn their techniques."

"Was your brother Patrick Lahey?" Finn asked.

She nodded. "He's gone now, just recently. God rest his soul."

"He was a friend of Eamon Byrnes?"

Mary poured three cups, handing one each to Finn and Hollis, then sitting on the couch next to Hollis while Finn continued to wander the room. "Did you know Patrick?"

"We met him. He was a lovely man," Hollis said. "Very charming."

"Oh he was that. Sometimes too charming for his own good. He and Eamon were so different. Good lads, both, but Eamon is so serious and steady in his business and Patrick was always looking for a bit of easy money. But they've been great friends for years. Eamon helped Patrick, especially in these last few years. It'll break poor Eamon's heart to know Patrick's gone."

Hollis bit the inside of her mouth to stop herself from crying. "Your brother did well as a painter."

"He did, in the past few years, anyway. He sold quite a few. Eamon introduced him to people in Dublin. The kind that buys paintings they never look at, that's what he said." She laughed. "How do you hang a painting on a wall and never look at it?"

She was such a sweet woman that Hollis felt doubly bad about Eamon sitting dead in his cottage not five minutes away. She didn't have the heart to ask about a manuscript. She looked over at Finn, who had started scanning her bookshelf, packed with hard covers and paperbacks and a few small collectibles. Maybe he would find something that would make such an awkward question easier.

"I teach literature in the States," Finn said. "I can see by all the classic novels you have that you love reading too."

"I did once," Mary said. "But my eyes are too weak now to enjoy a book anymore. Those are my nephew's books. Those are his too." She pointed to what looked like two Picasso sketches hanging on the wall. "He's not as good as Patrick was. Not yet anyway, but he's got talents."

"Patrick had a son?"

"No, not Patrick. We had a sister, Anne. She passed away years ago when the boy was only twelve." She stiffened a little, the memory of it seemed too much for her.

Finn poured more tea into her cup and sat across from her in an armchair. "I can't imagine raising a child alone, without his mother. I'd be lost."

Mary smiled at him, and he smiled back. His kindness and charisma worked, Hollis saw, because he was sincerely interested in other people, in hearing their stories, and knowing what made them tick. Mary sensed it too, because she sipped her tea, and relaxed. "His father meant well, I know, but he didn't understand him. He gave him everything money could buy, and little else. His father lost everything when the

Celtic Tiger lost its bite, and he put a gun in his mouth, Lord save us, leaving my nephew alone in the world, save for Patrick and me. And now it's just me, I suppose."

"I'm so sorry," Hollis said. "What's your nephew's name?" To her mind, there were only two choices—Declan and Kieran—and either would make sense.

But Mary ignored the question. She got up from her couch and wiped a tear from her eye. "It's been a sad week," she said.

Hollis could see she'd been too brusque. "You have lovely things," she said, hoping to get things back on track.

Mary glanced around the room. "Dust catchers. But you can't get rid of them," she said, turning misty-eyed once again. "Eamon gave me the crystal on the bookshelf." She pointed toward a paperweight in the shape of a half circle. "His poor late wife, Nora, loved her crystal, and Eamon thought it would be a reminder of her. And it is that." She paused. "I might have some ham left over from last night if you're hungry."

"We don't want to take up too much of your time."

"You want the cottage. I have a key somewhere. Give me a moment." She walked out of the room, heading toward the back of the house.

"I don't think Eamon just handed her a manuscript," Hollis said. "If he had, Declan and Kieran would have it by now."

"Then it's hidden somewhere."

"I'm not tearing this house apart."

Finn glanced around, frustrated, but not for long. "I don't think you have to." He walked over to the bookshelf and pointed to the small crystal paperweight Mary had mentioned. "Where do leprechauns keep their pots of gold?"

"At the end of a rainbow?"

He picked up the paperweight. Up close Hollis could see the half circle was really a rainbow, etched into the glass. He moved the paperweight to another shelf and grabbed a coffee table-sized book underneath it. The book was titled *The Tuatha De Dannan*.

Finn opened the book and took out a manila envelope, just the right size for a fake Behan play. He opened the envelope slowly, and Hollis dreaded the possibility that it was another clue. But it wasn't. Finn pulled out a surprisingly authentic-looking manuscript, typewritten, with age stains and notes in the margin.

They finally had what they'd been looking for across Ireland. It was almost too good to be true.

Sixty-Three

The luck of the Irish. And I always thought that was ironic."

She knew the voice immediately. "Were you just waiting for us to find it, Declan?" she asked.

"If you had told me what clues Eamon had left in the package, I'd have found it on my own, and you both would have been spared the journey to the Aran Islands," he said, walking into the parlor, his hand out toward Finn. "But that would have been a shame. It's a lovely place to see."

"It is," Hollis agreed. "And a lot of others wanted to see it too, like Lydia and Peter. They're on the island."

"Then I can't stay and chat. I'd like the manuscript now, please."

"Unfortunately, I can't do that," Finn said as he put the play back in the envelope. "This manuscript will prove that Hollis and I are not in TCT, I didn't authenticate a fake painting, and I'm not one of your gang listed in this document."

"We're not a gang. We're a loosely organized group of individuals pursuing both separate ambitions and cooperative strategies for the collective good."

"You sound like their PR guy," Finn said.

"It's a cause I believe in, and I know that the rest of TCT is just as committed. Even if I don't know them, I know that much."

"Don't know them? You all seem to be friends," Hollis said.

"Our little cell, yes, but we're just one small part of a larger movement." Declan walked closer to Finn. "Please, just give me the envelope."

"I can't."

Declan bit his bottom lip. He looked tired and more than a little annoyed. "Then I'll kill you."

Hollis moved toward Finn. "Your aunt is in the other room. How would she feel about two murdered Americans in her parlor?"

"There's a hundred and twenty-five million dollars waiting for whoever has the account number. At midnight the buyer of our fake painting will release the money into an account—"

"Set up under the name Liam Tierney," Hollis added.

He gave a slight nod. "One minute later, I'll move the money again, where it will be safe from nosey parkers like yourselves. Then I intend to take a nice long vacation somewhere warm. No one is getting in the way of that."

"I thought it was supposed to be split five ways," Finn said.

Declan rolled his eyes. "It was, until Eamon got greedy, trying to bail Siobhan out of some mess she got up to in Sydney. He leaked the name of one of our ... *group* as an incentive for the rest of us to let go of our shares. A small cog, a man working at a free port who got us photos of the original painting and confirmed it wasn't about to be sold or displayed. It was a cheap move on Eamon's part, but in his way he was protecting Patrick and me."

What kind of trouble could Siobhan have gotten into that required so much money, Hollis wondered. Even the world's most expensive rehab would have been covered by one-fifth of the painting's sale price. Whatever it was, it made Eamon desperate enough to betray his old friend Patrick. And keeping their share must have made someone else desperate enough to kill Eamon.

"Did you kill him?" Finn asked.

Declan let out a dry laugh. "Making that sale proved to the others at TCT that I was a serious player. That's what I wanted. I would have given Eamon the money, truth be told, if he'd only asked instead of demanded. Then he got himself killed, apparently, along with my uncle Patrick."

"But you know he's dead."

"Eamon's had more visitors today than he's had in his lifetime, poor man."

"So that's four people you've mentioned," Finn said. "You, Eamon, Patrick, and the cog at the free port. And number five is an authenticator that Interpol thinks is me. Who is it, really?"

"Someone Eamon knew. Someone out of the country. But he's not part of things. The authenticator works on a flat fee. It's good money for very little work, if you're ever looking to add to your retirement."

"Won't be much of a retirement if I'm in prison."

Declan was losing his patience. "I'll send a note to your jailers, I promise, Finn, if you just hand over the manuscript. I don't want to kill you, but don't count on my kindness. It has limits."

It was a funny thing. So many people had threatened their lives in forty-eight hours that it no longer had the same effect. Hollis was instead fixated on the identity of the fifth person. "Kieran?" she asked.

"I told you, he was an apprentice. I promised him five percent of my share if he could find the manuscript. He got poor old Eamon to send him some package on the promise that he would give it straight to Siobhan. The old man trusted him, which was right, I suppose. He did bring Siobhan into it. But she and Kieran share a common ... hobby. A stupid, self-destructive hobby. He gets a little too excited in pursuit of his cash and what he can put into his veins once he has it. It's dangerous to be excitable in this business."

"If it's not Kieran or the authenticator, that still leaves a fifth person," Hollis said. "Is it someone in Interpol? We heard there might be someone on the inside."

Declan just smiled.

"Because there are three people in the intelligence community pursuing this manuscript as much as you—Lydia, Peter, and David."

"Eamon put our little group together for this task. I was just out of the military a year ago, looking for some direction. Eamon was already helping Uncle Patrick find a way to make money and do good in the world. I asked him to help me too. He was like a father ..." His eyes misted over. "Hand to God, I couldn't tell you the name of the final person if I wanted to. That secret died with him."

"You don't know anything about the fifth person?"

He shook his head. "We all had nicknames."

"Eamon's was Liam Tierney," she said. "He was the agent, and he opened the account."

Declan bit his lip. "My nickname was Header, because I really do think one day I'd like to go back to school and get my PhD. Uncle Patrick was Leonardo, after daVinci. The poor cog was called Cheese, because he was Swiss. Eamon thought it was a bit of a laugh to keep calling him Swiss Cheese. And there was an intelligence person watching out for us in case Interpol cottoned on to what we were doing with the sale. It was an odd nickname. I'll tell you what it was if you give me the manuscript."

Mary walked back into the room with a key. "I think this is the right one. I'm a bit muddled."

Declan took it, putting his arm around the woman. "Thanks, Aunt Mary. You just rest now for a while and we'll get out of your way."

Hollis watched the tenderness he showed toward Mary, and it made her want to believe him. But part of being a spy, she knew, was never trusting anyone. While Mary gave them instructions on the house, Declan left the room. Before they had a chance to leave, he was back, wearing his jacket and holding a cane for Mary. "You shouldn't be without this," he said and kissed her lightly on the cheek.

"My nephew will show you Eamon's house," Mary said as they left. "You'll enjoy having a nice quiet place to rest."

Finn and Hollis walked outside, Finn clutching the manila envelope tight, with Declan behind them.

"We told her Uncle Patrick died of a heart attack in Dublin. It'll kill her when she finds out about Eamon. There's no pretending a bullet wound is natural causes. I'll have to disappear for a while too, and she'll have lost all of us. It's not fair to her, but it's what must be done. You need to give me the manuscript now. I've been fair to you, more than fair."

"We're going to go find Peter Moodley and give this to him," Finn said.

"What if he's your inside man?"

"You said he had a reputation for doing the right thing."

"And you believe me?"

"It's the best we've got," Finn said. "I'm sorry about the money, but it seems to me you can always make more."

Declan seemed to take the news well. Too well, Hollis thought.

"You'll give me time to get away?"

"You helped us get away from the cave this morning. Let's just say we're returning the favor."

"Decent of you." He reached out his hand, and Finn shook it, taking one hand off the envelope.

Declan grabbed it.

Hollis wasn't about the let him get away with that, so she took a step back and side-kicked Declan in the gut.

He collapsed on the ground, clutching his stomach, and dropped the envelope to the ground. "Jesus! Kieran wasn't kidding when he said you were lethal."

She scooped up the envelope, more than a little proud of herself. She and Finn walked quickly away, the sound of Declan still writhing in pain at their back.

Sixty-Four

Three police cars and half a dozen uniformed officers stood outside the church as Hollis and Finn walked toward it. It was the kind of commotion that's never supposed to touch such a lovely place, Hollis thought, a little sadly. But someone had brought it here. Someone had killed Eamon in his own cottage, and to her mind, it had to be the fifth member of the group—unwilling to give up their share of the loot or to be blackmailed by Eamon.

As they reached the church, Hollis could see that Siobhan and Kieran were still there, separated but still handcuffed, and Siobhan was sobbing against a Garda car. Word about Eamon had obviously reached them.

"Stay here, and I'll look for Peter," Finn said. "But stay right where the guards are. Don't move." He walked several feet then returned. "Not that you can't take care of yourself, because obviously you can."

"I've got the manuscript, though. Too valuable to take any chances with it." He kissed her cheek then moved his lips up to her ear. "I'm grateful for every moment with you, even the ones where you're nagging me and I'm ignoring you."

She wanted to grab him, hold tight, and never let go. But instead she moved her head so her lips grazed his. "When this is over, I promise I'm going to keeping nagging you."

"And I'm going to keep ignoring you."

It sounded like heaven. They kissed, and then Finn moved his head away. "Be safe," he said as he walked away.

"You too," she whispered as she watched him go.

Hollis was only a few steps away from the Garda car, but she decided to move closer. When she was about two feet from Siobhan, she caught her eye. "I'm sorry about your dad."

Siobhan leaned toward her. "It's my fault he's dead. All he wanted was a quiet life … to be here … and I ruined it for him."

Hollis could see that she was a slight woman. Her uncontrollable red hair seemed the biggest part of her. Years of drugs had made her eyes hollow and her skin drawn. On her arms there were little round scars. It seemed odd to Hollis until she realized what they were. "Someone burned cigarettes on your arms," she said. "That's a torture technique. Why would someone do that to you?"

Siobhan folded in on herself and kept crying.

"You were a drug mule," Hollis said suddenly, realizing it couldn't have been rehab money Eamon was after. And that the move to Australia wasn't for a fresh start, but for a much darker reason. "Did you lose the drugs? Is that what your father needed the money for?"

Siobhan let out a wail. "They said they would pour petrol over me, burn me alive as an example," she got out before the tears overtook her.

Hollis felt an urge to put her arm around the girl. "Your father was buying your freedom from some drug cartel?"

"It was my mess. He could have let me take the punishment for it. Instead he just got deeper and deeper into things trying to save me. And now look what's happened."

"How did you get out?"

"He put up some money, a down payment. He said he'd give them a hundred million dollars but they had to let me go first. They knew they could find me if he was cheating them. But I guess they got impatient and killed him first."

"It wasn't a drug cartel that killed him," Hollis said. "It was someone from TCT. I'm sure of it."

Siobhan stared at the churchyard where her mother was buried, and her father soon would be. "He made me promise I'd have a whiskey for him at Dun Aonghasa on the day he died, and I can't even do that much for him." She held up her handcuffed wrists. "Doubt I'll be able to even attend his mass."

"Maybe your brother will."

"I don't have a brother. It was just my parents and me."

"But there was a photo in the shop, with a little boy behind your dad's leg."

She smiled. "That was Declan. He was a bit of a stray my da wanted to help. He was always wanting to help ..." Her voice trailed off, replaced by tears. One of the guards touched Siobhan's arm and suggested she sit in the car. She meekly followed his suggestion. Whatever got her on the path that led here, she couldn't have imagined things would turn out like this. It was a feeling Hollis could relate to more than she wanted to admit.

Hollis swallowed her own desire to cry as she moved away from the Garda car. Another reason she wouldn't have liked being a spy. Real people, good people, get killed and so often there's nothing that can stop it.

"Look what you have there!" Lydia popped up, as had become her tiresome habit, and walked toward Hollis.

"Finn is looking for Peter," Hollis wrapped her arms tightly around the envelope. "We're giving this to him."

Lydia inched closer. Hollis could feel her muscles tighten. She got ready to punch, or run, or scream for the police.

"Peter is a decent choice for help," she said. "But he's also very ambitious. If anyone gets in his way ... You heard about Bangkok."

Hollis clung to the envelope. "What exactly happened in Bangkok?"

"Brad Thomas, the officer who was killed, he was a friend of yours, wasn't he? If I remember correctly, he trusted Peter too, which was a shame, obviously."

"And you can't trust anyone in your business." It was all Hollis could think to say. But she wasn't sure. And Finn had been gone a long time.

"No." Lydia stared off at the water for a moment, then seemed to shake off whatever disappointment she felt.

Hollis looked at her and saw that Lydia Dempsey was the path not taken. Strong, sure of herself, full of skills and courage. "Do you regret being in intelligence?" she asked.

Lydia lifted one corner of her mouth into a kind of half smile. "Only sometimes. How about you? Regret giving up something you would have been good at?"

Hollis let the question sink in. "Only sometimes," she answered.

"Now that we've bonded, can I have the manuscript?"

"I don't think we've bonded *that* much. Maybe the manuscript outs you as TCT's inside person at the CIA. Maybe you just want the money for yourself."

"Maybe I can use the information in the manuscript to help national security, without having to share credit with Interpol, and I might be able to redeem myself at Langley in the bargain."

Hollis shook her head.

"Why don't I prove to you that Peter is a liar," Lydia said.

Hollis saw Finn and Peter walking toward them. If Lydia knew something, there were only seconds before Peter would have the manuscript and it would be too late. "Prove it how?"

"Ask him how Thomas really died. Ask him what's in that manuscript that complicates his life."

"You're saying *he's* TCT's inside man?"

Peter and Finn reached them before Lydia could answer. Hollis looked to her for something—some clue that she knew Peter was actually working for TCT—but there was nothing.

"Let me see it," Peter said, his hand out to Hollis.

She looked at Finn. He nodded, but her hands still clung to the envelope.

"Give it up, Hollis," Peter said. "Your husband says this proves your innocence. You want me to believe you, then give me the manuscript."

Hollis looked over at the Garda standing just a few feet away. She could scream and the whole bunch of them would be taken into custody. What would happen then, she had no idea. Peter could still get the envelope, and she and Finn could still be mistaken for criminals. Or she could hand it over and hope that they'd picked the right person.

"Don't give it to him," Lydia said. "I'm CIA. You know that. I may have put your lives in danger a few times but my motives have been pure."

"Don't do it, Hols," David walked up to them.

Hollis pivoted. "Where have you been?"

"About four steps behind you every step of the way. You really are a good spy. A good team of spies, actually." He nodded toward Finn, who seemed disinclined to take any compliment from David.

"I suppose you want this too," Hollis said.

"I know you don't trust any of us at this point, nor should you." David took a business card out of his pocket. "This is my boss's address. Mail it to him."

"How do we know that's your boss's address?" Finn asked.

"How do you know that either of these bozos aren't TCT?" David snapped.

"That's enough," Peter said. "Just give me the envelope, Hollis, so I can be rid of the lot of you."

The three intelligence agents starting bickering like children, each accusing the other of being the inside man. Hollis's head was spinning, and her grasp on the envelope was causing it to bend in half. "I know," she said.

The others all stopped, and looked to her.

"The manuscript is supposed to have clues to the person's real identity. We all look together and between us, I'll bet we can figure out who it is." She looked at each of their faces one by one—Lydia, Peter, and David. They each had the same expression: annoyed. Finn put his arm around Hollis's shoulder.

"Let's do it here. Out in the open."

"I don't think that's a good idea," Peter said.

"I think it's brilliant," Lydia said.

"So do I," David chimed in.

Peter threw up his hands. "Do what you want."

Hollis opened the envelope and slowly pulled out a stack of paper. But it wasn't what she was expecting. There wasn't a typed manuscript of a fake unpublished play. There was just one paragraph printed on the top page. The rest of the paper was blank.

"'I have a total irreverence for anything connected with society,'" she read, "'except that which makes the roads safer, the beer stronger, the food cheaper, and the old men and old women warmer in the winter and happier in the summer.'"

"Brendan Behan," Finn said. "And, I suspect, Declan Murphy's personal mantra."

"*That's* what we've been chasing this whole time?" David asked.

Finn shook his head. "No. We saw the real manuscript. Declan went to get his aunt's cane. He put on a jacket. He must have put that in an envelope and then switched it with the real one somehow."

It stung to realize how easily she'd been fooled. "When I kicked him," Hollis said. "He dropped the manuscript and fell to the ground in pain. Or so I thought. He was probably just keeping the real envelope out of sight until after we left."

Peter ran to the Garda car and spoke to one of the officers, then he came back. "There's a ferry in ten minutes. I've told the guards to ground any helicopters that try to leave the island. He could take a private boat, but let's hope he doesn't." Then he pointed a long finger at Hollis. "You better not have switched the manuscript yourself."

"If we had, why wouldn't we have done a better job of faking a manuscript? Finn is an expert, remember. We could have written half a dozen fake Behan plays by now."

Peter seemed to consider it. "You know what he looks like, this Declan Murphy? The only time I saw his face was when his friend stuck a needle in my neck, and my memory is a little fuzzy on the details."

"We know him," Hollis said.

"Good. Then you point him out to me and you might be able to survive this."

"You do something for us first," Hollis said. "Tell me what happened in Bangkok."

He stared at her, then Finn. "What do you know about it?"

"I know that a friend of mine died when he was working with you."

Peter took a step forward, then stopped. His eyes squinted until his pupils almost disappeared. Hollis could see his throat move as he swallowed hard. The veins in his neck seemed twice as large as they had just seconds before. He moved again, this time faster, getting almost to her face. She braced herself for an explosion.

"Someone chose not to listen to me and died as a result." He spat each word out like a bullet. "Don't make that mistake, Dr. Larsson."

Finn stepped in front of Hollis. "We have less than ten minutes to find Declan," he reminded Peter.

That seemed to snap Peter out of his rage. "When you find Declan Murphy, point him out to me, and I'll take it from there." He turned and walked away.

Finn grabbed Hollis's elbow and pulled her back. "Why would you do that?"

"What if he's TCT? Lydia said—"

"Lydia? You trust her?"

"You trust him?"

Finn let go of her arm. "We had a plan, and then you just do whatever you want..." He looked around. He had the same expression he'd had days before when the idea of going to Ireland had first been mentioned. She could feel the distance between what they each wanted growing by the second. Hollis reached out to him.

"We're in this together, remember?" she asked.

He nodded. "Let's get to the ferry with the rest of them. I want to know which of them is the real bad guy."

"Finn," she said. "Declan isn't on the ferry. I think he has one stop to make before he leaves Inishmore."

Sixty-Five

Hollis and Finn walked back toward the ferry with the others, but instead of running for the boat, they flagged down a mini-van that offered tours of the island.

"Are you headed to Dun Aonghasa?" Finn asked the man.

"Sure, and where else would I be going?" was the answer.

They squeezed in among a group of German tourists, and watched out the windows. The others had obviously noticed their change of plan because Peter turned from the ferry and jumped into a police car to follow them, while David and Lydia were stuck sharing a pony cart.

The driver told the group that Dun Aonghasa was a prehistoric stone fort, with construction that went back to the Bronze Age.

"A pile of rocks, really," the driver said, "framing a sheer drop to the water below. One hundred meters from the cliff to the water. For you Americans, that's more than three hundred feet. There's no guard rails, so as not to spoil the view. Good idea to watch your step and not get too close to the edge."

It was only a five-mile journey, but the roads wound around and the van moved slowly, even stopping for a flock of sheep to cross the road. Hollis found herself willing the driver to speed, but that wasn't an option. In Ireland, everything—even a rush to catch a criminal—took its own time.

When they finally arrived, Dun Aonghasa seemed to Hollis so much more than a pile of rocks. The fort was in a semicircle, four concentric walls built just as Martin's wall had been on his farm—without cement to bond them.

Surrounding the concentric walls were stone slabs cut sharply and half buried on their sides, as if they were soldiers guarding the fort. She imagined their practical purpose in ancient times was to cut or even kill anyone dumb enough to attempt a raid. Though they were now little more than a backdrop for selfies, the stone slabs still looked capable of doing their original job.

She could hear a tour guide saying the original construction might have been an oval, but the rocks had fallen as, over the centuries, the water reclaimed the land. And seeing the crash of the waves far below, it made sense that nature was the only force powerful enough to bring down the fort.

"Let's head to the left," Finn said. "Fewer tourists over there. Seems more like a place to have a last whiskey for a dead friend."

They made their way through the crowds. Seagulls swooped overhead, cawing loudly and—to Hollis anyway—menacingly. The wind was sharp. She felt pulled toward the cliff, even as she and Finn held tight to each other amidst the crowd of tourists.

There were lots of people milling about taking photos and enjoying the scenery, but Declan wasn't among them. Maybe she'd been wrong about his coming here. Maybe he'd gotten on a private boat and left immediately. Or maybe he was chancing it, sitting with Mary and having a last cup of tea before a long goodbye.

But in her heart she knew either was unlikely. The police were watching the ports and helipad, and surely someone was at Mary's house by now. If Declan had been found, Peter wouldn't still be following them. And he was still following. She and Finn spent as much time trying to duck the three intelligence agents as they did looking for Declan.

Finn kept moving Hollis away from the crowd, looking for the quietest place on the cliff, but they'd almost run out of land.

Then an arm reached out from behind a stone wall and grabbed Finn. "Not that it isn't always a joy to see you," Declan said, drawing them both behind the shelter of a large pile of cut stones, "but I'm having a bit of a private moment."

"You switched the manuscripts," Finn told him.

"Look, Finn, this is no business for good people. Uncle Patrick was a good man. Eamon was a good man. Someone killed them looking for that stupid play. I tried to warn you from following in their footsteps." He opened the backpack at his feet, and Hollis immediately saw the gun Keiran had pointed at them earlier.

"You were the one who put the bullet in Finn's pocket?"

"For all the good it did. But you two don't take a hint." Declan pushed the gun aside and reached for a bottle of whiskey.

"Interpol, the CIA, and Garda are all over this place looking for you," Hollis told him. "They're going to catch you any second."

"Don't worry about me. I know a dozen ways off this island without running into anyone with a badge." Declan stared out at the water, seemed momentarily lost in his thoughts and then raised the bottle high. "To Patrick and Eamon. *Ar dheis De go raibh a anamnacha.*" He took a long swig and handed it to Finn.

"Rest in peace." Finn drank and handed it to Hollis, who—to heck with it—took a short swig as well. It was sweet, and sad, and it made clear that there were certain things more important than the rules. It was a moment that belonged perfectly in Ireland.

The sun had been bright, but as if in solidarity with Declan's mourning, it slipped behind the clouds. She could feel rain in the air, but unlike the sprinkles she'd gotten used to in Ireland, this time the sky threatened more than just a few drops.

Declan put the bottle back in his bag, zipped it, and slung it across his shoulder. "I've done all I can for the dead. And more than enough for you two."

"You can give us the real manuscript," Finn said. "It might tell us who killed Patrick and Eamon, and you can get justice for them."

"The manuscript is in the fire at Mary's. The account numbers are in my head. And as for justice, there's an old saying around here: 'May you get all of your wishes but one, so you'll always have something to strive for.'"

"There's an American saying," Hollis said. "Stop being such a jerk."

Declan smiled. "Poetic."

"You said all of you had nicknames. If you can't give us the manuscript at least you can tell us the nickname of the intelligence officer." She stood in front of him, blocking him from moving away from the wall.

"That can-do American spirit. It's a bit annoying, honestly."

"It's what kept me going when I was working on my black belt."

He laughed. "Okay then. I don't fancy another sample of your talents. But this is the last time I do you a favor. You've slowed me down time and again, and I'm in kind of a hurry now. The inside man's nickname was Hols."

Something caught Declan's eye, and he moved Hollis's shoulder until she was out of his way, then tipped backward toward the wall of the fort, and quickly disappeared into a crowd.

But Hollis didn't care. She felt her head ringing as the word played over and over in her mind. Hols. There was only one person who would think of that name, of her name. She looked to Finn, who had turned white.

"He was in our home," he said quietly. "He used us."

She had always thought she'd be the better agent, but David had outshone her from the start. The incompetence was a masquerade. He'd been watching them and manipulating them the whole time, while they led him to the manuscript that would reveal his identity— and nearly got killed for their trouble. She felt sick.

Sixty-Six

She knew. Even before she saw him, she knew that David had found them.

"I heard what your friend said. It's good news and bad," he said as he came around the stone wall, a gun pointed at Finn. "The manuscript is gone, so no one can prove I helped TCT, but you both know it was me."

"Why would you use my wife's name? Still holding a torch for her?"

"Hardly. She was my competition in training. I thought her old nickname would inspire me."

"Well, it's pathetic," Finn said. "And 'Hols' was never her nickname. She hates being called that."

Hollis grabbed Finn's hand. "Now is not the time." She edged away from the spot they'd been in, partially hidden from the crowds, and toward a more open space. David followed. She knew it would soon be impossible for him to hold a gun on them and keep out of view of the police. "Why would you get involved in a group like TCT? You're not a revolutionary."

He sighed. "I told you. I'm a middle-aged man with an expensive divorce and a career going nowhere. No one throws revolutions for people like me. I found some of TCT's cell groups on the back channels of the web. I penetrated one of them and helped break it up. But did I get any recognition? No sir. No promotion, no raise, no pat on the back. I was just some nobody at a computer while the field agents got the glory. So I figured since no one is looking at me anyway, why not help myself a little."

"So you forced Eamon to give you money?" she guessed.

"I didn't force him. I offered my services. It was a year ago. He was desperate. His daughter had gotten arrested in Dublin on drug charges. I made them go away and even helped pave the way for her to get a work visa in Sydney. Not that she did much with it. Then I kept an eye out for any Interpol stings that might interfere with his work. In return I got a share of the proceeds. It was never much, but we had a nice thing going."

"And then he needed to help his daughter. Surely you understood the situation he was in?" Hollis asked.

"I matter too," he shouted. "I have plans. I have dreams. That Bacon painting was real cash. Our first shot at the kind of money that matters. But it was drawing CIA attention. I knew it was going to have to be my last score. My chance to lie on a beach in Belize and finally have the kind of life I deserve."

"But his daughter was being tortured…"

"So? I'm supposed to put my career in danger so his stupid daughter can keep getting bailed out?" He gestured wildly. Hollis saw a woman notice the gun, point to someone, and run. It would only be another minute, she hoped, until Peter and Lydia found them. She and Finn just needed to keep David talking. She glanced over at her husband, who seemed annoyed. She did her best to convey that talking, not arguing, was their way out of this, but his eye twitch was back.

"He blackmailed the group by faking a manuscript with all your information in it, with the account numbers," Finn said. "But the money from the sale wasn't going to be in the fake account until Monday."

"We were to hand over a hundred thousand euro each, plus agree to let go of our share of the Bacon money, or he sends the manuscript to Interpol. I could have ended up in prison like some common criminal." David let out a dry laugh. "And you want to know the worst part? The moron sent me the threat on an email from his own home Internet service. I hack into emails for a living and he doesn't have enough respect for me to hide his IPO. People are such idiots."

Hollis felt a momentary twinge of sadness for the man she'd once known, as she finally realized the bitterness and delusion that had overcome him. "So, you found Eamon," she said. "And he wouldn't tell you where the manuscript was."

David shook his head. "I searched the house after he ... after I killed him. Then when you guys couldn't find it anywhere else, I figured I must have missed it so I searched again." He was swallowing hard, waving his gun to punctuate each sentence. Several tourists were taking pictures of him with their smartphones rather than running for safety. David had a point about people being idiots.

"Where did we fit in?" Finn asked.

"I tracked down Leonardo—Patrick. He said if I gave him fifty thousand euros, he'd get me the manuscript. He couldn't afford to give Eamon his share, he said. But he didn't mind taking my money. These people are so greedy ..." he said. "But I couldn't go get it myself. What if I were seen?"

"There wasn't anyone who was supposed to meet us at Bewley's," Finn said. "You hired someone to steal the manuscript from us. Or at least the money if we didn't get the play. The mugger."

"Who knew she kept up with her martial arts training? All you had to do was give up the damn purse and at least I'd have my fifty grand. But I don't even have that."

"You were already in Ireland when we arrived, watching us. Patrick didn't have the manuscript, so you killed him at the Abbey Theatre. A loose end," Hollis said.

She realized she and Finn were taking turns speaking, forcing David to keep turning his head from side to side. She glanced over at Finn. He was studying David, moving slowly to his left, while she moved to his right, as if they'd choreographed it. David had to move slightly farther back to keep both of them in range. It would only be seconds more, she told herself, before help arrived. Just one more question, just one more step.

"Patrick was Eamon's friend. He was supposed to know where Eamon had hidden the manuscript, but he didn't. But by then he knew who I was. So I had no choice." David was shouting now, the gun swinging even more wildly. "I've been chasing this stupid thing all over Ireland and it doesn't even matter anymore. Because it's gone. The money is gone. And you know who I am."

Peter and Lydia, followed by a half dozen uniformed officers began moving across the rocks, through the spiky stone slabs, toward David. Several of the officers took over pulling the tourists back, while Peter and Lydia kept coming. David finally noticed them. He kept his gun pointed toward Hollis and Finn but shot furtive looks at Peter and Lydia every few seconds.

"Does he have the manuscript?" Peter yelled.

"It's kindling for a nice turf fire," David yelled back.

"So there's nothing stopping me from shooting your head off if you don't put down that gun?"

David moved fast, grabbing Hollis and locking her neck in the crook of his arm. He began pulling her toward the edge of the cliff, his gun pointed to her temple. "I'm not going to survive this," he said into her ear, resigned now. "So neither will you. You deserve to die with me."

"I'm not responsible for your life not working out, David. If you want things to be better, you have to do something yourself."

"Who's the life coach now, Hols?"

The wind was getting stronger. It had begun to howl, low and sad, whirling around her. A banshee wind. She looked for a way to steady her footing. David was so close to the edge that a wrong move could put them both over. She needed to get out of his grip.

Finn was moving toward her. His eyes locked with hers. She had imagined that one day those eyes would be the last thing she'd see in this world. But that day was not today.

"Stay back, Finn," David yelled. He pointed the gun at Finn and squeezed. *Ping.* The shot hit a rock a few feet from Finn. David was always a terrible shot, Hollis remembered. That was good news for keeping Finn safe.

Finn, though, wasn't interested in keeping safe. As David and Hollis moved closer to the cliff, he moved too. "Wherever she goes, I go," he said.

Ping. Another rock exploded.

"How romantic," Lydia chimed in. She grabbed Finn's arm from behind but kept her gun pointed at David. "Should have killed you in the hotel and saved us all a lot of trouble."

"No one has to die," Peter said, his voice the steady one in a group full of people shouting. "Listen to me, David. We all make mistakes. I've made them. Big ones. But I survived. So can you."

David moved closer to the edge of the cliff, pulling Hollis with him. She could sense the ocean behind her. A rock slipped underneath her feet and she could hear it break against the wall as it made the three-hundred-foot drop to the water.

"Without that manuscript, I don't have anything to bargain with. As soon as I put my gun down, you'll put me in prison."

"You have Hollis," Finn said. "I'll give you anything if you give me my wife back."

Finn touched his hand to his chest, as if he were pledging allegiance, but he widened his eyes as he did it. He's telling me something, Hollis thought. He's telling me ... what?

She glanced over at David's chest. A light. A tiny reflection of light. But the sun was behind the clouds. She looked up toward the fort. There was a man standing there, a sniper rifle in his hand.

One more step back and they would go over. It was now or never. Hollis took a deep breath, wondered if it was her last, then punched her elbow back into David's ribs. He screamed and let go long enough for Hollis to move a few inches. But he grabbed onto her hair, held it tight.

Ping.

David coughed. Bent over, his fingers still wrapped around her hair.

Finn ran forward. He dove onto the grass, pulled at Hollis.

David moved his gun just inches from Finn. Even a terrible shot couldn't miss at that distance.

Ping.

David stood up, letting go of Hollis. He looked toward the fort, confused. Then stumbled back and over the cliff.

Finn wrapped his arms around Hollis, pulling her away from the edge, while Peter and the others ran toward the spot where David had disappeared.

Hollis looked toward the fort. The sniper was gone.

Sixty-Seven

Finn ordered a round of drinks, passing them back to Peter and Hollis. The pub was crowded, several patrons were playing music, and the rest were singing along or engaged in loud conversations. Even though it was well past closing and the bartender had locked the door, no one seemed to be in a hurry to leave.

"*Slainte*," Peter said. "To a job well done. At least on your end. Poor Lydia has a lot to answer for at Langley for getting involved with a member of a criminal organization and letting him get the best of her."

"I think she'll survive. She's smart and tough," Hollis said. She thought of the sniper and smiled. "And she wasn't *entirely* wrong about Declan."

"I hope so." Peter clinked glasses with her. "Two murders, a criminal mastermind, and a hundred and twenty-five million dollars gone. And the worst part is, the only way we got as far as we did is because of two American college professors. I've got some explaining to do myself once I get back in the office."

"Which agency is your office?" Finn asked. "MI6, Interpol, or Blue, which I gather is a super-secret spy agency within Interpol?"

"I'm Interpol." Peter took a swig of his beer. "And Blue doesn't exist. Doesn't do missions around the world that are not strictly police matters. But if it did, this mission would be a success, even without the money, because we identified a mole in our ranks, thanks to you two."

"And you have the address book." Hollis grabbed a chip from Finn's plate of fish and chips. She was beginning to understand why no meal was complete without a potato.

"That address book will help identify more TCT members, if we can break the code," Peter said. "How did you get it?"

"I stole it from Eamon's shop in Dublin."

He laughed. "And you've spent this whole time telling me you're not a criminal." He took a swig of his beer. "Too bad we weren't able to stop the transaction or catch Declan Murphy, but we did salvage something." He took a piece of paper out of his jacket pocket. "I have an inventory of your things that were found in the van. You two don't travel light."

Finn took the paper and began reading through it. "They have your blanket from O'Maille's, Holly, and all our clothes. What's this?" he asked. "'Fifty L.T.'"

"Legal tender. I assume that was payoff money for poor old Patrick."

Hollis laughed. "L.T. … Liam Tierney. It was a joke, I guess, to put that as the name on the account. Legal tender."

Peter jumped up. "Liam Tierney. You're sure? Why didn't you tell me this before?"

"It didn't mean anything to us before now," Finn said. "It was the name Patrick Lahey called himself when we met in Dublin. For most of the time we've been running around the country we thought it was the missing Interpol agent."

"I'll call it in. Maybe we can stop the transfer if we have the name. Declan may have memorized the account number, but we have the name." Peter pulled his cell out of his pocket and walked outside.

They watched him go, then Finn turned to Hollis. "Should we tell him that Declan already knew the account was under Liam Tierney?"

"It's almost twelve thirty, so it's Monday now. My guess is Declan transferred that money at the stroke of midnight. If we tell Peter now, he'll probably charge us with aiding and abetting."

"I don't care." Finn gently stroked Hollis's hair. "I owe Declan everything."

"I think our flight is at noon tomorrow," Hollis said. "I don't know how we'll get a ferry to Doolin and then a train to Dublin in time."

"We definitely won't." Finn nodded to the bartender, who began pouring another round of Guinness. "I was thinking that we might want to stay a few days in the west country. Didn't Declan tell us Connemara was beautiful? There's a little town called Spiddal with lots of artists living there, and Kylemore Abbey, which is supposed to be out of this world. Lydia said they make really great jam."

"You sure?"

"I have two weeks before my summer class, and Ireland isn't the sort of place you should rush through. We need to do everything you're supposed to do when visiting Ireland. All the really important stuff anyway, don't you agree?"

"'The most important things to do in the world are to get something to eat, something to drink, and have somebody to love you,'" Hollis said.

He smiled. "That's Brendan Behan."

"Yes, it is."

Finn leaned in to kiss her. "Then I have everything I need."

© Logan Conner, Oomphotography

About the Author

Clare O'Donohue is the author of the Kate Conway Mysteries and the Someday Quilts Mysteries. She is also a TV writer and producer, and has worked on *After the First 48*, *Deadline Crime*, and documentaries for CNN, History Channel, A&E, and Investigative Discovery. An avid traveler, and dual Irish and American citizen, she got her first passport stamp at the age of two.